Praise for Anne Carter

POINT SURRENDER

"A quiet coastal town with a stormy past tows the reader in from the very first page.   Unresolved mysteries and a passionate romance keep the pages turning."

–Molly Evans, author of
The Surgeon's Proposal (Harlequin)

"Truly a wonderful read…ghosts…mystery…A truly heart touching story and one with an ending that will surprise. I truly enjoyed reading this story and the suspense kept me hooked to the very last page."

–Coffee Time Reviews

STARFIRE

"…a powerful tale of morality versus destiny…. With unerring passion and heart-pounding perfection, Ms. Carter weaves an intricate drama…truly captivating…"

–Dawn Whitmire, author of
Heart First

"*Starfire* by Anne Carter is almost scary. It takes a part of your own life, intermingles it with your dreams, and creates reality. I absolutely love her story. Pens raised to Anne Carter."

–Romance Reviewer Brett Scott

"Imaging in your wildest dreams…Anne Carter captures the ultimate romantic fantasy, in *Starfire*. A touching story…fireworks…one emotionally charged, satisfying tale. *Starfire* is a must read for ALL romance lovers."

–Susan R. Sweet, author of
A Deadly Agent

Also by

Anne Carter

Echelon Press Publishing

☙   ❧

Starfire
(*eBook*)

When Harry Met Soli
(*eBook*)

Other Books by Anne Carter

☙   ❧

Star Crossed Hearts

In Too Deep

A Hero's Promise

Point Surrender

By

Anne Carter

Echelon Press

Publishing

POINT SURRENDER

An Echelon Press Book

First Echelon Press paperback printing / April 2007

Cover © Nathalie Moore
Photograph for Artwork © JT Mac Photography

Echelon Press
9735 Country Meadows Lane 1-D
Laurel, MD 20723
www.echelonpress.com

ISBN 978-1-59080-514-5
10 Digit ISBN: 1-59080-514-3

PRINTED IN THE UNITED STATES OF AMERICA
10 9 8 7 6 5 4 3 2 1

To Laura:
For always supporting,
Always encouraging,
Always being there.
You helped more with this book than you know.

To Mike:
For believing in this book
from the start and giving
me the freedom to write it.

Prologue

CASE MCKENNA stood by as they lifted the manatee from the water. Amanda's massive, lifeless form looked slightly bent, as if still in pain, even though he knew she was finally free of the agony. Gently, they laid her on a tarp beside the pool, and Case hoisted himself onto the deck to sit beside her. She looked so serene.

Later, in the locker room, Case tried in vain to extract his duffel bag from his locker, its looped handle caught on the coat hook inside. Suddenly it didn't matter. He slammed the locker door so violently that the force rattled the high glass transom windows and left the steel locker door dented.

"Hey! Cool it, man. You need to take it easy. It wasn't your fault, you know." Jack clapped him firmly on the shoulder and squeezed. "Let's go get a drink."

Case looked at his friend through narrowed, pained eyes. "A drink. Sure. That's the answer. A drink!" His voice rising to a shout, he turned and again slammed the heel of his hand against the locker door.

Jack sighed, crossed his arms, and leaned against the opposite bank of lockers. "Sorry," he murmured.

Case sat down on the narrow wooden bench and dropped his head into his hands. After a few moments, he turned back to Jack. "She was so much better on Monday. I just can't believe…"

Jack nodded and ran a hand through his own dripping hair. "I know you cared about her. But sometimes, no matter what we do, we can't change the things that have to happen."

"Don't give me any of that destiny crap. She didn't have to die. There must have been something we could have done."

"We did everything possible. You know it; I know it. She was so banged up–hell, she had eight-inch lacerations from some damned boat propeller! It's a miracle she lived as long as she did after that Mexican resort shipped her up here. You're a vet, dammit, not a god."

At last Case stood up, his face drained of color, and his anger spent. His eyes fixed on Jack's, seeking solace, but knowing he'd find no comfort for Amanda's death.

"Look. Why don't you take some time off? Take the boat out; go down south or something? Or go see your mom," Jack suggested.

Sarcasm turned a bitter smile onto Case's lips. "My mom. Oh, that's good. Real good."

"Okay, so maybe that's a stupid idea. But you gotta get out of here for a while. Everyone thinks so. I don't have any time coming or I'd go with you."

The duffel came out easily now. Quiet, defeated, Case packed his personal items and left the locker room, leaving Jack to watch him go, with sorrow-filled eyes.

For it wasn't just the loss of a manatee haunting Casey McKenna.

Chapter One

"That's impossible!"

"I'm afraid not. Both tests came back positive." The doctor's words from the week before resonated in Amy's head as she hurriedly stuffed clothes, shoes, and toiletries into her bag. She couldn't think about what to take; she didn't even know where she was going. She only knew that she had to get away, and fast. It didn't really matter whether she had matching pumps and handbag.

There'd been no warning. No symptoms, not even the infamous 'morning sickness' about which she'd always been told. Sure, her monthly cycle was erratic, but that was nothing new. She had been under stress.

Stress? Amy smiled. A smile borne, perhaps, of certain madness. A woman who'd been through what she had was entitled to a little craziness.

Oh, she'd been happy at first. Thrilled, even. But the call this morning from an old friend had set her world terribly askew.

The phone rang. She ignored it. Amy zipped the overfull bag, catching delicate lace in the zipper as she forced it closed. In the small kitchen, she pawed through her purse and retrieved two credit cards, which she placed in plain view on the counter. From her key ring, she hurriedly wrestled the house keys. *At least I own my own car.* Clutching the remaining keys, she made her way to the door, taking a nostalgic look around the small duplex she had called home for the last three years. She'd unlikely ever sleep here again. She turned the knob and started to go, then paused. Lifting her left hand, she stared at the two-carat diamond ring and watched it blur as her eyes filled. Blinking several times, she quickly slipped it off her finger and went back to the counter where she slapped it down beside the credit cards. *Lying two-timing bastard.*

Outside, Mr. Franks knelt on his hands and knees in the flowerbed next door.

"Amy! Say, you don't happen to have any rose food, do ya?"

Amy forced a brief smile. "Not on me," she called, wishing she could say goodbye and stifling a pang of guilt because she couldn't. "They do look beautiful," she added as she popped open her trunk and tossed in her bag.

"Off to New York again?" the elderly man asked, rising with effort and dusting off the knees of his pants.

"Not this time. You take care, Mr. Franks." Amy waved and again blinked back her tears, hoping they didn't run beyond the bottom of her dark glasses.

The streets of Carmel, California bustled with tourists. Amy gazed over the top of the steering wheel, watching families saunter across the street, ice cream cones in hand. Melancholy filled her heart. It wasn't supposed to feel this way. She had always fantasized about having a baby, a baby conceived in love and devotion, with one who shared her hopes and dreams. Yet the child within her was a mistake. Innocent of all, created in a moment of irresponsibility with a man who didn't love her. No, it wasn't supposed to be this way.

It was not until she got onto the highway leading out of town that she fully exhaled.

She stopped in Monterey for gasoline. While waiting for the tank to fill, she dialed her brother's number on the cell phone for the fifth time.

"Hello, it's Brian, you know what to do..." the answering machine repeated. This time she left a message.

"Hey Bri, it's me... I...I was just wondering when...uh...when you'd be home." Amy looked out the windshield, slowly panning the station for anyone who might be watching her. "I'll just...just call you later. Bye." Slowly she closed the phone and let it slide from her fingers into her lap. It would be another two hours or so to Brian's flat. She could only hope he'd be home by then.

San Francisco was a big town. Not New York or L.A., but certainly a metropolis compared to the tiny burg in Santa Paula Valley where Amy Winslow and her brother Brian had played cowboys and Indians. Also much bigger than the coastal haven of Carmel-By-The-Sea from which Amy fled when her life there had unraveled so completely.

Stopped at a red light near Golden Gate Park, Amy tightened her seatbelt across her tummy. She was reminded of the life inside her and she shivered. A baby. Drew's baby. *Oh God.*

Trying to clear her thoughts, Amy concentrated on finding Brian's apartment. He answered on the third knock and Amy all but fell into his startled arms.

"So. You feeling better?"

Amy nodded, her fingers curling around a warm mug of herbal tea. "I'm just glad you were home. I don't know what I would have done. I called, like, ten times, but I kept getting your machine."

"You were just calling at the wrong time." Brian reached across the counter to where Amy sat on a barstool and lightly cuffed her on the chin. "What happened to your brain down there? And for that matter, what happened to your hair?"

Amy pushed her hair away from her face. Brian hadn't changed, but she had. "Thought I'd try something new, that's all." Self-conscious fingers plucked at the strands brushing her shoulders, strands that used to wave down to her mid-back.

"Had to find out if blondes really have more fun? They don't. Or so I've heard," Brian said with a chuckle. "It'll grow out." The touch of merriment in his eyes waned. "So did Drew make you do that?"

The sound of Drew's name on Brian's tongue renewed the quaking within. *Yes. No.* Drew *had* encouraged her to chop the thick chestnut locks into a more modern style. And, believing he had a penchant for blondes, Amy had doused her tresses with peroxide–throwing caution and, perhaps, common sense, to the wind.

14

Amy didn't answer Brian's question, so he turned and put his mug into the sink, his disappointment evident. "If you want to clean it off, you can sleep on that Futon. I'm not working tomorrow, so there's a good chance we can both sleep in."

Later, he covered her with a sleeping bag and tousled her hair. "Just holler if you need anything, Aim. I'm a light sleeper."

"That, I know." Amy looked up at her brother's warm smile and sympathetic eyes. "Thanks again." Despite the two years she had on him, she felt the younger sibling to his responsible, solid ways. Her own conduct was anything but responsible these days.

Amy lay awake long after she supposed her brother fell asleep. Emotion rested heavily upon her, much heavier than the thick sleeping bag draped across her body. With no clock nearby to focus upon, she finally closed her eyes sometime near dawn.

The teakettle's shrill whistle brought Amy around like smelling salts under her nose. The sun streaming through the gap between the living room draperies brought the day on with a harshness for which she was not prepared.

"Decaf?" Brian called from behind the counter, the hot kettle poised over a mug bearing the words *Tom's Transmissions*.

"I guess." Amy struggled to sit up, her limbs tangled in the sleeping bag, her hair hanging over her eyes. What she really needed was a good shot of caffeine. "What time is it?"

"Ten o'clock, not that it matters," Brian answered. He brought her the mug, carefully turning it so that she could see 'Tom's' smiling likeness. "Just milk, right?"

"You remembered."

Brian returned to the stove. "We lived together for a long time, Aim."

"I wouldn't blame you for forgetting everything about me."

"That would take major surgery." Brian ran his hand over his close-cropped, sand colored hair. "I'm not ready for that yet. But I'm up for some breakfast, how about you?"

Amy finally managed to disengage herself from the covers and got to her feet. Having slept in her clothes, she looked down in dismay. "Just toast would be fine."

"No good. You need something nourishing after your little excursion last night. *Heart's*, across the street, has great breakfast specials." Brian took a big gulp of his coffee and issued a satisfied sigh. "Come on."

"I need to at least clean up a little…"

"Whatever. But you look fine. Except for the hair, of course." Despite the subtle insult, Brian's eyes shown with warmth.

Amy stared into the small bathroom cabinet mirror. Leaning closer, she scowled at the faint darkness below her brown eyes and uttered a soft moan. Well, Brian had seen her worse. Much worse. She washed her face and ran a brush through her hair, wishing with every stroke that she could make it longer. But what did it matter, anyway?

* * *

With a fresh cup of hot coffee warming her hands, Amy stared across the booth at Brian's dark eyes and shook her head. "You never change."

"Is that a bad thing?"

"No. It's a very good thing." Amy lowered her chin, focusing for a moment on nothing in particular as she remembered days when she would have given anything for Brian to be different.

"You always change," he said, his voice soft and non-accusing.

"Is that a bad thing?"

"No." Brian's eyes were suddenly keen on hers. "Except when you don't talk about it."

"What should I be talking about?" Amy picked up a sugar packet and began working it over.

"What happened with Drew. Why you're here suddenly after all this time. Why you shacked up with him in the first place."

Amy leaned back in the booth and took in a deep breath. Of course he would ask. And he was entitled to answers. She wondered about how much to tell, but knew that in the end she would tell him everything. "Drew…isn't the man I thought he was."

"Oh really? Gee, what a surprise."

"I had that coming, didn't I?"

"Couldn't help it. I never understood how you ended up with a stuffed shirt like Andrew Richards in the first place. And why it took you so long to realize he would never change."

"I knew it from the beginning." Amy paused,

searching for the right words to explain. "It was me I wanted to change. I wanted to be the kind of woman who could live with him. I thought I wanted the sophistication, the glamour. But as time went on, I found myself wanting to change him instead. It wasn't really his fault." Her words dissipated into the thick atmosphere of the diner, clouded by the smell of burnt toast and frying bacon.

"You wanted to be like *him*? With his Beemer and his Pod-phone and his lifetime membership at the Athletic Circle? That's not you, Amy. That's never been you, or me. Dad didn't raise us with glitz."

Amy felt helpless under her brother's gaze. "It's not really *glitz*," she defended, but knew her brother was right.

As if sensing her discomfort, Brian looked down as he refolded his napkin."Well. Anyway. You're here now. What are you going to do? Does he know where you are? Is he still commuting to the East?"

"I sent him an email. He's in New York, again. I'm on summer break right now, I've been teaching second grade, you know. But I don't think I can go back."

Brian was watching her closely. "Why not? Carmel's a great town. Pass the pepper?"

"I love Carmel. And the kids are fun. But..." Amy swallowed hard. The sugar packet began to fall apart in her fingers. "There's something else."

"Like?"

"Like, a baby. I just found out I'm pregnant."

Pepper shaker in hand, Brian paused momentarily to absorb Amy's admission. But only for a moment. "Oh."

Eggs seasoned, Brian proceeded to eat them.

"Just, 'oh?' That's all?"

"Well it's certainly interesting news. Big change in *your* life, that's for sure." Brian flagged the waitress. "Could we have some orange juice here, please?"

"I don't know what to do. It's just so awful." Amy pushed aside her plate, and Brian pushed it back.

"I don't suppose you mentioned the baby in the email."

"No."

"Eat your breakfast. Do you have a doctor?"

"Not really."

"Insurance?"

"Yeah, for awhile. Until I formally quit my job."

"Hmmm." Brian spread strawberry jam on his toast. "Love this stuff," he murmured, then sighed. "Well. I think you should get as much medical care as you can before you have to quit. You can convert to private insurance if you can afford it. You know you're welcome to stay with me as long as you want," he said. "As long as you can stand it. But you'll have to tell *Druid* eventually. He should be part of this, at least financially."

"I'll have to find some kind of work here. I have no cash left of my own."

"Amy. Drew is responsible–or at least half responsible–for this situation. He needs to support you through this. Do you have a joint checking account?"

"Well, sort of. We pooled all our funds when we moved in together. But he still has his own, for his New York expenses. It seemed like the right thing to do at the time. I'm not ready to talk to him yet." Amy shook her head slowly. "I do have my car."

"Great. Mine's a piece of crap. But you know what? I don't care. It gets me around. Now if you want to talk about boats..."

Amy smiled. Brian had never cared about cars or expensive toys, other than boats. She thought about Drew, about his lavish playthings and lifestyle. He couldn't understand Brian's simple ways. They had clashed from the start.

"So anyway, why the big change? I'm still not clear about what turned the tide. Last time I saw you, you were dizzy with hormonal affection over that jerk. Frankly, I would've thought you'd be happy to be so...so intimately connected now."

"I might have been." Amy lowered her eyes, memories beginning to flood her mind. The tightness in her throat threatened to prevent her confession. "You might as well know it all. Do you remember Jessica Taylor?"

"Sure. You went to college with her. She married that movie star guy."

"Jess and her husband went to New York recently, and thought they'd stop in and surprise Drew at his flat. We were all so close in school, you know, Jessie, me, and our roommates... Jessie even went out with Drew, once."

"Another woman with lousy judgment. Go on."

Amy paused to formulate her words, wishing she could find an easier way to say it. "Anyway, Drew wasn't home, but his girlfriend was."

Brian's eyes narrowed and he trained them on his sister's for several moments before looking away to the street. "This was before, or after, you found out about the baby?"

"A couple of days after. I was going to surprise Drew with the news the following weekend. *This* weekend. Jess called me yesterday."

Brian let out a long breath through pursed lips. "That's rough, Sis. What an asshole."

They let the sounds of the diner overtake the space between them for a time, each sipping coffee and avoiding the pain of further discussion. Finally, Brian put his cup down. "Do you ever talk to Dad?"

"Oh yes. He's still chasing the widows around Santa Paula. He's particularly smitten with a woman he met at the senior center. She's okay, I guess. But I haven't called him about this…yet. I don't want to upset him. You know he's almost seventy-nine."

Brian drew in a deep breath. "Yeah. I know."

Amy splayed her fingers on the table, her eyes cast down. As mortifying as her situation proved, she was infinitely glad to have Brian. "I really loved it when you sent those Coast Guard posters to my class last fall, by the way. The kids told me how lucky I am to have such a really cool brother."

Brian looked up. "I'm going to be a really cool uncle, too." He picked up the check. "Let's go. I've got something wonderful to show you."

They drove Amy's small compact out of the city and

down the coast highway. Brian kept up a steady stream of chatter about his work with the Coast Guard.

"They own a lot of the lighthouses, you know. All of them are automated now. They don't have real 'keepers' anymore. The older stations are being systematically replaced with modern, high-tech jobs. Mostly ugly steel things."

"I remember once, Dad took us to the lighthouse in Santa Cruz. Built out of brick, I believe."

"Yup. It's a beauty. I've got a log going now of all the California lighthouses I've visited–got pictures, too. Anyway, the CG–the Coast Guard–sells them off when they become a problem. You know, a liability."

Amy nodded, comfortable with her brother's careful maneuvering of her car as they drove south. Brian pointed out the sights along the way.

"Look! There's one right there!" Amy pointed out.

"That's Point Montara Lighthouse. It's a youth hostel now, and they rent it out for special occasion type stuff. One of the guys got married there earlier this year."

They continued on in silence for several miles, passing the turnoff to the small coastal town of Newburg. Amy was just beginning to wonder if they would end up back in Carmel when Brian exited onto a gravel road leading toward a bluff above the sea. They soon came to a ramshackle wooden garage, once white, but now bearing signs of splintering neglect. Brian got out and trotted around to assist his sister.

"Check out this view! I love it up here." Brian led her toward the bluff, where they paused to scan the salty blue horizon of the Pacific. "And there's more." Brian took Amy's hand and pulled her toward the now visible top of a rough stairway leading down the precipice. Large, flat stones had been imbedded to create the steep path. "See?"

"Oh, my…" Amy's eyes were drawn to a white tower perched on a secondary cliff below them. The tower rose from the back of a small, one-story house. She turned to look into Brian's grinning face. "Is it real?"

"Oh, it's real enough. And soon it will be mine. Welcome to Point Surrender."

Chapter Two

"Wow, I've never been *inside* a lighthouse before! Look at that stairway!"

"It's at least four stories high. Come up to the top; you won't believe how incredible it is."

They climbed the spiraling iron stairs together, their laughter echoing like that of eager schoolchildren. The stairway seemed to end against a solid wood plank roof. Brian gave it a sharp push at one end, flipping over a hinged trapdoor to gain access to the lantern room.

"Not much room up here, is there?" Amy said as she followed her brother into the narrow space encircling the lens.

"Technically, no—but just look around you! We can go outside if you want."

"*Outside*?"

"The rim. It's called the gallery. You have to be able to go outside, to clean and maintain the glass."

Brian opened a narrow glass door and Amy followed him out, immediately grasping the iron railing that wrapped around the light. The brisk wind forced her hair back away from her face, made her eyes water. Looking over the edge, she was amazed at the elevation.

"If you're wondering, we're about 140 feet above sea level. Cool, huh?"

"What did you mean, it will soon be yours?"

"The CG is selling it to me! I can't wait. Judy and I are going to fix this place up just like when it was new. We'll get the light working again, and refurbish the house, and live here."

"Judy?" Amy practically shouted as the wind threatened to carry her words away.

"My fiancée! Didn't I tell you?"

"I think I would remember something like that! Let's go inside. I don't want to miss a word!"

Amy took her time descending the steps while she tried to prepare herself for Brian's news. Why hadn't he told her before now?

They sat down together at a small wooden table in the kitchen.

"It was built in 1856, and re-built in 1912. Some of this furniture has been here almost that long. Isn't it beautiful?"

Amy looked around at the cracked, peeling paint on the walls, the blackened, fieldstone fireplace that was missing more than a few stones, the rough-hewn wooden floor, uneven and heavily battered.

The sink looked like it had been dripping for a number of years. A long rust plume marred the once-white porcelain. The kitchen windows were fogged from decades of salt spray, a couple of them cracked. The small house harbored an odor of must and mildew that was hard to miss.

"It-it's interesting," Amy said, nodding vaguely.

"I know it needs a lot of work, but over time…"

"Tell me about Judy."

Brian smiled, his lips pressed together comically. "I know I should have called you. I just didn't want to get *him* on the phone."

Amy nodded, softly biting her lower lip at Brian's reference to Drew.

"She's great, Sis. She's a flight attendant for Trans-Con Airlines. But she's tired of it, so after we're married she'll stay at home and help fix this place up and have babies."

Amy stood up and turned toward the open kitchen door, facing the sea.

Brian stood also and scratched at his forehead with his thumb. "I'm sorry."

"No! No need. It just takes getting used to." Amy forced an over-bright smile. "So when's the big day?"

"December 15th. We're hoping to have this place ready by then. At least partly."

Amy looked at her brother with fondness. Brian, actually getting married! Overcome with a potpourri of emotions, she rushed him with a hug.

"That's just wonderful. Congratulations. I can't wait to meet her."

Amy was quiet on the drive back to the city. Despite her brother's joyful news, a melancholy spread over her. She knew she should be thrilled for Brian, and yet…there was a sense of foreboding. It all sounded just too good. Too neat. Too happy.

Back in the apartment, Brian peeked into the near-empty refrigerator, dismay on his face. "I've gotta get to the store, otherwise we'll starve. Anything in particular you want? Still love macaroni and cheese?"

Amy turned a bleak smile upon her brother.

"Okay, how about tuna salad? PB and J?"

"I guess your cooking skills haven't improved," Amy said, shaking her head. "I hope Judy's good in the kitchen."

Brian grinned. "So what if I ate 366 granola bars last year. At least I gave up French fries." He began searching through the kitchen cabinets. "Hey, here's some spaghetti. We're saved."

"In a *can*?"

"Of course. Why, you suddenly allergic to cans or something?"

Amy smiled to herself. Drew would go hungry to avoid eating anything from a can. The closest he ever got to spaghetti was eating pasta *Prima Vera* at Mario's in the high-rent district.

"It's okay. I was just kidding."

Brian looked closely at the label for a moment before announcing, "Hey, it's got little meatballs in it." But after another glance at his sister's face, he put the can back on the shelf and grabbed his keys from the counter. "I'll be back in awhile. You take a nap or something."

While he was away, Amy read the newspaper. She went directly to the classifieds, hoping to spot an opening for a part time teaching job nearby. Yet nothing fit. Discouraged and unsettled, Amy lay down on the couch and stared at the ceiling.

What was it about Brian's lighthouse that she found so disturbing? She recalled her brother's bright, exuberant smile as he ran his hands along the cracked walls, the chipping paint, the pocked breadboard in the kitchen. Why should she be anything but delighted for him, that he had discovered such an obvious treasure? Surely it wasn't the news of his engagement that depressed her. Brian had to be the most deserving person she knew.

Closing her eyes, she recalled climbing the black, narrow staircase to the top. She could almost feel the crisp wind against her cheeks; feel the stinging in her eyes as she squinted into the breeze.

Amy wasn't even aware that she had fallen asleep until her cell phone roused her thirty minutes later. The sound of Drew's voice had her sitting bolt upright in an instant.

"*Why*, Amy? Why did you do this? Is there some way we can work this out?"

Amy clutched at her stomach, leaning over it in an attempt to stop the quivering inside.

"There's really nothing to work out, Drew. Let's just leave it at that."

"Are you in the city? I can be there by dinner. Meet me. Meet me at the St. Francis Hotel."

"Don't make this difficult. You-you just stay there on your side of the country and I'll stay here. The duplex is available if you want to rent it out or maybe give it to someone else."

"That place is *ours*. Why would I want someone else there? Come on, Amy." Irritation crept into Drew's voice.

"You tell me. Or doesn't your new girlfriend like California?"

There was silence on the line. Amy covered her mouth briefly to stifle a sob. "Anyway, I won't be going back. Your credit cards and keys, and wine rack and skis are all there. Your 'A-list' address book of California buddies is there. You won't see any signs that I've ever been there."

"I don't understand any of this."

"Well that makes two of us. Jessie didn't understand, either, when she stopped by last week. To see you. She brought her husband, you know. Or didn't your little friend mention that? Too bad. Jessie always liked you, Drew."

"Jessie? She was *here*?"

"You've never been very good at playing dumb. Good-bye Drew. I wish things could be different."

Amy pressed her forehead against the phone after hanging up, as if afraid it would rise back up somehow. Hot tears flooded her eyes. At least it was over.

Her college days seemed eons ago, and yet Amy remembered with disquieting clarity the day Andrew Richards had stopped her in the parking lot to ask directions. His smile was sweet, his expression sincere. She hadn't hesitated to give him her phone number. Jessie and Roxanne had chided her for it later.

"What does it hurt?" she had asked, coyly reminding them both that any man pursuing an MBA had to be a good catch. Their stunned expressions made her laugh.

"I hope you're not serious," Jessie had warned her.

I guess I was. Serious and stupid.

Amy laid her arm across her eyes and sighed, still reminiscing and regretting. How many times had she and Drew broken up? Her teaching credential had seemed so meager next to that shining MBA. Her young pupils were so full of eager promise, yet so insignificant in the shadow of Drew's brokerage opportunities. Still, his youthful smile had charmed her. And when Wall Street offered Drew that prestigious address, he swept her off to a candlelight dinner at Chasen's and proposed. Then he went to New York. They'd never found time to get married.

She'd tried the East Coast scene, spending her summer vacation walking and riding taxis all over Manhattan. Boldly and optimistically filed a change of address card at the post office. And as if to emphasize her commitment to Drew and his new life, she'd cut and bleached her hair.

But it didn't work for her. By September she was back in California, in the cute little duplex in Carmel. Drew didn't seem to mind the every-other-weekend commute, and Amy spent holidays in New York when she could get away. It was a tentative arrangement, with neither of them talking too much about the future. Maybe they should have.

If I had pinned him down, I would have found out sooner. Before this awful situation. Before this...

Amy could not bring herself to blame the baby, but she did blame herself. These days, there was no excuse for an unwanted pregnancy. She couldn't even blame

Drew. It was as much her own responsibility as it was his. But she could blame him for his infidelity.

She thought she would feel better in the morning, but when Monday dawned over the bay, Amy only felt worse. Brian's note on the counter reminded her that someone had to work to keep the lights on and spaghetti in the cabinet.

Half-heartedly again perusing the classifieds and sipping coffee, Amy's mind wandered back to the coast and the aging white sentry on the cliff. In Brian's stack of mail were the escrow papers he had shown her the night before, naming him and Judy as the purchasers of the lighthouse. The mortgage would be 75% of the purchase price, and he had already put up a significant deposit. Still, the balance of the down payment was hefty. *It's in the bank.* Almost all of it, he had assured her, One more paycheck and he would close escrow.

Perhaps if she went back into the lighthouse, she could come to terms with her misgivings.

It wasn't long before Amy found herself back at the coast, her tires crunching over the gravel drive leading to the old wooden clapboard garage on the bluff.

The key still hung on the bent nail under the front porch risers. Nearly frozen with powdery rust, the lock turned crankily and Amy swung open the heavy wooden front door, taking a step backward rather than inside as a rush of stale air clouded around her. Coughing a little, she boldly crossed the threshold.

Passing up the kitchen and eating area, Amy toured the smallest bedroom first. The room was nearly bare, with a twin bed in one corner and ladder-back chair against the wall. A tattered braided rug roughly centered on the floor, and faded cotton curtains hung tiredly at the two small windows. The closet appeared empty except for a couple of disintegrating boxes amidst copious spider webs.

Not much larger than the first, the other bedroom housed a double bed, a small boudoir dresser and mirror, and a rocking chair. This room, on the back of the house, contained only one bare window facing the sea.

The closet door was closed. Although she considered her own curiosity absurd, Amy tugged hard on the closet doorknob, forcing groans and creaks from ancient hinges that had been sleeping for a very long time. She was rewarded with a surprising sight.

"Whoa..." Expecting the small space to be occupied by dust bunnies and eight-legged creatures, Amy was astounded to find half the closet space still filled with clothing. Women's dresses, blouses, and pants hung from the rod, surprisingly clean despite the fact that they had obviously been hanging a very long time. Amy pulled one, then another, out for inspection, her eyes wide in amazement. Small flowered prints, high-waisted gowns her Aunt Lucy used to call "granny" dresses when Amy was a child. Bell-bottomed trousers with colorful trim around the cuffs; loose cotton day dresses in Hawaiian prints; a fur-trimmed vest.

Holding one particularly gaudy dress up against her

chest, Amy turned toward the foggy vanity mirror and stooped to get a look at herself. Her own silly reflection made her laugh. Tossing the dress to the bed, she pulled the fur vest from its hanger and hurriedly slipped it on, still grinning at herself in the mirror.

"These are authentic," she murmured, turning from side to side. "They must be almost forty years old…"

She wasn't sure if she really saw something in the mirror, or if it was just the overwhelming feeling of being watched that made her spin around and face the window behind her. Although its pane was clouded with crusted sea salt and debris, Amy could see nothing amiss with the view, no spectators watching her modeling debut. Still, her uneasiness remained and she quickly re-hung the clothing before closing the closet door.

The kitchen was the same as she remembered it. What she didn't recall was a small nook off the eating area, adjacent to the door leading up the tower steps. The nook housed a small, built-in desk, and Amy was intrigued by its design. It seemed a higher quality than the other parts of the house, possibly added after the completion of the main structure. Definitely a different craftsman had designed and constructed the desk, shelves, and drawers. Even the chair was honed from the same beautiful mahogany wood. She made a mental note to ask Brian about it.

Eyeing the tower door with dread, Amy turned the doorknob and was surprised to find it locked. She did not remember Brian locking it when they left. Still, a sense of relief spread over her. She didn't really want to climb those steps today.

Back on the bluff, she stared down at the tower for several minutes, letting the breeze rush against her face. The lighthouse held a mystical, hypnotizing aura of its own, despite its ominous stature. And although the feeling of disquiet remained, Amy knew she was captivated. Point Surrender was drawing her in.

Chapter Three

The wind had held steady since *the Fancy Dream* lifted her sails at Grogan's Head, California. Case normally would not have begun such an ambitious journey on his own, but then he wasn't doing many things quite the usual way these days. Still, his initial doubts faded as the Pacific made calm her waters and the boat nearly sailed herself south.

Strenuous, yes; but it was good, physical work and the salt air cleared his head. Navigating around San Francisco Bay, usually a dreaded challenge, seemed effortless and before long the *Dream* was drifting lazily toward Monterey. He'd put in there for the night and a hot meal. Some of that famous chowder, perhaps. Sourdough bread. Case's stomach rumbled its approval. Breathing deep, Case scrutinized the western horizon, where the sun would soon dip into the sea with a loud hiss and lots of steam…a childhood fantasy he hadn't thought about in years. He closed his eyes and tried to recall the picture book depicting that boiling seawater bubbling around the descending ball of fire.

The wind died. A sudden death, so sudden that Case's eyes blinked open and he abruptly stood. Looking around, he saw the waters around the boat smoothing out like lake water. *The Dream* came to a near halt.

"Well, shit." Looking up at the limp mainsail and jib,

he started to trim them. He'd wait it out and relax a bit. There was no current, no waves, nothing to take him off course. He could motor for a while, if the wind didn't return soon. Pulling a Rolling Rock from the ice chest, he laid back on the bench cushions and closed his eyes.

He must have dozed. For when he next opened his eyes, they fixed upon a steep, craggy cliff with the setting sun at his back. He didn't move at first, so complete was his shock and confusion. The boat's proximity to the coast alarmed him, yet still Case remained frozen to the spot. The water no longer looked like glass. It churned and roiled around him, pushing the *Dream* closer to the huge jutting rocks at the base of the cliff. How could this be? Still no wind. Nothing made sense.

Suddenly propelled into action, Case quickly made his way to the helm and started the engine. He had to get the sailboat away from the rocks and back out to sea. Struggling, sputtering, the motor whirled to life. Case grabbed the wheel, turning the *Dream* about and motoring away from the dangerous shoreline. Once he was several yards away, he turned to look back at the treacherous cliffs. His breath caught in his chest. There, about halfway to the top of the cliff, stood a blindingly white lighthouse perched on an outcropping below the bluff. Case's eyes widened in awe.

"How the hell did I get *here*?" he muttered, staring hard at the lighthouse. Behind him, the engine quietly died, and the waters around the boat once again flattened into an aqua silk sheet. *This is nuts.* Case shook himself free of the trance and turned to restart the motor. After

Anne Carter

three fruitless attempts, Case pushed the hair from his forehead and sat down. He was sweating, frustrated and disoriented. Unable to resist, he again looked back to the high bluff and the lighthouse, and felt himself shudder. "Of all the damned places I could end up." He was about to retry the ignition when a movement drew his attention back to the grounds surrounding the lighthouse. A figure, a man perhaps, stood on the bluff, his back to the sea. Case squinted his eyes, hand poised on the key. *What the hell?* Case watched in horror as the man felt backwards with such force that he literally flew off the cliff, soaring in a great arc, over and down, down, down into the swirling waters at the bottom of the cliff. Stunned for the second time in minutes, Case frantically twisted the key. "Come on! Come on, you sonuvabitch!" Finally the engine came to life.

Still incredulous, Case hurriedly maneuvered his boat around and back toward the rocks. He dropped anchor as close to the bluff as he dared, then dove into the water. Swimming hard to the spot where he thought the man entered the surf, he dove beneath the surface and scanned the murky water, turning left, right, coming up for air, and then diving again. He had to be here. Finding nothing, he swam south, thinking perhaps the current had carried the man away. Still there was no one, no body, no flailing swimmer. Only the churning, heaving waves, cloudy with sand as they crashed over the jagged rocks at the base of the cliffs.

Finally, realizing he could do no more, Case made his way back to the sloop and hurled himself onto her deck.

He rested only a moment, then turned and sat up to face the coast. His breathing was heavy, labored. He reached for and grabbed a towel to drag across his face.

It didn't take him long to notice that the *Dream* was listing to starboard. The probable reasons brought a sick feeling to his stomach. Once again he dropped himself over the side, this time swimming down to inspect the hull of his boat. His fears were realized; he could have pitched a softball through the hole he found in the hull, and there was a chunk out of the keel.

Unable to curse adequately underwater, Case let out a string of mental obscenities before returning to the surface. Once again hoisting himself aboard, he quickly gathered together the items he would need to provide a temporary patch. This time he snagged his mask and snorkel before diving, taking an extra moment to damn the fates that had messed with his day. Messed with it bad.

It was an hour past sunset when the *Fancy Dream* limped into Newburg Harbor. As soon as she was safely moored, Case reported the scene on the cliff and his own attempts to recover the victim. The Sheriff's deputy, however, seemed unimpressed. "We sent a coupl'a guys down there when you called from the marina. Didn't see nothin' much...now you say this guy just tumbled backward off the cliff?"

"He...either stumbled or was pushed."

"Um-hmm. Did you see anyone else on the cliff?"

"No. I didn't."

"Okay. What was this purported victim wearing?"

Case paused, trying to bring the memory into focus. "Uh…nothing remarkable, nothing bright, maybe gray or tan, blue jeans, you know, like anyone off the street."

"Did you hear anything? Any voices?"

"I was out about 100 yards. There's wind. No, I didn't hear anything." There hadn't been any wind, Case remembered. But it didn't seem prudent to share that tidbit of information.

"You, uh, doing any drinking out there, Mr. McKenna?"

"No. Well, yeah, earlier in the day I had one beer. Sea was calm, I was waiting for some wind, sails were flat. I took a nap."

"How long had you been awake when you saw this…this incident?"

"I'd just woken up. Look, if you don't want to believe me, fine. I'll go on my way. I just thought, in case someone turns up missing, or turns up *dead*, for that matter, you ought to know about it."

The deputy narrowed his eyes slightly, tilted his head. "You from Southern California?"

"No. I'm just down from Grogan's Head. Near Crescent City."

"I see. Well we do appreciate your making the report. You staying here in town?"

"No longer than tonight if I can help it. My hull looks like a cannon ball went through it."

The deputy was writing and did not look up. "We'll do some more checking at Point Surrender. Look for clues, that sort of stuff. Just do us a favor and let us know where we can reach you, in case we have any more questions."

"Fine." Case picked up his duffel and walked out the door. He had to find a place where he could change out of his still soaking wet Levi's.

It was late afternoon when Amy parked her car in the near-empty lot at Riley's Rib Place on Coast Highway. Only a mile back from the turn-off to Point Surrender, Riley's was popular with the locals, according to Brian. Amy decided to check it out.

She picked a small table in the corner and sat. The tables were knotty pine, heavily varnished and shiny.

"What can I get you?" the man called Riley asked, as he approached her table. "Looks like you could use a brew."

Amy smiled. "Nope. Not today. I'd love some lemonade if you have it."

"You got it."

Riley quickly brought her drink and stood expectantly while Amy took a sip.

"*Mmmm.* It's great."

"Anything else? A sandwich? Chili? Some soup, maybe?"

Amy looked up and smiled, immediately liking the big man with the tired but kindly eyes. "I was thinking about taking some of those ribs home," she offered, gesturing toward the wide plastic banner hanging above the bar. "That 'Bucket-O'-Ribs' sounds great. My brother is eternally hungry."

Riley grinned. "A man after my own heart. Do I know your brother?"

"Brian Winslow. He's an ensign with the Coast Guard. He lives–*we live*–in the city."

"Yeah, I know Brian. Comes in here with his girlfriend. Nice guy. Always talking about the lighthouse."

"You're telling me. Did you know he and Judy are buying it?"

"Point Surrender up for sale? Wow. That's weird." Riley shook his head slowly. "They gonna live there?"

"Eventually, I guess. They want to fix it up."

Riley shrugged. "Well. To each his own. You want the large bucket or the trough?"

"Whichever is bigger."

Amy watched as Riley made his way back to the bar, calling into the kitchen for the ribs and picking up the lemonade pitcher off the counter. In moments he was back, refilling her glass.

"Nobody's lived there for a long, long time," he said, almost to himself. "Wouldn't want to, m'self."

"Why is that? It has a lot of potential. You know, the view is stunning."

"Man died there, right in the house, been almost twenty-five years. The keeper."

"Really?" Amy's eyes grew round and she put her glass down. "How?"

"Fell. Down the stairs. Terrible accident. 'Course, folks around here say he was drunk. The Coast Guard, they came in and motorized the whole deal, y'know, computerized it or something, so no one's had to live there. Then, 'bout 5 years ago, they built a second light station down the way a little. Turned this one off, and there it sits."

"My..." Amy whispered. Maybe that explained the aura, the uneasiness she felt in the house. "That's just awful. Did he have any family?"

"Not sure. I never heard the whole story. Miz Hastings mighta lived here then. She might know a thing or two. I know one thing, the sailors been complaining they never shoulda turned it off. That new light isn't much good, they say."

"I wonder if Brian knows about that."

Riley shrugged. "Could be. Probably don't matter to him. And by rights, it shouldn't. It's all in the past. If he can make that place work again, more power to him, right?"

"Right," Amy agreed, if unenthusiastically. "Right."

An hour later Amy tiredly climbed the steps to the front door of Brian's second floor apartment. The shoes were off before she reached the kitchen. Setting the oven on "warm," she deposited the cardboard bucket of ribs and then wandered to the living room. The large, worn easy chair invited her to collapse. Forcing her thoughts toward dinner, she wondered what she could put with the ribs from the odd assortment of groceries that Brian had bought. For just a moment, she longed for the nights when she and Drew would 'paint the town,' wining and dining their way through the best restaurants money could buy.

Indeed, being a New York stockbroker had its perks, and Amy had often felt like royalty at his side.

She shook her head. She could not afford to think about that now. Amy closed her eyes and laid her head back. Her thoughts returned to the conversation with Riley and the history of Point Surrender. Mentally she again traveled back to the house, saw the closet door and the women's clothing; they must have belonged to the keeper's wife. *But why are they still hanging there?* She shivered a little, remembering the feeling of being watched and the shadow that had passed by the window. Riley's story had given her fear legs.

She couldn't wait for Brian to get home so she could tell him, and quiz him about what he knew. There was more to Point Surrender than met the eye, and she was suddenly determined to find out the rest.

On the kitchen counter she found a scratch pad and pen. Frowning, Amy fought to remember the details of Riley's tale. There was a woman who knew...Hastings! Quickly Amy jotted the name down, and then retrieved the telephone directory from Brian's small desk. She scoured the 'H' page, and found only one listing in Newburg, that of Hastings House Bed and Breakfast. She copied the address and phone number down, and went looking for a map.

"Good evening, Mr. McKenna. I took the liberty of putting your clean laundry in your room. I hope you don't mind."

Case McKenna forced a quick grin. "Thanks, Miss

Hastings. I appreciate that." He started up the stairs, but paused when the innkeeper spoke again.

"Can I fix you something to eat? You look pretty tired."

"Thanks, no, I..."

"Got some leftover beef stroganoff in the kitchen. The other guests have all gone out for dinner. Why don't I just heat it up, with maybe a little buttered bread? And a nice glass of some local wine. Do you good."

Case rubbed his forehead. She was such a nice lady, one who should be somebody's mother. With a short sigh, he acquiesced. "I'll just wash up then. Thanks."

It didn't take him long to return to the dining room, his stomach leading the way.

"You looking for work, Mr. McKenna?" she asked, putting the steaming plate down on the lace-covered dining table before him.

"Quite the contrary. Running from it, I'm afraid." The smell of the stroganoff made him feel like he hadn't eaten for days. Maybe he hadn't. After mooring his boat in disgust, he'd spent the rest of the day walking off his anger. "This looks great."

"So you're on vacation?"

"In a manner of speaking, yes. I'm taking a month off. Thought I'd sail on down the coast to San Diego, maybe Mexico. Unfortunately, my boat isn't as seaworthy as when I started out. Had to dock her down at the marina. Gonna have to do a little repair work before I can go on."

"Well, our gain then. Your first time in Newburg?"

"Ah, no. Stayed here once briefly as a kid. You been

here long?"

"My brother, Matthew, used to own this house. Been in the family for over a hundred and fifty years. I moved here from Colorado, oh, twenty-some years ago. Matthew's since passed away. After he died, it got too quiet and I started taking in borders."

Case nodded, eyeing the antique-filled dining room as he ate. His attention was particularly captured by a small piano tucked into the bay window at the front of the room.

"Isn't it beautiful? Matthew brought it home from the local school when it burned down. It was damaged and the school didn't want it anymore. He did some lovely restoration work on it."

"It's in great shape. Your brother lived here all his life?"

"Yessir. He was a custodian at the school, and then he worked as a craftsman. Quiet man, but kind."

"I'm sorry for your loss."

"What kind of work do you do, Mr. McKenna?"

"I'm a professional wanderer."

Miss Hastings smiled but waited patiently for a better answer. Case ran his fingers through his shaggy brown locks.

"When I'm not running, I guess they call me an oceanographer. I'm the guy who figures out how many little fish it takes to feed a bigger fish, the guy who's always fighting the oil companies, and the guy they call when there's a beached whale in San Francisco."

"Ooh, how exciting!"

Case nodded. "Sometimes it is. Sometimes it's...no fun." Of course, his mind flashed on Amanda and her last few minutes. He remembered the moment, the exact second when she had gone from a living, breathing creature to a still, lifeless body. He shook his head. "There are times when I wish I was a bartender, or maybe the guy who paints the Golden Gate Bridge. I don't know."

"I'm sure you love what you do, Mr. McKenna. And I'll just bet you're sorely missed when you're not there."

He smiled. He wondered what his hostess would say if she knew he'd been asked to take a leave of absence.

As usual, the minute he fell asleep he began to dream. He had gotten pretty good at dodging the nightmares in recent years. But that all changed when Amanda died. Died in his arms, no less. Only the most recent in a long series of losses, and he had hoped it would get easier somehow.

He wondered if surviving loss would ever become commonplace, something to be proud of. No, he thought, I'll never get over it, will never accept that death is a part of life.

Now, in his sleep, he was swimming. Graceful, his body sleek and well defined as he cut cleanly through the water, following Amanda as she swam ahead of him. Playfully spinning onto her back, then spinning again in a water ballet reminiscent of mermaids in days of old. Whoever said mermaids were mythical had never seen a manatee diving and whirling beneath the surface.

But Case had. He marveled at her agility, her sense of

fun despite the injuries that had brought her to be under his care. Amanda had to be in pain, he knew, and yet she traveled around the tank in apparent joy. In no hurry, seemingly happy to be alive, Amanda took Case as her playmate and savior.

He smiled, his dream comforting and serene; so real, so like the days just two weeks before when he thought Amanda was truly on the mend. And then the water began to brighten.

A light, blindingly bright, shone in his face. Murky clouds swirled up out of nowhere, blurring his view of the mermaid swimming before him. Gray clouds, now pink and turning red all around him. He stopped swimming and began thrashing about, trying to catch a glimpse of the manatee as she began drifting down. Down to the bottom of the sea. Panic overtook him, his arms flailing, as if he could stop the redness from spreading. As if he could push away the darkness. As if he could save Amanda from certain death.

Sweating, heart pounding, Case opened his eyes once more only to see the dim shape of the small glass ceiling lamp in his rented room. Amanda was gone, and with her had gone his newly found peace of mind.

Thursday afternoon brought rain, snarling San Francisco's traffic and delaying flights both in and out of SFO. It was a wonder, Amy thought, that people continued to visit the city by the bay with its reputation for such bad weather. Still, Judy arrived in time for dinner and the three splurged on a nice restaurant in town.

"So what do you think of our lighthouse?" Judy asked her soon-to-be sister-in-law. "Isn't it beautiful?"

"*Mmm*. Yes. Wonderful," Amy said, nodding and taking a quick sip of water. "It's a real treasure."

"Well, we know there's a lot of work ahead of us, but it's just so exciting."

Brian grinned at Judy, clearly adoring her. And Amy could see why. From her natural, flowing, auburn locks to her sensible but stylish low-heeled shoes, Judy was Brian's ideal woman. Clear thinking, genuinely friendly, not a vain bone in her slender body.

"I was wondering," Amy began, keeping her tone nonchalant, "do you know much about the history of Point Surrender?"

"History? Sure. There are all kinds of legends and lore about the place, dating back to the mid-nineteenth century. Something about a famous privateer and his fiancée leaping to their deaths from the bluff, back in...oh, 1864, I think. You know the original tower was damaged in the 1906 quake, but pretty well restored. In the seventies one of the local carpenters built that cool little desk in there."

"How about later history? I mean, recently–the last keepers. Do you know who they were?"

"Oh, you mean the *Jenners*. Yeah. We know about them." Brian took a moment to push some food around his plate. "That's a weird story. I guess the guy had some real problems. It's not uncommon, you know–the 'keeps' were so isolated. They used to be, anyway–and people would get into some bad habits. When we get done cleaning the place up, you won't know that anything ever happened there." Brian reached across the table and covered Judy's hand with his own, and she smiled.

"Did he–did he have any family? A wife, maybe?" Amy's need for answers pushed aside her usual decorum.

Brian turned his gaze upon his sister. "Yes. But she wasn't living there at the time of the...accident."

"Oh. I just wondered because there are some women's clothes in one of the closets."

"Really? I don't remember seeing them." He turned toward Judy. "Weren't the closets empty last week?"

Judy nodded. "Bare except for cobwebs. I thought."

Brian sighed, shrugged. "Who knows. One of the lieutenants' families stayed there last year for a short spell. Maybe they left them there. Maybe we missed them. Maybe...hell, someone could be shacked up there."

"I hope not." Amy decided not to question her brother further. It seemed wrong. Perhaps she wouldn't contact the Hastings woman after all.

She thought she would feel awkward with Judy spending the night in Brian's bed, but was pleased to discover that nothing seemed more natural than the two of them turning in together. It reminded her, however, that eventually she would have to find her own lodging, which ultimately meant that unless she returned to Carmel, she would have to find a job. A job she could do while pregnant. Amy could think that far in advance, but when she envisioned herself trying to work and support an infant, her imagination locked up.

It was a vision she could not conjure, and she fell asleep engulfed in unhappy dread.

Amy slept later than usual, despite the discomfort of the lumpy Futon. Drearily she read a good-bye note from Judy, whom by now had left on a flight to Paris. Brian had buoy inspection duty and would check in later. The newspaper lay already open on the kitchen bar. Amy thumbed lazily through it, wishing she could motivate herself to look harder for a job. She had decided that going back to Carmel alone was not an option.

Her eyes casually sought the "part time" column, and there it was: an ad for a waitress, some experience necessary. The job would not have normally caught her eye except for the name of the restaurant needing help. Riley's Ribs in Newburg.

Case didn't feel like working on the boat. After a fitful night and a huge ration of Hastings House hotcakes, he decided to walk through Newburg and down to the wharf. He hoped the sights of the small seaport would help clear his troubled mind, and gratefully accepted the Thermos bottle of hot coffee thrust on him by Miss Hastings.

Despite the mid-morning hour, the town was sleepy and slow. Still, it seemed like any ordinary day. Early fishermen were making their way back with the catch of the day.

Wandering along the wharf, Case found himself in front of the small boat rental booth. He pulled his wallet from his hip pocket and spread it open.

"How 'bout that little dinghy over there. Motor work?"

"Yep. You gonna do some fishin'? Kinda late."

"Nope. No fishing. Just a little speculating."

"Suit yerself. Back by five."

"Got it."

Case motored out to the edge of the small bay, where the water was still reasonably calm, and dropped anchor. Amid the clanging of buoys and screaming of gulls, he settled back and poured out a cup of steaming java.

From his vantage point in the bay, he could see his sailboat, *Fancy Dream*, moored near the dock. The temporary patch on the hull was just that: temporary. Good enough to keep her from sinking, not good enough to last him to Mexico. And he didn't feel like spending his vacation with his sleeves rolled up.

In fact, he didn't really feel like sailing south now. He didn't feel like doing anything at all.

The clouds above him drifted by, and he imagined them to be like the segments of his life, moving slowly but definitely, changing shape and density with the breeze that drove them.

He again looked back at the *Dream*. Why here? What unseen force prevailed, causing him to land here? Newburg. A place he had never wanted to see again.

With some difficulty, Case arranged the dirty blanket in the bottom of the dinghy so that he could lie back and close his eyes. Removing his sunglasses, he threw his arm across his eyes and tried to relax. Indeed, the gentle rocking of the boat, the calling of the birds and the sunshiny breeze created a sanctitude he sorely needed.

The smell of the ocean worked on him like a tonic. His thoughts invariably returned to the oceanarium, his pal Jack and the lost manatee. Jack was right, he decided. *We did all we could for Amanda. I can't take responsibility for that too.*

Maybe veterinary medicine was the wrong business. Trying to patch together those innocent creatures, maimed by the dregs of mankind, was painful. He got too involved, too personal. After all, he had long ago decided that people could not be trusted to be there when you needed them. He now realized, not even his cherished sea animals could fill the void he felt inside. He was alone. He would always be alone, and the sooner he accepted that fact, the better.

Case drifted in and out of twilight, dreaming about his brief years in Idaho when he had truly been happy; wishing he could somehow return to those days.

Just after noon, his reverie was interrupted by the sound of approaching boats.

"Sure, I've got lots of experience. My mother died when I was twelve, and I practically raised my father and my brother."

Riley Paul grinned at her from across the varnished bar counter, immaculately clean but dull from years of scrubbing.

"Twelve, you say? My mom died just after I turned thirteen. I got a little brother too." Riley gave her a searching perusal, and then slapped the counter. "You've got the job. When did you say the baby's due?"

Amy colored at his frankness. "I'm–I'm just newly pregnant. It'll be awhile. I'd rather people didn't know, if you don't mind."

"No problem. You can start anytime you want, the sooner the better. My wife, well, maybe you know–she's sick and the doc doesn't want her working too much. You know how it is."

"No, I didn't know. I'm sorry."

"She's getting chemo and all that stuff, and Lord knows she's a strong woman. She'll be okay."

Amy nodded. Everyone had a story. But she liked Riley and was immensely thankful for the job. Five hours a day, five days a week, with Tuesdays and Thursdays off.

"I'll see you Sunday, then."

Amy gave her new employer a little salute and a smile, and then trotted out to her car. Once behind the wheel, she sighed before starting the ignition. It was a long trek back to the city.

On a whim, she drove slowly through Newburg instead of taking the turnoff to the highway back to San Francisco. The population had to be less than 3,500, she decided, eyeing the single gas station, the two stop signals and the small, original McDonald's. It had to be the lone fast-food place in town.

Highwater Street seemed to be the main drag off of Coast Highway. Home-based businesses included a beauty-and-barber shop, an insurance, notary, and real estate office, and a psychic/tarot card reader. The house at the end of the block was a large, three-story Victorian with a weathered, hand-painted sign in the front garden.

Amy stopped her car in front of Hastings House. She leaned forward and peered up at the beautiful but aging home housing Newburg's only bed and breakfast, reckoning it had to be the same Hastings Riley had told her about. Yet she hesitated. Perhaps the secrets of the lighthouse were meant to stay secret. And anyway, the woman would most likely think she was crazy even to care. Reluctantly, Amy put the car back into gear and headed home.

On route back to the city, she thought about Riley's wife. She did not remember seeing a woman in the place before, and wondered how long she had been ill. Even though Riley seemed entirely open and approachable, she felt uncomfortable asking–at least for now. But she was reminded that she had one more thing on her agenda, to find a local doctor. Like it or not, she had an unborn child to take care of, and take care of it she would.

Amy knew that she would eventually have to face Drew and tell him about the baby. But the longer she could keep that information from him, the better. She needed time to adjust, to get used to the concept of being a mother, albeit a single one.

Perhaps Judy could recommend a doctor. She made a mental note to ask her when she returned to the city.

In the mail was an envelope from Drew. Overnight delivery, of course. Inside, a note informed her that he would arrive in a few days. The "market" was in chaos, as usual, but he needed to see her right away.

Her stomach lurched. *Is this morning sickness, or am I just reacting to Drew?* The kitchen clock read 6:30 P.M. Not morning, she mused.

Steeling herself against the nausea, Amy began unpacking the tubs of fried chicken and potato salad Riley had sent home with his newest employee.

"Brian is going to love this," she murmured, again glancing at the clock. But where was he?

As if in answer, the phone on the counter rang. Pressing one hand to her stomach, Amy lifted the receiver to her ear.

Chapter Four

The wreckage was still burning as Case McKenna pulled full throttle and pointed his struggling rental boat toward the harbor. Still reeling from the fact that he'd witnessed two accidents–or two crimes–within twenty-four hours, he kept one eye trained on the latest victim. The groan from the man curled against the hull beside him was at least temporary evidence that he had survived the collision. Glancing briefly behind him, Case could see the remains of the smoking patrol boat sinking into the depths of the Pacific. The other vessel, a high-speed ski boat, had disappeared.

"Hang on, buddy. We'll get you some help. Hang on." Case gripped the rudder tightly with false confidence. He prayed he could get help for the young sailor in time.

"So, Mr. McKenna, you tryin' out for the part of super hero these days?" the deputy asked, just a hint of sarcasm in his high-pitched voice.

"I told you. I was just out for a little R & R. I heard the boats coming, I turned around, they crashed together, and the ski boat took off. I pulled the kid out of the water and brought him in. That's all there is to tell." Case stared, his blue eyes level and unflinching as the deputy jotted still more words into his small notepad. "Are we done?"

"Almost, Mr. McKenna. Now, the color of the ski

boat was?"

"Black. Or dark purple."

"Two people aboard?"

"Two. I think. It happened so fast, and I was tired. I'd been out awhile, taking a nap."

"Tired? Had you been drinking again, Mr. McKenna?"

"No! Of course not." Case dragged his fingers through his dark sienna hair and sighed, a sardonic smile coming to his lips. "Well, actually, yes. I'd put away a whole Thermos full of joe."

The deputy looked up from his notes. "You said you're new in town?"

"You might recall I'm only here until my boat is repaired. I'm staying in Newburg right now. You can get me at the Hastings House."

"Fine. Thanks, McKenna. By the way, what do you do?"

"I'm a vet."

"Middle East?"

Case chuckled to himself and stood. "No. I doctor-up sick sea mammals. But that doesn't usually include humans."

The deputy nodded, eyebrows raised. "Oh. Well. We'll be in touch."

Case nodded and headed for the door, pausing before exiting the police station. "Any word on the kid?"

"His name is Brian Winslow, he's with the Coast Guard. I guess he was giving chase to a couple of alleged vandals. The ski boat's outboard donked him pretty good as it went over. Too bad. Only twenty-four years old, too."

Case groaned inwardly. Ten years younger than himself. "Anybody catch the jerks?"

"Nope. Not yet."

Case shook his head and left the station.

He walked the few blocks to the front doors at Roth General Hospital.

"Mr. Winslow is still in surgery. You can have a seat in the waiting room if you'd like," the receptionist told him. Case nodded. He liked small towns. Big city hospitals were cold and indifferent, adhering a little too close to the letter of the privacy law.

Grabbing a cup of all day, industrial strength coffee from the pot in the corner, he settled into the empty waiting room and picked up a two-year-old copy of *Managing Your Health*. He skipped the unconvincing article about why he should give up carbs and began reading the praises of laser eye surgery.

He wasn't alone for long. The petite woman joining him had layered, almost-shoulder-length ash blonde hair. He couldn't see her eyes clearly behind the small, oval, tinted lenses she wore, but her pink nose belied the fact that she had been crying. She, too, picked up a magazine and flipped through it nervously, occasionally glancing his way. Her obvious anxiety made Case tense also, and he struggled to concentrate.

A nurse had appeared in the doorway, causing both the young woman and Case to start. "Amy Winslow?"

"I'm Amy."

"Doctor Barnett would like to talk to you. He'll be out in just a moment." The nurse smiled and turned.

"Wait. Is Brian–is he okay?"

"He's out of surgery, and holding his own. That's all I can tell you." The nurse smiled a smile that said she knew more, and took her leave.

Amy stood and walked to the window, staring out while clenching her laced fingers together. Case stole a look at her, noticing she had finally removed the sunglasses. She caught him looking and absently brushed her hair from her face.

"Are you here for Brian?" she asked, her voice tentative and quivering.

"Sort of. I just wanted to hear that he's going to make it."

"You must be the man who rescued him. I don't know how to thank you."

"It's not something that deserves thanks. Anyone would have done it." Case closed the magazine and stood up.

"You saved his life. In my book, that deserves all sorts of thanks," Amy said. For a moment it looked as if she might smile, but instead she moistened her lips before speaking again. "He was lucky you were there."

"Yes he was. He shouldn't have been out there chasing those heathens alone. Damned fool thing to do."

Amy tilted her head slightly, her jaw dropping subtly in surprise. "Excuse me?"

Caught in her accusing gaze, Case peered into her eyes and then looked to the floor. Suddenly he felt angry, and he didn't really know why. Maybe it was because her eyes were that rich, chocolaty-brown like his mother's–eyes that could adore you one minute and destroy you the next. Or maybe it was just that a nice guy like Brian Winslow shouldn't be having surgery on his head at twenty-four, with his life, and a beautiful woman to boot, hanging in the balance.

Dragging his fingers across the stubble on his chin, Case tried to prepare a retraction. Surely this grieving woman didn't deserve his bad manners at a time like this. But he was spared from, or maybe cheated out of, his apology. Dr. Barnett beckoned to Amy from the doorway, and she followed without a word.

Case sat back down, this time on the edge of the seat. He hoped for good news. If not good, at least decent. I did the right thing, he reminded himself. *He was unconscious. He would have drowned.* Replaying the scene in his mind, he saw the floating wreckage, the blue and white cushions, the shattered windshield, and the broken hull. He saw Winslow hanging into the water, one foot caught in the semi-coiled tie rope on what was left of the small craft. There had been no time to spare in getting Brian out of the water–he may have already filled his lungs with water. No time to worry about spinal cord injuries or punctured organs, broken ribs or skull fractures. Case knew, in more detail than he cared to remember, about all those possible traumas, but his training also taught him to make quick assessments and to act swiftly.

A small shriek from the office across the hall pierced the memory like an arrow through a balloon. It was followed by sobbing, the heart-wrenching despair of a woman grieving the fate of her beloved.

Case stood and left the hospital.

Amy didn't remember driving to Roth General Hospital. In fact, she later remembered almost nothing of the time between the phone call and the moment she entered Brian's hospital room where he lay swathed in bandages and connected to tubes. He was nearly unrecognizable.

"He's had a pretty severe head trauma," the doctor said. "He's going back into surgery in just a moment. You can wait and we'll advise you the minute he's out."

Trance-like, Amy had watched helplessly as they wheeled her brother quickly down the hall and through the double swinging doors into the operating room.

A man seated on a bench in the hallway stood and cleared his throat.

"Miss Winslow? I'm Deputy Sheriff Carnahan. I just need to ask you a few questions."

Amy nodded. Her knees threatening to give way, she sat down on the bench and listened to the deputy's queries, answering the best she could.

"He's lived in San Francisco since he left home. Maybe seven years."

"Anybody gunning for him? Did he make anyone mad that you know of?"

Amy sniffed and straightened her back. "Everybody loves Brian. He doesn't have an enemy in the world. I can't imagine anyone trying to..." Unable to complete her thought, she pressed her lips together.

"He was actually pretty lucky. A guy in a nearby boat pulled him out of the drink. He would have drowned for sure. You visit him very much?"

Amy shook her head, feeling more than a little numb. "Not as much as I should. Our lives are... different. I'm a...*was* a teacher. Our hours are sort of...not compatible." Never mind that Brian would prefer crawling across broken glass to seeing her with Drew.

"Would you like some coffee? Some water maybe?"

"No, thank you. I just need to sit for awhile."

The deputy helped Amy back to the empty waiting room and left her there. The duty nurse looked in on her from time to time, but Amy barely noticed. Her thoughts were jumbled and without continuity. The only clear picture in her mind was that of Brian's lacerated face, partially bandaged as they tore him away from her.

"Are you alone? I mean, do you have other relatives on their way?" The nurse asked her eventually.

"No. No one I can call right now." Amy thought of her father and how he might react to the news. No, better wait until she had something positive to say. But who else? *Judy!*

"Oh, my gosh. I do have to make a call. His fiancée. But I don't know how to reach her."

"Did the admitting clerk give you your brother's things? His wallet, perhaps?"

Of course. Brian's wallet. With shaking fingers, Amy struggled to open the still-soaking wet wallet and quickly reviewed its contents. Finally, a soggy airline card appeared with Judy's name and a number where she could receive voice mail.

"Brian. Brian, it's Amy. Come on, Brian. It's me. Wake up!"

Amy squeezed her brother's hand insistently, hoping for even the slightest sign that he could hear her. But the fact remained: Brian was still unconscious, still unresponsive to any outside stimulation.

"Miss Winslow, why don't you go on home and get some rest? You've been here all day. I promise, if he even so much as twitches his little finger, I'll call you."

Amy looked at the nurse whose faded blue eyes held sympathy and a touch of sadness.

"I'll go, soon. I just wanted to stay a little while longer. I keep thinking that maybe something I say will touch him somehow, snap him out of it. They say he can hear everything we say, even if he's in a coma."

"That may be true, but it's also true that *you* can only take so much in one day."

With a deep sigh, Amy nodded, then leaned down to kiss Brian's forehead. "I'll be back, you stubborn boy, you."

She crumbled onto the Futon within a half-hour of arriving back at the apartment. Judy's message on her voice mail assured that she would get there as soon as she could, possibly by tomorrow afternoon. Amy hoped so; she had promised Riley she would start work tomorrow, and someone had to be at the hospital in case Brian woke up.

* * *

Waiting tables was no more and no less than Amy thought it would be. The local customers were friendly, but kept pretty much to themselves. The menu was simple, the food served up on time, and overall, she had no complaints. Except for the fact that by Monday evening, her feet were killing her, her fingernails stained a telltale barbecue sauce orange.

She spent every available minute sitting by Brian's side. Judy stayed as long as she could without putting her job in jeopardy, switching flights with friends and using precious few 'sick' days.

Friday night proved the busiest for Riley's. Fortunately, Judy was in for the weekend so Amy could work her first full stint. Harried but always optimistic, Riley nodded his approval whenever he caught her expectant eye. In the kitchen he pulled her aside.

"The fans love ya," he said as Amy prepared to lift a large tray full of potato skins, onion rings and fried zucchini. "How you holding up?"

"Fine. Thanks," she replied, backing through the swinging door with the tray held high. "Watch your back!"

The dining room was crowded. "Here you go." Amy placed the tray in the center of a group of six patrons, all men, amid their cheers and grunts of pleasure. "More beer?"

She counted hands of those assenting, thinking whimsically of her second graders back in Carmel. As she turned toward the bar to fill their orders, an almost familiar face caught her eye. The dark haired stranger from the hospital sat alone in the corner booth, the same booth she had chosen her first time in. She motioned that she would be with him momentarily and he responded with a slight nod.

Amy watched the man from the corner of her eye as she refilled the beer mugs for her customers. Subtly, he seemed to be watching her as well, a fact that unnerved her. She didn't know why.

"What can I get you?" she asked at last, standing before the brooding patron who now turned his face toward hers.

His eyes were a clear, startling blue, his face slightly thin. His hair, a warm, solid brown, fell in unintentional, wavy layers that curled slightly over his collar in the back. Just the shadow of a trim, Gable-esque moustache seemed penciled in on his upper lip. His gaze fixed on her eyes briefly before returning to the plastic coated menu in his hands.

"I'll have a steak sandwich, medium, easy on the mayo, no onions…and whatever light beer you have on tap." Handing the menu to Amy, his eyes again seemed to lock onto hers. She struggled to pull away from the fixation.

"Uh…it stays on the table." She took the menu anyway, reaching across him to slip it into the chrome holder behind the salt and pepper shakers. The move put her close to the man, closer than she had intended, and she hastened to straighten up and back off. "Any fries?"

He shook his head. Amy nodded and awkwardly

wandered back to the kitchen.

"Ri!" she called, once behind the door. "That guy in the corner. You ever see him before?"

Riley peered through the small round window in the kitchen door. "Maybe. Maybe once before, not sure. Not from around here, I can tell you that."

Amy found herself pacing while waiting for the newcomer's sandwich. When at last it was ready, she hurried to bring it to his table. "Can I get you anything else? Ketchup?"

"Uh, I think I have ketchup right here," he said, gesturing to the full condiment rack on the table. "Thanks anyway." He offered a tight, brief smile and Amy smiled back, trying to think of some reason not to walk away. Finding none, she smiled again and turned to go.

"How's Brian doing?" the man asked to her retreating back. Amy spun so quickly she upset a wooden chair at the next table. Comically she reached out to catch the toppling chair, tripping herself in the process and very nearly landing in the booth across from her customer.

Flustered and breathless, Amy steadied herself against the table, then swept the hair from her forehead in enlightenment.

"The hospital. I knew we'd met somewhere before."

"We didn't actually meet. I'm Case McKenna." Case held out his hand, which Amy regarded in surprise before finally grasping it in hers.

"Amy. Amy Winslow. Sorry. I, uh, didn't expect to see you again. Here, I mean. Hi." She looked around at the men at the center table, then to the still bare order window. Their pizza wouldn't be up for another five minutes at least.

"So how is he?"

"Who? Oh! Brian! He's...the same. He hasn't regained consciousness."

"That's tough. I'm sorry."

"Yeah. I, um...well, thank you again for, you know, getting him out so fast. They say he wouldn't have made it at all if you hadn't."

Case shrugged, looking down at his sandwich. Amy glanced over her shoulder again, her mind abuzz with conflicting thoughts and feelings. She felt flushed and confused, and the man sitting in the booth was the cause. She gripped the table for support.

"I guess I could use some steak sauce," he said at last, and Amy hastened back to the counter.

"Ri! Could you take this to table 17?"

Riley looked puzzled but took the A-1 over to Case. Amy busied herself serving pizza and more beer to the Newburg Pin Kings.

Try as she might, Amy could not stop herself from glancing across the room at the corner booth. She hoped that Case did not notice her attention as he finished his meal. Cleaning the bar for the fifth time today, she called to mind the scene in the hospital waiting room and remembered Case's subtle arrogance with chagrin. Still, she was undeniably attracted to those striking, blatantly honest blue eyes. He had, after all, asked after her brother. And now Riley was sitting with the man.

She wished she had taken the steak sauce.

"Hey Amy! Got any more of that apple pie?"

Apple pie? After pizza and beer? Amy forced a smile and nodded brightly at the bowling team captain. "Coming up." As she cut the pie into slices, she wondered how she could get back into Case's gaze. With a grin to herself, she cut one more piece of pie.

After a deep, cleansing breath, Amy dried her moist palms on her jeans and took the pie to the corner booth.

"Here you are, Mr. McKenna. Would you like ice cream with that?"

"I didn't order pie," he said politely, glancing at Riley and then back to Amy.

"Oh, didn't I tell you? It comes with your steak sandwich. Friday nights only, no extra charge."

Case smiled and shook his head. "I'm pretty full…"

"Come on, you gotta try it. Riley's wife made it fresh this afternoon."

Riley grinned at her, now in on the game, and headed back toward the kitchen.

"Well, maybe just a bite. You, uh, want to join me?"

"Me? Oh, no, sorry, I've got customers, but thank you. Maybe another time."

The blue eyes looked right past her fluster, past her scheme, past her resolve. Amy felt like her inner self was on display. Grasping her own elbows, she backed away. "Enjoy your pie."

"What did you talk about?" she quizzed Riley after Case McKenna left the restaurant.

Riley beamed, a burger in mid-flip. "Nothing, really.

He asked who was good at repairing boats. And something else, it's weird. He wanted to know if anyone lived at Point Surrender."

Amy stopped slicing tomatoes and turned to face the boss. "What did you tell him?"

"I told him no, of course."

"Did you mention that Brian was buying it?"

"I said I thought it had been sold. That's all. I figure it's none of his business. He's a stranger. Just passing through town."

Amy went back to slicing, but Riley continued.

"Lighthouses are always a curiosity, but the thing about Surrender is, you can't see the dang thing from the highway. You have to *know* it's there. He knew that."

"But he's got a boat, right? So he probably saw it coming into Newburg Bay."

"Maybe. If he came in from the south. But it's on the other side of the point, so you can't see it from the north if you're very close to shore. He, uh, said he's from Northern California."

"How come you know so much?" Amy asked with what she hoped was a suspicious grin.

"You gotta know I get a lot of sailors in here. They talk. I listen."

Amy nodded, pensive as her thoughts drifted past the aging white beacon.

"I'm not sure what will happen now. I don't know if Brian has to have the money in by a certain time, or if he can even still buy it. He might not even be able to work when he comes out of this."

"Let's keep the faith, Amy. Brian's a strong guy. He'll make it. You'll see. We gotta have faith."

Amy looked at Riley with grateful sympathy. She knew he was talking about much more than her brother's recovery.

Case walked south on Coast Highway, away from Riley's and away from Newburg. The sun had just taken its daily dip into the Pacific, and the sky was weaving all spectrums of color into its evening blanket. Consciously, he knew he wasn't ready to meet the past head on. Subconsciously, he had no choice.

After about a mile, he saw the gravel road leading off to the right, down to the bluff where the small white garage stood. He stopped walking and stared at the old structure, his hands thrust deep into his pockets.

What kind of person would want a lighthouse? He took a couple of tentative steps onto the gravel. *A recluse, maybe. A loner. Someone...anti-social.*

A wry smile formed on his lips.

Someone like me.

Chapter Five

Judy Cashion crossed and uncrossed her legs as she sat across from Amy in the airport coffee shop. She reached for the salt shaker and held it above her coffee cup. "God! I hate to leave. I don't know what to do. I haven't slept since you called me."

Amy placed her hand over Judy's and gently pulled the shaker away from the cup. She knew all too well about sleepless nights. "He *will* get better, Judy. You know he will. Nothing keeps Brian down for long." She smiled through glistening eyes. "I remember once, when he was about seven, he fell out of our tree house. Trying to be Robin Hood, I think. Got the wind knocked clean out of him. I ran up to him, scolding him all the way because I knew Dad would have a fit at me for letting it happen. Brian just lay there, staring up at me. Of course I didn't realize he couldn't even catch his breath, much less defend himself..."

Judy sniffed and uttered a melancholy chuckle.

"But he was back in front of the TV an hour later, watching that Robin Hood movie, trying to figure out what he did wrong."

"He's the best thing that ever happened to me. We were meant to grow old together; we both felt it as soon as we met." Judy wiped an errant tear, then twisted the watch on her wrist to read the time. "I've gotta go. I'm off to Paris, again. Last time. They switched me to domestic flights only beginning Wednesday so that I can get back here easier."

Amy walked Judy as far as the security gate, then headed back to the parking lot and the lonely drive back to the small apartment in the city. Once more climbing the stairs, she forced her key to turn the lock. She dreaded having to get right back into her car and drive out to Newburg within an hour.

There was nothing of interest in the refrigerator, but Brian had stocked up on "healthy" frozen cuisine dinners and Amy held one in her hand, not really seeing its colorful box as she dragged the tear strip from the edge. While it heated in the microwave, she methodically changed into a clean, forest green "Riley's" polo shirt and fresh blue jeans, noting that the pants didn't zip quite as easily as before.

Her new life becoming a labor of love, Amy refused to think about the past or the future, choosing to focus only on the moment as she dished out ribs, read magazines to Brian, and grilled the doctors about his recovery. The only deviation from routine was her one stop at the sheriff's office to ask about the hoodlums who had nearly killed her beloved brother.

"I'm sorry, Miz Winslow. We have very little to go on. Brian was patrolling the area around buoy 26 when he apparently spotted the hooligans firing a rifle into the water. He radioed that he would investigate their activities. And according to Mr. McKenna, when he looked up, the go-fast was speeding directly at your brother's boat."

"Go-fast? Is that what you call speeding marauders?"

Deputy Carnahan shrugged, looking down at the papers on his desk. "I wish there was more. It happened pretty quickly. We've got bulletins out all up and down the coast in case they put the boat in for repairs. We figure it had to have sustained some damaged when it hit the CG patrol boat."

Amy nodded, her eyes cast down. "You'll let me know if–if you hear anything else."

"Of course. We have your number in San Francisco."

"I'm hardly ever there. You can call my cell. Oh, and I'm working at Riley's."

"Commuting? That's crazy," Carnahan commented, shaking his head. "You outta find someplace closer to stay for awhile. Are they going to transfer Brian to a city hospital?"

"No, not to my knowledge."

"Have you tried Hastings House? She just might have room for you for a while. Beats that drive every day."

Amy considered the deputy's suggestion. Staying in Newburg made all the sense in the world. But could she afford it? Of course not.

"Thanks. I'll look into that."

Amy got into the car and slowly fastened her seatbelt. It had been nine days since the accident. Nineteen days since she'd found out about the baby. Two weeks since Jessie's heart-rending phone call…

"*I would want you to tell me if the situation was*

reversed," Jessica began, her words pushing a crease into Amy's forehead.

"*Tell you what?*"

"*Tell me if something was going on I should know about. Aim, Mac and I just got back from New York. We stopped by to see Drew...*"

Amy squeezed her eyes tightly closed as if she could wring the memory from her mind. He'd been calling, too, once a day for the past week. She carefully checked the "caller I.D." before answering her cell phone. Heated with renewed humiliation and remorse, she fought for the strength to quell her building anger. It would do neither herself nor her baby any good. Yet she held the steering wheel in a death grip as she drove slowly, blindly, through the quiet streets of Newburg, stopping her car once again at the curb before Hastings House.

The sofa was as uncomfortable as it was formal, but Amy ignored the over-firm cushions and the stiff brocade. A dead ringer for the late Katharine Hepburn, the elderly proprietress poured her a cup of tea.

"Right now I only have one room, dear. Jacelyn's Room. It's small, real pretty, and very feminine. It's actually my favorite, but unfortunately it doesn't have a private bath," Irena Hastings said, her tone apologetic.

"That wouldn't bother me," Amy found herself saying, bringing the trembling china cup to her lips.

"Better hear the rest. It's a shared bath, at the end of the hall. Shares with Morgan's Room."

"Morgan?"

"Captain Morgan Hastings. Jacelyn's lover. Historic figures. Why, he built this house. What a tragedy. Late 1800's, I think...or was it mid 1800's?"

"You were related, I take it?"

"He was my grandfather's brother. Quite a rogue, I understand. Liked to call himself a 'southern gentleman,' although most folks called him a pirate."

Amy shifted her position.

"Anyway, there's a nice man staying in Morgan's room. I don't know how you'd feel about sharing a bath with a gentleman. I can tell you he's very neat."

Amy put down her cup. She could not remember a time when she didn't share a bathroom with a man. The rent turned out to be far less than she expected, and the way she felt right now, anything was better than driving back to the city. If she had to, she could borrow some money from Brian when he recovered.

"May I see the room?"

Case drew in a deep breath and blew it out through his lips in disgust. Arms crossed, he stood to the side as Emery Davis hunched over the damaged rudder they had just pulled off the *Fancy Dream*.

"Don't reckon it's a total loss. We can fix the shaft here, but see how all these threads are stripped? I think Ted might have one out behind his garage, but it might not fit...maybe, maybe not..."

Case lifted his eyes to the buttermilk sky above, then dropped them back upon the crusty, but highly recommended, boat builder beside him.

"Whatever it takes. I gotta move on."

Newburg was sapping him, somehow. The little town with its single stoplight, its quiet townspeople carrying on with their pre-set lives–each knowing their tomorrows as well as they knew their yesterdays. For Case, a man who preferred not knowing either, it was unnerving.

He began to question the wisdom of his flight from Grogan's Head. Like a doctor who had gotten too involved with a patient, he had suffered a personal loss when the Florida manatee had succumbed to the injuries inflicted upon her by his fellow man.

Jack's words came back to him. While his friend had come just short of saying so, Case knew Jack regarded Amanda's death as just another part of life, certainly tragic but not with the devastation Case felt. Now, standing on the dock beside his crippled sailboat in a gray little town that gave him the willies, Case decided that he had, indeed, overreacted to the manatee's passing. When the *Dream* was back in action, he would turn her sails to the wind and head back north, back to his small cabin above Grogan's Head.

Amy threw all the perishables into the trash, then bagged up the granola bars, crackers and cereals and put the bag beside her suitcase. Quickly she walked through the apartment once more, turning off all the lights and re-checking the locked windows. A neighbor had taken Brian's meager collection of houseplants.

She was almost out the door when the phone rang. Thinking it might be the hospital, Amy dropped her bags and picked up the receiver. Drew's unwelcome greeting knocked the wind from her sails.

"Hey, Aims. I'm here. In town. You're not answering your cell."

Amy sank slowly into Brian's easy chair. "You shouldn't have come."

"I had no choice. We have to talk."

Amy closed her eyes and pressed her hand against her forehead. "I told you before, there's nothing to talk about."

"Just stay put. I'm on my way."

"Drew, no. Please. This is not a good time."

"How can it not be a good time? We need to talk! Is your brother there? Afraid he might toss me out on my ass?"

"No. Brian's not here. He's in the hospital. A boating accident."

There was a decided pause on the other end of the line. "I'm sorry. Is there anything I can do? Anything at all?"

"Just...just leave me alone." Amy could hear Drew breathing while he considered her request. At last, he continued.

"I'll be in town until Friday. I'm at the Prescott Hotel. At least write down the number. Please let me know if you need anything, Amy. I'm really sorry. Honest."

Amy sat for fifteen minutes with the phone, and the gasoline receipt on which she had jotted the Prescott's number, in her lap. Tears again threatened her eyes, pain closing on her throat. She had to talk to someone. Still not ready to bring her father into the scenario, Amy dialed Roth General Hospital and asked for Brian's room.

Judy answered on the first ring.

"How's the patient today?" Amy asked with false cheer. Her query was answered with an audible sigh.

"His color is good." Judy's voice was small and distant.

"Judy, what's wrong?"

"I got a call from the escrow company today. We only have until Monday to get the money in to close. Technically, they don't want to know that Brian's out of commission. Since we've already signed all the loan papers, if they were officially advised that Brian might not be able to carry out the obligations...they would have to let the bank know, the bank giving us the loan, you know, and..." Judy's voice quivered.

Amy, too, shuddered at the thought of Brian losing his precious lighthouse. She shuddered again when Judy spelled out the amount needed to close the escrow.

"I have a third of it ready to put in, but we need Brian's share and there's no way I can get to it with him in–in a coma."

Amy swallowed hard. Faced with Brian's apartment rent, her own lodging expenses and unknown medical costs, she almost laughed at the memory of her first paltry paycheck from Riley's.

How could this be happening?

"Judy, does Brian need to sign anything else to close escrow?"

"No. We signed everything in advance. We were just

waiting for his last paycheck to be deposited."

"I'm on my way back. I'll see you in a little while. Don't worry, okay?" Amy didn't recognize her own voice, let alone the confident tone she had managed. "Give him a kiss for me."

Replacing the receiver on the phone, Amy stood up and squared her shoulders while drawing in a deep breath. She blinked several times and uncrumpled the receipt in her hand, smoothing it out between her palms.

The two women entered the diner and quietly moved into the corner booth. Riley looked up, puzzled, and trod heavily across the sawdust covered plank floor.

"That's pretty sad when you gotta come in here on your night off," he said gaily, a welcoming smile on his face.

"This is the closest place to home, right now," Amy replied. "Besides, Judy would like a beer. And I would love a beer. But bring me one of those fake beers. I can pretend."

"You got it, ladies. Any news?"

"Not really." Judy's hand trembled as she took a sip of water. "Thanks for asking."

With their drinks in front of them, the women sat in silence while each formulated their thoughts. It was Amy who spoke next.

"Okay. I've made a decision. I'm going to ask Drew for the money."

Judy looked up, her expression one of horror. "Are you crazy? You can't get hooked up with that creep again.

Especially not now!"

"What choice do I have? It's only temporary, right? Brian will be well soon, we *know* that. When he comes out of this, he'll pay Drew back. Drew's loaded, anyway. It's a drop in the bucket for him."

"I don't know."

"He offered. He made me promise to let him help somehow."

"He doesn't even like Brian. He's only doing it so he can manipulate you."

Amy thought about Judy's comment, then nodded. "You're probably right. But why should I care? I'd be using him, using his money. In fact, it would be kind of fun. If he thinks he can buy me back, he's got another thing coming. It will be a joy to see the look on his face."

"Are you going to tell him about–?"

"No. No way. Not yet."

"Are you sure you want to do this, Amy? I mean, maybe there's some other... Maybe between the two of us, we can think of someone else we can borrow it from."

"Maybe, but it would take a miracle to get it together by Friday. Drew can write us a check today, if we ask. If I ask. So. We'll deposit the funds, they'll close escrow, and the place will be yours and Brian's. Brian will wake up, pay Drew back, you kids will get married and Point Surrender will shine its light for all to see that we did it."

Judy reached across the table and grasped both of Amy's hands in her own, squeezing them tightly. "If you're sure."

Amy smiled brightly. "I'm sure."

I must be crazy.

Amy came to consciousness slowly, having slept soundly for the first time in days. The rose print chintz comforter draped warmly around her, the ample feather pillow shaped to the back of her head made her feel like a little girl again, a little girl with a mother who tucked her in at night and looked in on her before going to bed. She stretched, noticing as she did so the tiniest squeak of the bedsprings beneath her.

The sunlight illuminated the matching rose patterned curtains. There was no phone in the room, but she had her cell and Miss Hastings had promised to summon her should the hospital call the house. Reluctant to rise, Amy rolled off the side of the antique brass bed and snatched her thin summer robe from her as-yet-unpacked suitcase.

The suitcase. Was this the sum total of her life, the contents of a single piece of luggage? As she shrugged into her robe, she pondered the question. She did have possessions at home, at her father's house in Santa Paula. But they were childhood treasures. Dolls, books, videos. A few pieces of clothing. Special items that had belonged to her mother.

Where was her adult life? Slowly tying her belt, she turned to the window without really seeing the street below. Her classroom appeared in her mind, her desk, her bud vase with the artificial rose. A wooden apple, a notepad with her name on every sheet, and a couple of picture frames.

They would box it all up and put it in the storeroom.

Her kids would stop by to see her the first week of school, all full of joys and fears about third grade, and find her gone. A new teacher would be sitting at that desk.

Looking back at the yawning suitcase on the floor, Amy shook her head slowly. The balance of her life she left behind in the duplex. The kitchen towels so carefully picked out. The new sewing machine Drew had bought her for Christmas. The artwork they'd chosen together. Left behind. But she'd come away with something new, hadn't she?

Her hands went to her abdomen, a smooth, caressing gesture she'd become accustomed to. Was it really true? A baby, a tiny, living being, growing inside her?

A mental slap was due. No time now for sappy and disturbing thoughts. Raising her arms, Amy pushed all the hair away from her face and sighed. *Gotta get into the shower.*

The bathroom door stood open. Once inside, she turned the large skeleton key in the lock and began unpacking a few toiletries onto the modest shelf space above the pedestal sink. Her smile was involuntary and brief as she noticed the twin-bladed razor on the shelf, still gleaming from recent use. It reminded her of the one Drew left in their bathroom back in Carmel.

Glancing around the room, Amy decided that aside from the razor and the steam on the small window above the john, there wasn't a shred of evidence that she was sharing the bath.

Miss Hastings had invited her to breakfast, even though the meal was usually provided to guests on weekends only. Amy decided to accept the offer, prompted by her hunger and growing weariness of cafeteria food. Besides, anything she could do to save money would be prudent.

She didn't expect quite the spread at the table. There were freshly baked banana nut muffins, not the skimpy, elfin sized ones Brian bought at the supermarket; each of these could be a meal in itself, Amy decided. Yogurt with fresh berries and real granola followed by a cheese and herb omelet and slices of Canadian bacon. Hot coffee and fresh squeezed orange juice completed the meal.

"Gosh, do I feel pampered or what," she murmured, spreading butter on one of the hot muffins.

"Eat up. You're the last this morning."

"I'm sorry, should I have been here sooner?" Amy looked up at the innkeeper's smile.

"No. It was better that you got a good rest." Miss Hastings refilled Amy's coffee.

Amy nodded. "The bed is heavenly. I didn't want to get up at all."

"Sometimes I feel like that too," Miss Hastings agreed, pouring a cup for herself and sitting down across from Amy. "But I figure, if I don't get up, I could miss something wonderful."

Amy paused, fork in hand, trying to decide if her benefactor was being serious. Satisfied that Miss Hastings' optimism was genuine, Amy smiled back at the older woman.

"You've probably seen a lot happen here, huh?"

"Oh, not really. My brother, Matthew, told me a lot

of the local stories before he died, though, so I feel like I've been here longer than I have."

Behind her was a large antique sideboard, crafted of rich cherry wood. Its elegant brass handles had long been tarnished, but its presence added a royal feeling to the dining room. Above it on the wall hung a framed photograph, and Amy narrowed her eyes to examine its aging scene.

In the picture was a man, probably thirty years old, and a boy of eight or nine, standing together and squinting into the sun. The man had long, dark hair that hung in waves past his shoulders, and a wide moustache that curled at the ends. The boy was unremarkable except for the decided pout on his lips. Their faces seemed vaguely familiar, but Amy could not place them. The black and white photo was taken on a bluff, the ocean behind in the distance. And in the background, just to the right of the subjects, was the unmistakable white tower of Point Surrender Light.

"Is something the matter dear?"

Amy didn't realize she had frozen so completely at the sight of the lighthouse in the photo. She cleared her throat and took a sip of orange juice.

"No, no, nothing. I was just looking at the picture."

"Oh, that's Matt. It's the only decent picture I have of my brother. It used to be in my bedroom, but I brought it down here this morning. That's Point Surrender there in the background. Kinda pretty, then."

"Your brother was a handsome man. When was it taken?"

"Oh, around '81 or '82, not sure–I wasn't here then. He knew the folks that lived there, and once or twice helped out there, I think. He dabbled in carpentry." Trying not to stare, Amy tore her eyes away and concentrated on cutting her bacon. But soon she felt compelled to look again. "Look familiar, does he? He played in one of those popular San Francisco bands back then. Once I remember they closed off a whole street near Golden Gate Park for a free concert."

"So he had a son?" Amy asked, forcing her voice to stay calm and unaffected.

"Oh gosh no. Matt never married. Wasn't the marrying kind, you know."

"Oh! Really."

"Not sure who the boy in the picture is, probably a neighbor boy, someone from the school where Matthew worked."

Amy nodded. "Do you, did you ever hear much about the lighthouse?" Amy managed, puzzling over Miss Hastings' curious admission about her brother.

"Oh, there's talk, there's always talk, always will be, you know. The Jenners were odd people. Moved down here from Washington State–Seattle I think. I don't know too much except that he worked for the Coast Guard, and that bit about him falling down the stairs…"

"His wife must have been devastated," Amy murmured softly.

"Wife? Way I heard it, she wasn't home."

"She had gone out?" Amy's eyes were wide with

unbridled curiosity.

"No, I mean, she wasn't living there at the time. There was talk she took off with another man." Miss Hastings rose and took her cup to the kitchen.

"Goodness," Amy whispered. No wonder the husband drank! Infidelity was a particularly sore subject for her. Instead of satisfying her curiosity, Miss Hastings' tale only fueled her need for more of the story. It was clear, however, that the innkeeper didn't intend on imparting more today.

Despite the delicious meal, Amy's appetite waned quickly. She had a very important meeting to get ready for, a meeting that would change the course of her life. Climbing the stairs back to Jacelyn's Room, Amy thought about what she would wear to the Prescott Hotel.

Chapter Six

Emery Davis sat on the end of the dock and popped the ring on another can of stout.

"Don't know how a fella could ever git out of a sink hole like Newburg if he tried. I been here all my damn life."

Case took a sip from his can and pressed his shirt cuff to his lips. "Oh, I think a person could leave if they really set their mind to it." Case gestured subtly toward Coast Highway. "Road's down that a-way."

"Sure, easy for someone like you. You got money, you're young, you ain't got roots growin' outta your shoes."

Case chuckled, shook his head, and looked down at his dangling feet. He could imagine tiny tendrils creeping from edges of his soles. "Maybe," he murmured. "Funny, back home I was beginning to think I had barnacles stuck to my backside."

"Guess that kinda feelin' can come 'round any ol' time, huh? Like you just ain't movin' fast enough. An' pretty soon, you just ain't good for nuthin' no more. Like that ol' lighthouse 'round the point, there. One day, they jus' up an' turned her off. Locked the cursed door and there she sits."

"You know anything about someone trying to buy that lighthouse?" Case asked.

"Lotsa folks allahs ask 'bout it, now I heared the Coas' Guard's a-sellin' it to one a their own guys. A kid. You know that kid that got dinged up out there last week. He the one s'posta be buyin' that ol' light."

The three-quarter moon shone with a brightness unknown to city dwellers; the sea passed the brightness on into Case McKenna's eyes as he listened to the old codger talk. So it was true. And more than that, it was Brian Winslow who had purchased Point Surrender. Brian and Amy Winslow.

Amy pushed the hangers back and forth in the small closet, looking for the "little black dress" she had purchased just before leaving Carmel. Seemed appropriate, she thought, holding it at arm's length for approval. It was to have been the dress she would wear when she gave Drew the big news. *Ha! The big news.*

Now, he wouldn't hear that news. He didn't deserve to know that she carried his child. And even though she knew he would one day find out, she hoped her attempts to conceal the fact would hurt him.

She hated to stiff Riley on a Friday night, but Riley had been more than happy to help her out after she'd confided her intention. Amy would make it up to him, somehow.

Carefully slipping the dress over her head, Amy held her breath while fumbling with the zipper. She turned to the mirror and exhaled. A perfect fit. The sweeping, round neckline exposed more bosom than she was accustomed to showing, but then, she had more bosom than normal.

She grimaced; too bad she didn't look this good when she wasn't pregnant and so uncomfortable!

The antique vanity mirror swiveled coquettishly, and Amy leaned forward to apply her make-up with expert strokes. She forced herself to remain focused on the reason for her date with Drew; the goal was money, not reconciliation *nor* retribution. Still, she wanted to knock him out. She wanted to look gorgeous, luscious, and seductive.

Lipstick applied, she smiled at herself, lowering her eyelashes and purposely causing the smile to fade. She knew Drew's hot buttons, his weaknesses, and his drive for perfection. And tonight, she would be perfect. The perfect prize for the perfect swine.

Amy left her car with the valet and walked into Postrio's Restaurant inside the Prescott at exactly 7:00 P.M. The maitre d' escorted her to Drew's table. He was already seated and talking into a cell phone, but stood when Amy arrived.

"I *know* the NASDAQ tanked again today. You gotta trust me, Bob, just sit tight for awhile." He paused, his eyes devouring Amy as she slowly sank into her seat across from him. "Uh, yeah, that's a Dow component...look pal, I gotta go. Have a drink and call me in the morning."

Ignoring the obvious frowns of other patrons, Drew snapped the cell phone closed and dropped it into his inside breast pocket. "You...look awesome. Wow."

"Thank you," Amy said softly, her eyes drifting from

Drew's almost vulgar stare to the wine captain who had just appeared beside the table. Drew also broke his gaze and accepted the wine list, hurriedly selecting a pricey Chardonnay and turning his attention back to Amy.

"We have a lot to talk about," he began, reaching for her hand, but Amy withdrew and instead grasped her water glass.

"If you say so."

"Amy, I know I screwed up. It was..." Drew swallowed, glancing around the room as if searching for words. "It was a fleeting thing. A stupid thing. Just an attraction, nothing more. Something I immediately regretted. It's over."

Amy didn't answer, her face expressionless.

"Please. Can we just get back to the way things were? Maybe we should make some plans, spend more time together. I could take an office here in the city, and divide my time more evenly with New York. You–you don't even have to work if you don't want to. Come on, can we give it a shot?"

"You seem to be forgetting something. You were unfaithful to me, Drew. *You cheated.* I'm not sure I can get past that. Where you spend your time is one thing, but with whom is quite another. Frankly, I'm still reeling from this...this situation." *That was true enough.* Amy adjusted the burgundy cloth napkin in her lap.

"Okay, okay. I know this is awkward. I can understand your reluctance to...trust me again. I really blew it." Drew failed to make eye contact with Amy as he squirmed uncomfortably in his seat. "All I can do is ask you to give me a chance to make it up to you. To prove how much I–I love you and want you with me."

Amy, too, looked around the room. Dimly lit by chandeliers, the room was elegant and filled with monetary ambiance. Crowded, but not noisy. Exactly Drew's style. She decided not to answer.

Drew sighed and finally looked at her. "You're wearing the diamond pendant." He leaned forward slightly, his finger sliding beneath the single, tear-shaped diamond and caressing Amy's skin in the process. She drew back.

"Two carets, isn't it? Yeah, I thought I'd wear it one more time."

Drew frowned. The wine captain poured a scant sip into Drew's glass for his approval. "This is fine. What do you mean, one more time?"

"Well, unless you want it back, I'm probably going to sell it. I'm in need of some funds, and it should bring a pretty good price."

"What? Sell it? Do you know how much that little trinket is worth?" Drew colored, apparently at the thought that Amy would hawk the diamond.

"No, not really, but whatever it is, I can put it to good use. Unless you want it back."

Drew took a moderate gulp of the wine, nearly choking in the process. "What in God's name do you need that kind of money for?"

Amy pretended to take a dainty sip of wine, then sat back in her chair. Her plan was going perfectly. "Brian."

"Surely the Guard is picking up his medical

expenses?"

"Of course. It's something else. Brian put a deposit on a piece of property. It means everything to him to acquire this real estate, but he's...he's in a coma, Drew. He'll lose the deal if we don't deposit the closing funds by Friday. I want to help him. Hopefully, when he comes around and can get to his own money, I can get the necklace back."

Drew drummed his fingers lightly on the tablecloth. "Why didn't you just ask me for the money?"

"Ask *you*? Are you kidding?" Amy offered Drew a level stare.

"How much are we talking about?"

Amy responded with a six-figure amount, but Drew did not blink an eye.

"Call Patricia tomorrow morning with the wire information. You'll have the money by 2 P.M."

"Absolutely not." Amy opened her menu, eclipsing her view of the man across from her. The man she once loved, the man who had cheated. This was easier than she thought it would be.

"Come on, Amy. Don't sell the necklace. Let me help. Not to sound crass, but that's not that much money. If it will help Brian–"

Amy snapped the menu closed. "Help Brian? That's rich."

"I know we don't always agree, but Brian's a good guy. He deserves a shot. I'm impressed that he's investing in real estate. Is it a marketable property?"

"You could say that. Custom. Non-conforming. Incredible ocean view."

"Ah. Fabulous. Look. I'll tell Patty you'll be calling. We'll work out the details about repayment later. Let me do this, Amy. If not for Brian, then for you."

Amy smiled slightly, grinding her teeth inside. "I don't know. Are you sure?"

"Of course I'm sure. I don't lend money lightly."

"I'll sleep on it."

"Why don't you come back to New York with me? You're on vacation, right? We need to spend some time together."

Yeah, right. You horny bastard. Can't keep your eyes off my cleavage, can you?

"I just need some time, Drew. I need time to think about all this, to recover from...the shock..."

Drew's face again reddened and he opened his menu.

"And besides," Amy continued, "I need to be here with Brian."

"Of course. I understand."

The waiter stood by expectantly. Amy again opened her menu, and despite the fact that she knew the food would be excellent and Drew's tab deliciously exorbitant, she knew she could not eat a bite without becoming ill.

Closing the menu, she put her napkin on the table.

"I'm not feeling real well, Drew. I have to go. Thanks for your generous offer; I'll let you know in the morning if I'm going to take it. Good night."

Amy stood before Drew could protest. She knew once she was on the move, he'd be loathe to make a scene.

"I'll walk you out," he began, hastily getting to his feet.

93

"Don't bother. Thank you, Andrew."

The three-story Victorian inn on Highwater Street was lit against the inky night sky as Amy parked her car and got out. It looked like a haven. She saw Miss Hastings through the kitchen window, still up and moving about.

She didn't feel like more conversation, so went straight up to the second floor and down the hall to Jacelyn's Room. She truly did feel nauseous, and thought a warm bath might do her good.

She grabbed her robe and toiletries and locked herself in the bathroom, filling the claw-foot tub with bubbles and water. Sinking into the bath, she immediately felt better. The 'dinner' had gone much better than expected; she had gotten Drew to commit to the loan without eating dinner with him. Without going home with him. Without having sex with him. Not that she would have! She would call Drew's secretary in the morning and the money would be wired to the escrow company in time to close. On Friday afternoon, Brian and Judy would own Point Surrender. And then maybe, just maybe, Brian would wake up.

Case walked the five or six blocks back to Hastings House in the dark, his mind abuzz with the information he'd gleaned from his new friend. He wondered what Brian Winslow had in mind for the property on the bluff, and found himself wishing he'd gotten to it first. His own thoughts surprised him; what would he do with a broken down old lighthouse? *Especially that one.*

Maybe he didn't need to *own* it. Maybe he wanted a look inside. Or maybe just wanted to tear it down.

The house was quiet, save for the groans of the risers beneath his feet as he climbed the stairs to the second floor. In the hall outside his room he encountered Miss Hastings.

"Still up?" he queried, the ale in his system mellowing his usually subdued demeanor.

"Oh! Good evening. I was just putting some clean linen in the cupboard for tomorrow."

"I'm glad I caught you. Do you know any local real estate agents here?"

"Interested in settling here in Newburg, Mr. McKenna?"

McKenna? Amy remained motionless in the tub, listening with interest to the voices just outside the bathroom door.

"There's a specific property I'm interested in," Case said. Amy was barely breathing.

"Well, Joe Franzman up the street here, he's also the local tax man and notary, he does some real estate selling."

"Franzman. Thank you. Well, I guess I'll turn in."

Amy remained stock-still until she heard the door to Morgan's Room snap shut and Miss Hastings's footfalls die away down the hall.

So Case McKenna was her bathroom mate. Silently she got out of the tub and dried off, then hastily gathered up her discarded clothes and pulled the plug on the tub. As quietly as possible, she retreated to her room.

Amy climbed into her bed and pulled the comforter up to her chin. For a reason she could not explain even to herself, her heart was thumping loudly in her chest. Frozen to her spot, she listened intently to the sounds of the old house. Upstairs, Miss Hastings called to her cat. Below, the ancient coal-oil furnace creaked and struggled to heat the drafty rooms. She heard the sound of the water running in the bathroom sink. It was the latter that interested her the most, because she could not shake the image of Case McKenna's searching blue eyes.

Case removed his shirt, his shoes and socks then retrieved his shaving kit from the top of the highboy dresser. He'd thought he heard someone vacate the bathroom, and he was badly in need of its use.

Once in the over-sized bathroom, he noticed the small mounds of bubbles still sliding down the drain and the scent of tangerines surrounding the tub. Swiftly closing the door behind him, the back of his hand was slapped with a flying garment hanging on the door hook; a woman's lacy black bra swung back across his arm.

Cocking his head to one side, Case drew his arm slowly away, letting the brassiere fall gently back against the door. It had been awhile, a long while, since he'd been in the presence of a lady's finery, and the sight stirred something inside. Something nearly gone.

In his slightly inebriated state, Case cracked a winsome smile unseen by anyone except himself in the oval mirror over the sink. While he'd known he was sharing a bathroom, it hadn't occurred to him that the 'someone' might be female; he somehow couldn't believe the black satin demi-cup belonged to Irena Hastings.

Chapter Seven

Independence Day in Newburg was nothing like the July Fourths of Amy's childhood. Despite the fact that she had the day off, Amy spent the day and evening alone, fighting depression. From her bedroom's bay window, she watched a mediocre skyrocket display over Newburg's small harbor.

Even Judy's cheerful voice on Wednesday morning did little to improve her mood.

"I've got the keys! I'm taking them to the hospital to show Brian."

Amy smiled into the phone. Like herself, Judy was hopeful that Point Surrender would somehow revive Brian. But at what cost? Getting the money from Drew had taken its toll on her emotional equilibrium.

"Great. I'll meet you over there."

Judy was pressing the keys into Brian's palm when Amy arrived. Two nurses patiently waited to change the linen on Brian's bed.

"It's ours, darling. All ours. See? The keys, Brian. We've finally got the keys to Point Surrender."

From the corner of Brian's private room, Amy leaned against the wall, her pain masked by an expressionless face. The scene was more than sad. Judy touched Brian's face, rattled the keys, and squeezed his wrists. When he didn't respond, Judy collapsed against the bed, her sobs

uncontrolled in utter disappointment. Amy went to her
and gently pulled her away from Brian's still form.

"I know, I know...just give it a little more time.
These things take time," she murmured, trying to comfort
her sister-in-law to-be.

"Oh Amy, what am I going to do? What can I do with
a stupid old lighthouse, by myself?"

On any other day, her question might have brought
smiles, but now, crying into Amy's shoulder, Judy's plea
only brought pity to the faces around them. For the fact
remained: Brian Winslow might never wake up.

Amy managed to get Judy into her car and together
they drove down the highway to the lighthouse.

Her eyes still swollen, Judy unlocked the thick, solid
wooden door and led Amy inside the small living
quarters. "Well, here we are," she began, looking around
at the musty, vacant living room.

"Yup. Here we are." Amy unconsciously held her
hand against her abdomen. The disquiet within the
structure was still present, still ominous.

"Needs a lot of work," Judy said, running her fingers
along the rough, dust-laden mantel above the fireplace. "A
lot of work."

Amy nodded, pushing a stray wisp of hair away from
her forehead. "I guess we should put together some kind
of plan."

"Plan? Like what?"

"Like what we're going to fix first, and where we can
get some help. I don't know about you, but I'm not real

good at stucco or plumbing."

Judy's face finally broke into a smile as she followed Amy into the kitchen, where the latter toggled the light switch up and down.

"Looks like we need to get the utilities going. No power, no water..."

"Gosh. I hadn't thought about that. Who do we call?"

Amy leaned back against the sink counter and regarded Judy, a whimsical smile curling her lips. "I'll get a local phone book from Riley. Maybe he knows of a carpenter, or a handyman who could do a little work here. I hate to ask, but do you have any money left?"

Judy rubbed her forehead, giving Amy an embarrassed nod. "About a hundred bucks."

Amy chuckled. "That's more than I have. But I'm not worried. We'll get it together somehow."

"I think we should just focus on getting the light working. That's all Brian talked about, *before*...he kept saying how important it would be, how just ass-kicking impressive it would be to see the big light shine again."

Amy's eyes went immediately to the door at the base of the tower, and a shiver passed over her. "Maybe you're right. I'd love for you to be able to tell Brian the light was on."

"I don't know the first thing about it, though," Judy admitted. She walked to the tower door and turned the knob.

"Don't!" Amy's single word escaped her lips without thought, and her gaze flashed to the bottom of the door. Had it been open that night? Where, exactly, had the body ended its fall? How had he looked to those who'd found him? Amy crossed her arms across her chest and absently rubbed her forearms.

Judy drew back from the door as if burned by the knob. "What? Is something wrong?"

Now embarrassed by her outburst, Amy forced a smile. "Let's just *not*, right now. I...I need to get something to eat."

"You okay?" Judy came quickly back into the kitchen, to Amy's side.

"Sure. Just–too much is going on. I'm feeling a little light-headed."

"Have you been to a doctor since you moved up here?"

"Not yet," Amy replied, walking past Judy, toward the front door.

"You'd better. It's important."

"I know. I will. That's something else I have to look into."

"I have a friend who lives in the city. I'll get the name of a good OB/GYN from her."

Amy nodded her thanks and subtly urged Judy out the front door, suddenly feeling like she could not spend another minute inside the lighthouse.

"WANTED: HANDYMAN TO WORK AT POINT SURRENDER. MUST BE WILLING TO WORK FOR FOOD!" Riley grinned as he pinned the card to the bulletin board beside the payphone in the back. Flanked by the restrooms, the board was often perused by the

101

locals, looking for jobs.

"Thanks, Ri. I don't even know where to begin."

"Well, we'll see if it dredges anyone up."

"I'm wondering if anyone will venture inside, after what you told me about its history."

"Sailors are a superstitious lot, but some of 'em have a soft spot for Surrender, seein' it from the waterside for so many years. Somebody will come forward. Maybe one of your bowling team buddies."

Amy shook her head with a laugh. She couldn't think of one customer she'd open the front door to. Her thought was immediately amended, however, as she watched Case McKenna stride easily into Riley's dining room. He offered her a non-committal nod and gave his order to Riley, who had practically met him at the corner table with an order pad.

The restaurant was fairly busy for a Wednesday night, and Amy looked forward to her day off. She had already stashed a local telephone directory under her purse to take back to the inn. Yet thoughts of finding an electrician and a doctor seemed far away, pushed aside by her desire to talk to the intriguing Mr. McKenna.

Intriguing? Did she really think that? She didn't even know the man. Except for the fact that he sailed in on a boat, rescued her brother, and was sharing her bathroom, she knew very little about the blue-eyed stranger. Even now, he watched her put together salads for the folks in booth number eight. Yet, there was something about him, a force field that both attracted and repelled–*come here, but not too close…*

Amy had no reason to stop by his table, and before she knew it, he'd gone. It was difficult to hide her disappointment.

"How's our Mr. McKenna tonight?" Amy tried to keep her tone nonchalant, but Riley offered a wink with his response.

"I think he would have preferred you wait on him."

"Why do you say that?"

"Just a hunch. And the fact that he didn't take his eyes off of you from the time he came in. Except for while he was in the john, that is."

"Oh." Amy hid a secret smile. What was she thinking? The last thing, the *very last thing* she needed in her life was another man.

Still, she could not avoid the thought that she wanted to know more about Case McKenna. More than just the brand of razor he used.

Okay. Here we go. Amy rolled up the sleeves of her blue chambray shirt and sprinkled cleanser on the stained sink basin, then tackled it with a scrubbing sponge. The electrician would be there at around noon, and the water company had already been out. Judy was somewhere over Iowa by now, but Amy didn't mind being on her own. She had resigned herself to the fact that working on the lighthouse was for Brian, like it or not, no matter that someone had died here. No matter that the house gave her the heebie-jeebies.

The rust stain went deeper than the scouring powder. Amy sighed. At least the water was running, and she rinsed the sink out the best she could. She turned her attention to the window over the sink. Climbing on the short kitchen ladder she had borrowed from Irena Hastings, she began cleaning the glass. The weather was changeable; sunny now, but thick, cotton-ball clouds were congregating overhead, a building breeze prodding them along. The sea reflected a deep jade, with whitecaps here and there as if the water longed to join the offshore breeze. Amy paused to scan the scene outside, perusing the rough, craggy edge of the cliff dropping away to the tide below.

A movement caught her eye. A man stood at the edge, his back to her as he stared out at the ocean below. He wore a gray plaid Pendleton-type shirt and blue jeans, his hands casually resting on his hips. Mesmerized, she descended the ladder and headed out the side door, only to find the lot empty. The man was gone.

Amy looked both directions along the edge of the bluff. There was no place for a man to hide, and he would have had to walk past her to get back up to the road. *Unless he'd fallen.*

It was less than forty feet from the door to the drop off. The tower stood majestically behind her. As if it's watching me, Amy thought, as she crept closer to the edge. Getting as close as she dared, she peered over, seeing nothing but the crashing surf and rocks below.

This is how it looked, how it's always looked. How it looked to them, the people who lived here before. And to him. The man who died.

"Hypnotizing, isn't it?"

Amy was still standing too close to the edge, and nearly leapt at the sound of the voice behind her. The man who'd spoken grasped her shoulders in an effort to stay her fall.

"Sorry, I didn't mean to startle you," Case McKenna said as Amy whirled around to face him, her face blanched and her pulse racing.

"My God," she murmured, trying to catch her breath. "I didn't hear you come up."

"The sea has a way of absorbing your mind, I think," Case said, turning his eyes back to the water momentarily.

"You weren't standing out here a minute ago, were you?" she asked, but knew the answer before Case shook his head. The man who'd stood on the bluff had longer, lighter, curlier brown hair. Case McKenna was wearing a sleeveless white t-shirt emblazoned with the likeness of Bruce Springsteen. No heavy woolen shirt on a warm July day. "Did you...see anyone else?"

"Just you."

Amy walked back toward the kitchen door. She hadn't imagined the man on the cliff. *Probably just a tourist.* She couldn't quite focus on the whys and wherefores with her visitor standing so close. "Is there something I can do for you or are you just sight-seeing?" She glanced over her shoulder to see Case looking up at the tower, shielding his eyes from the bright sunlight with his hand, before turning to catch up with her.

"Understand you could use some help out here," he called from the porch.

Amy snatched up her rag from the counter and started

up the ladder to resume her window cleaning. "You that hungry?" she asked, looking back at Case with a brief smile.

"May I come in?"

"Of course. But I should warn you, it's not pretty in here."

"Not pretty," Case repeated softly, nodding his head as he entered the small kitchen. "It, uh, has potential."

"You're too kind. Brian's wild about this place, but I think it's going to be a monster to fix up. So what kind of work are you offering, Mr. McKenna?"

"Case, please. I'm pretty good with my hands. I can fix things, as long as it doesn't involve electricity, plumbing, pipes, wires or gas..."

Amy turned around at his offer, and was met with an expectant grin. "In that case, you'll have to start in the painting department," she told him, taking a last appraising look at the window before coming down from the ladder. "Would you like a soda? Water?"

"Sure." Case helped himself to a can from a small Styrofoam ice chest and leaned against the wall, occupying the space where a refrigerator had obviously once stood.

"You folks gonna live here?" he asked after taking a long draught of soda.

"It will be a long time before this place is livable," Amy responded, scanning the cracked kitchen ceiling with a critical eye. "But that's the idea."

Case, too, gazed around the room, taking in the decaying plaster and evidence of earthquake damage.

"Not exactly seismically sound," he agreed.

"Nope." Amy continued to bustle about, opening kitchen cabinets and tossing various forms of debris into a trash bag.

"Mind if I look around?"

"Go right ahead. You can't really get lost, if you know what I mean."

Case wandered out into the living room and Amy paused to watch him. In the worn but clean white T-shirt, standard-issue blue jeans and blue and white athletic shoes, Case McKenna might have been a misplaced soap opera hero. The uneven chestnut brown locks, hastily brushed away from his face, invited her lonely fingers to play.

Amy blinked several times and smiled to herself. *Let it alone, girl. You've got other problems to worry about.*

Meanwhile, Case studied the fireplace. Arm outstretched, his fingers just short of touching the concave spots where several fieldstones were missing, he withdrew his hand when Amy joined him.

"Ever seen a fireplace like this one before?" she asked. "It's about the only thing in here I like."

"It's...quaint." Case rubbed his chin, his expression thoughtful. "A lot of missing stones."

"It's like everywhere you look, something needs to be fixed. Did you see this little nook?"

"Nook?" Case turned and strode the few steps toward the built-in desk area Amy pointed to.

"It's the only really nice thing in here. Obviously, someone built it more recently than the rest."

Dusty but mostly unscathed, the mahogany desk was a bright spot in the otherwise slightly shabby room. Shelves and cubbyholes surrounded the area above the desk, and drawers were installed beneath. A finely crafted swivel chair waited to be rolled out.

"Unique. Do you mind?" Case asked, pulling the chair out.

"Go right ahead. But if it breaks into pieces, I hope you have insurance."

Case took the dust rag Amy handed him and swiped it once across the chair's seat, then sat down, swiveling to face Amy.

"How is it?"

"Hard as slate. But not bad." Case ran his hands down the arms of the chair, tracing their curves and dips.

"Case? Is that short for something?"

Case looked up at Amy, mischief crinkling his eyes. "Oh, *suit*, *brief–federal* if you're in court with politicians..." He swiveled some more. "*Hard* case, if you're into parolees..."

Amy clamped her hands onto her hips. "Okay."

"Or just plain Casey, if you're Irish."

"Ah." Amy tried to hide her smile, but gave up. It felt too good.

Case stood, resumed his tour. He paused before the door leading to the tower, and the atmosphere instantly intensified. "Been up there, yet?"

"Yeah."

"What did you think?" Case crossed his arms across his chest. His actions seemed uncharacteristic, even with what little she knew about him. Amy expected him to at least try to open the door.

"Uh, I'm not particularly anxious to go up there again," she finally answered.

"Afraid of heights?"

"Not really. It's just...a feeling. I can't explain. You'll think I'm nuts."

Case's eyes once more fixed on hers, not unlike the first time they had met. He was inside her again. "Probably not."

"It's like something is waiting here, or unfinished or unsettled..." She could not bring herself to mention the word displayed in neon lights across her brain: *haunted*.

"I might ask you, then, why did you buy this place if it makes you so uneasy?"

"I didn't buy it," Amy replied softly. "Brian did."

Case's eyebrows lifted only slightly. He continued to stare at her for a few moments, then turned. "Two bedrooms?"

Amy followed him wordlessly into the larger bedroom.

"Are you keeping the furniture?" Case asked, squatting to examine the vanity dresser with the hinged mirror.

"I–probably. Some of it. I don't know for sure. We haven't had a chance, you know, to really look at it, with Brian still..."

Case stood. "I'm sorry. How's he doing?"

Amy forced a smile. "Okay. He's stable. Losing weight, though. But I have a feeling he'll be coming around soon."

Case nodded and grasped the closet doorknob, then looked at Amy.

"Go ahead. There were some old clothes in there."

Case stared into the closet, his face unreadable. Slowly he reached in and removed one of the hangers, withdrawing a long, flowered print dress. Taking a deep breath, he held it for several seconds before bunching it around the waist with his other hand.

Fascinated by his actions, Amy stood beside the door and watched as Case slowly brought the garment to his face as if to breathe in its aura. The moment seemed intimate; eerie.

Breaking the uncomfortable silence, Amy stepped closer. "Pretty musty, huh? Judging from the style, I'd say those clothes are from the 70's."

Whatever spell had befallen Case evaporated. He hastily put the dress back into the closet and carefully closed the door.

"So when do I start?" he asked, stuffing his hands into his hip pockets.

"What are you doing the next four hours?"

At Case's request, Amy drove him down to the harbor.

"The tools are locked in the galley. I'll just be a minute, unless you want to take a look inside?"

"Sure! Wow, it's a beautiful boat," Amy offered, accepting Case's steadying hand as she stepped onto the *Fancy Dream.*

"Guess I'm a frustrated sailor at heart." Case unlocked the hatch door and lifted it out, exposing a brief stairway leading into the interior of the large boat. "Watch your step."

Amy followed him inside the salon, amazed and impressed by the detail and quality of the sailboat. A complete kitchen, though three-quarter sized, filled almost a third of the hull. A built-in eating booth, desk, and twin bed completed the appointments, with a folding door hiding a very small bathroom.

"This is nice," Amy murmured, while Case repacked his toolbox.

"Nice but out of commission. I've got a guy working on the rudder. I guess I made a bad turn on the way down here."

"Down from?"

"Oh, up north. Near the Oregon border."

Amy gestured toward Case's T-shirt; the Boss' concert venue was in Gainesville, Florida.

"I thought you were maybe from the South."

Case snapped the box shut and stood up. "That's one of the places I'm from, yeah. Also Idaho. Mostly Idaho, actually."

"Idaho? I've never been there."

They walked back to Amy's car. Case stowed the toolbox in the trunk. "Idaho's beautiful, about half the year. I'm kind of a water-guy, though."

"Actually, I'm kind of a water-girl," Amy said with a grin. She slipped behind the steering wheel as Case got into the passenger side.

"Then you're in the right place."

Amy pushed the key into the ignition, then paused. "Yeah, but...I've always wanted to live in the forest, too. Weird, huh?"

"Not weird at all."

After a stop at the only hardware store in town, Amy and Case returned to Point Surrender.

"The first thing you want to do is secure all the doors and windows. You'll be keeping things here now; you don't want vandals getting in."

Amy nodded, feeling an immense comfort in Case's presence. As he started to turn his attention toward the front door, Amy grasped his arm.

"Casey, I know the deal was work for meals, but I want you to know, I do intend to pay you after...after Brian gets well. But please, don't feel obligated if you decide it isn't worth the wait."

Case's attention drifted from Amy's face down to where her hand rested on his arm, then back to her eyes.

"*Case*, if you don't mind. And I'm on paid vacation time, so don't worry about it. I'll probably ship out when my boat's done, but until then, I'm yours."

Amy slowly pulled her hand away, but the feeling of his warm flesh remained imprinted on her fingertips. He stood for just a moment studying her eyes before moving toward the door.

Amy and Case worked apart the rest of the day. Electricity was restored in the afternoon, and by five o'clock Case had all the locks cleaned and repaired and the windows secured.

"I'm gonna shove off now. Are you staying?"

"I can quit if you need a ride back to town."

"Not necessary. I'll walk. You be here tomorrow?"

"I work the next four days, but I'll be here in the mornings."

"See you then."

Case took his time walking back into Newburg and then retired early. The events of the past few days had put a decided wrinkle in his life. His fixation on Point Surrender aside, he had to admit it was his fascination with Mrs. Amy Winslow that bothered him the most.

He admired her stamina in the face of the tragedy that had befallen her husband, yet there was vulnerability, a defenselessness that tugged at him. She needed protecting, but her man was not there for her, might never again be there for her.

She posed a real problem for him.

"Damn." Case turned in his bed, cursing the sleep that eluded him.

It didn't help that she was attractive. Didn't help that her brown eyes held so much warmth, so much honest truth about herself. Truth she didn't even know she conveyed.

Tossing the other way, Case realized that no matter what his position, Amy's face appeared before him, inside his head. Sensibilities were stuffed into a bag and thrown into the sea to perish. It was useless denying the fact that he couldn't wait to see her again. Useless to remind himself that she had a husband barely clinging to life in a nearby hospital.

It had been–how many years? Five, six maybe, since he'd had a serious relationship with a woman. *That* one had gotten him almost to the altar, but commitment wasn't his thing.

No, Case McKenna had long ago discovered that there was no permanency to the emotion he mockingly thought of as 'love.' And trust? A virtue granted only to saints. If there was one thing, and one thing only, his parents had taught him, it was to never, ever trust anyone with your heart.

What of his aunt and uncle? True, they'd had a good, solid marriage. But even their love succumbed to fate.

The fact remained that love was not for everyone.

Certainly not for me.

Chapter Eight

"Riley thinks we should have a party," Amy announced from atop the ladder inside the small bedroom closet. Just outside the bedroom door, Case worked to replace a broken light switch on the wall.

"What kind of party?"

"A 'Save Point Surrender' fundraiser. He says maybe local folks will donate cash and goods and services to help us. Man this shelf is dirty!" She took a swipe at the shelf with her rag, coughed.

"That sounds like a plan. I suppose he'll donate the eats?"

"Of course. Which is no small thing, I can tell you. Could you come in here and hand me that scraper? There's something spilled on this shelf. Looks like paint."

Case came to the bedroom door threshold, but paused before entering.

"It's over by the window. Please?"

"Sure," Case muttered, briskly strode across the room, retrieved the tool, then handed it to Amy. Before Amy could level the tool against the shelf, a small movement caught her eye. From the darkest corner of the closet shelf rolled a tiny object. But how?

"What the–" she murmured as the small metal car stopped when it touched her hand. *I must have hit it with my rag.* She really didn't remember doing so.

"This might have been a child's room," Amy said, looking back down the ladder. "I found this up here." Opening her hand, she displayed the tiny blue toy car. "I'd say it's a '69 Camaro, what do you think?"

Case, leaving the room, called over his shoulder, "Couldn't say. I don't know much about toys."

Perplexed, Amy pocketed the car and resumed her task.

At around noon they broke for lunch, diving into turkey sandwiches Riley had put together from yesterday's leftovers. They sat at the kitchen table.

"Any news on Brian?" Case asked, keeping his tone routine but polite, suspecting he already knew the answer.

"Not really. Some eye movement, which is good. Dreaming maybe. Boy, he had some wild dreams as a kid."

"You grew up together. Where at?"

"Southern California, in an orange grove–Santa Paula. It's near Ventura, Oxnard–you know?"

"Heard of it."

"Great place for kids. At least back then. I hope someday…"

Case picked up on what he thought was her train of thought. "You and Brian planning to have kids?"

Amy's face broke into a confused grin. "*Me and Brian?* Well, Brian certainly wants kids, and so does Judy, his fiancée. And me, well, someday…I know my brother will make a wonderful father, but I'm not sure about *my* chances of finding such a guy to have children with."

Case's eyes widened involuntarily. *Her brother?* Hoping to hide his surprise, Case took a sip of cola and cleared his throat.

Amy cocked her head to the side and smiled. "How about you? You married? Engaged?"

Case chuckled nervously. "No on both accounts. Haven't had time for it, frankly."

"That's a cop out, McKenna. If and when love finds you, you make time for it."

"Spoken like a woman of great experience. I'll let you know when 'it' finds me."

"You do that," Amy said with a short laugh.

Between that laugh and the last glimpse of her car turning onto Coast Highway, Case McKenna hit his thumb with a hammer, dropped a box of 3-penny nails on his foot, and closed the medicine cabinet door on his finger.

"You're humming."

"I am not. It's your imagination," Amy accused Riley in the kitchen that afternoon.

"*Oh, touch me, touch me again with your sweetness...*" Riley sang as he swayed through the swinging doors to the kitchen.

Amy couldn't help but grin to herself as she pushed a huge tray of biscuits into the oven.

"Any big parties tonight?" she called over her shoulder.

"Nope. In fact, I been thinkin' about giving you the

night off. Wendy kinda wanted to help out tonight. She's going nuts sitting around at home. Wouldja mind?"

"Mind?" Amy looked up, a winsome smile spreading across her face. While she definitely needed the money, there was somewhere else she wanted to spend some time. "I'm thrilled that she feels well enough to work! I'll find something to do."

"That's what I thought. Oh, and I just happen to have some excess chicken parts if you're interested."

It took her no time to pack a picnic basket with Riley's offering. She stopped at the new convenience store at the edge of town and picked up beer, sodas, and ice. When she parked on the bluff at the Point, she sat in her car for a moment, wondering about her motives, questioning the giddy feeling inside. A voice she could only barely hear chastised, warned her not to get any closer. Taking in a deep breath, she listened for the other voice. The one urging her to go. To have fun. To live.

"What the heck. It's just chicken."

Amy trotted down the rough hillside steps leading to the lighthouse door, which stood open to the breeze. From inside came the intermittent sound of an electric drill.

"Hello!" Amy called during a quiet moment.

"In here," Case yelled from the kitchen where he was tightening new screws on the side door hinges.

"Riley sent lunch."

"That guy's going to go broke feeding us." Case stood and unplugged the drill, crossed to the picnic basket and reached inside. Amy noticed he wore cut-offs, his legs firm and tan. It was obvious that he rarely wore long pants. "Hey, Coors. Cool."

"I called the phone company. They can't get out here for at least a week. They said to decide where we want the lines. The house will have to be all re-wired anyway. I think one outlet on the little desk, don't you?"

Case nodded. He pulled a drumstick from the picnic basket and took a bite.

Amy took a long draught of black cherry soda, then pointed upward. Case followed her gaze, swallowed.

"The tower? You think we need a phone up there?"

"What if you were up there and it rang?"

"You take a cordless with you." Case wiped his mouth with a paper napkin. He took a moment to study Amy's face.

Amy looked away, embarrassed by his words and his stare. "Oh, yeah, you're right. I hadn't thought of that. Which reminds me. We...haven't been up there yet."

Case paused, drumstick in hand, his eyes cast down. Amy watched him carefully. Could it be that Case dreaded those steps as much as she did?

"All in good time," he murmured at last. "The living quarters are more important right now."

"Yeah, but, I *would* like to have someone look at the light. I want to know if it's even possible for it to work again. I don't have a clue, and I don't think Brian really did–*does*, either. The parts might not all be there."

Case tossed the chicken bone into the trash and reached for a biscuit. "These are the best rolls I've had in a long time."

Amy made a mock curtsey. "Why thank you, sir."
"You made them?"
"Like it was hard."
"Anything more than instant coffee is hard to me."
They finished lunch and Case showed Amy the items he had worked on before her arrival. Together they examined the desk area, marking with masking tape where they agreed the phone line should be installed.

Amy sat this time, opening the many drawers in turn, finding little but paper scraps and a few paper clips. Nearly missed in the back of the bottom drawer was a thin book. Amy pulled it out and placed it on the desk, looking up at Case in excitement. "Did you see this before?"
"Nope."
Without hesitation, she opened the untitled book. It was immediately clear that the handwritten words were part of a journal or diary, each entry written at different times, some in different colors of ink. Some painstakingly proper, others hurried and sketchy. "Wow..." Amy whispered, drawing her fingertips down the first page. "Listen to this..."

"Seattle, June 19, 1968...I can't believe we are finally leaving. Since the time the CG wrote me, we've packed and unpacked and repacked, waiting and waiting. My dream has finally arrived. Leta is excited too. I just hope there's a place nearby where she can buy records. I told her, keepers' wives usually plant vegetables and sew clothes. She looks at me like I'm crazy. I probably am.

"They say the tower is over 50 feet tall. Not as big as Pigeon Point, that's for sure. Big enough, though. I wonder how many steps that is?

"William R. Jenner,U.S.C.G., Civilian Keeper."

Amy took a breath, then continued.

"Oh my gosh. This must have belonged to *him*. The last keeper." She turned her head to find Case's reaction, but he no longer stood behind her. Instead, sunshine outlined his silhouette from the open front doorway, his back to Amy and the journal. "Case? Is something wrong?"

He turned around, his expression somber. "No. It's just kinda weird, that's all. It's somebody's personal diary. I feel like I shouldn't be hearing it."

"Oh." Amy closed the journal and slid it away from her on the desktop. "Well." She stood up and retreated to the kitchen. Soon, Case appeared at the open side door, his persona shuttered and cool.

"I forgot to tell you," Amy began brightly. "Riley's putting out flyers for our open house next Saturday. Can you make it?"

"Sure." Case rubbed the back of his neck, turned toward the sea. "Look, I need to get some air for a little while. I'm gonna…" He gestured toward the road with his thumb and Amy nodded.

"See ya." Amy was beset with melancholy as Case walked away. She found it hard to continue working without him. She considered following, but decided he needed to be alone for some reason. Instead, she went back to the desk and retrieved the journal, tucking it into her purse to take back to the inn.

* * *

Case walked south until he came to a path leading down to the beach. Taking the 'low road,' he jogged down the rugged, makeshift path, stopping when he reached the narrow sandy strip between the bottom of the bluff and the water. Quickly ditching his shoes and socks, he continued to jog down to the wet sand and then along the edge of the surf until he became winded and slowed to a walk.

Amy Winslow permeated his thoughts.

Not only was she intelligent, cute and witty, she was single. Seemingly unattached to anyone but her brother, satisfied to be a waitress in a one horse beach town full of retired people and fishermen.

There was more. She sensed something, something about Point Surrender, not unlike his own uneasiness. He had serious misgivings about being there, with good reason. But why would she?

Her discovery of the journal troubled him. Its contents could do no good, not now, not after all these years. When did it begin? 1968? Nearly forty years had passed since the words had been written. Case hoped Amy would just let it be.

Forty years. It wasn't like ancient history; the words did not recount the horrors of the 1906 earthquake, or the bombing of Pearl Harbor. What Amy probably didn't realize was that some of the people about whom the author wrote might still be around. They might be private citizens whose pasts were best kept private.

Tired of walking, Case sat down on the sand and watched the waves. Turning his head to the north, Point

Surrender looked like a piece of child's chalk standing on end, perched precariously on the rocky cliff. He thought about Amy still inside, wondering about his change of mood and quick departure. Her face had been crestfallen, maybe even fearful as he excused himself and fled down the coast. Once again, he chastised himself for his bad manners. Try as he might, he could find nothing wrong with Amy Winslow. It had been easier to push aside her charm when he believed her to be married. But now, there was no reason not to enjoy her company. Moreover, other than his own emotional baggage, no reason in the world not to fall in love with her.

Amy found herself glancing up more than once at the small portion of road she could see from the house. Case would be back; what his mood would be was another thing. She began to see that there was another side to Case McKenna, a mysterious and possibly troubled side that only occasionally revealed itself. Still, the man had her attention.

Amy put her chin down on her crossed arms at the table. How could this be happening? If she was smart–and she wasn't feeling too smart these days–she would dismiss Case McKenna and find someone else to help out. Someone older, less attractive. Someone without intriguing blue eyes and a surprising, alarming smile. Someone whose life was an open book and who wasn't afraid to go into the tower.

"Penny for your thoughts."

Amy sat up and turned around to see Case re-enter the kitchen through the new side door. "Have a nice walk?"

"Don't mind me. My mother was scared by a lighthouse when she was pregnant with me."

Amy laughed out loud at his joke and put her hands on her hips. "Anything to get out of going up there," she chided, pointing toward the tower.

Case raked a hand through his hair and, with a smile, shook his head. "If you want to go up, let's go up. But you might have to hold my hand."

Amy turned away before Case could see the blush rising to her cheeks. From a kitchen drawer she picked out a key, then led Case to the door leading to the tower steps.

The door unlocked easily and Amy pulled it open wide, then turned expectantly toward Case. "Ready?"

"After you, lady," he said with a grand gesture, and Amy started hesitantly up the iron steps.

"Warm in here," Amy said, grasping the iron handrail as she climbed.

"Yeah," Case muttered, from behind her.

There was a small landing halfway up, and Amy paused to catch her breath. The clatter of their footsteps on the tight, curving stairway echoed loudly. Looking back down, the spiraled steps resembled a seashell. She uttered a nervous laugh and continued the climb.

"They say this tower is a bit narrower than most of the others," she said. "These steps are really nerve-wracking, aren't they?"

"Yeah, I guess."

When Amy reached the top, she pushed against the wooden ceiling the way she had seen Brian gain access to the light, but nothing moved.

"I know it's here somewhere, but it's dark…"

"Here. Let me." Case, beside her in the narrow stairwell, reached past her and gave the door a firm shove in exactly the right spot. The trapdoor flipped open and light poured down upon them.

"How did you know where to push?"

"Easy. The hinges are over here, so…"

Amy pushed out her lower lip in a mock pout and moved past him, climbing into the lantern room on her own. Case followed, then closed the trapdoor behind him.

The view silenced them both. It was some time before either ventured to speak. Case walked the circumference of the light, looking first outside and then at the lens. "Still in place after almost ninety years. Wow." Fingers splayed, he caressed the glass enclosing the lens almost reverently. Amy watched in fascination as Case admired the craftsmanship.

"Do you know anything about these things?" she asked, her fingers still tightly wrapped around the interior handrail.

His spell momentarily broken, Case diverted his eyes to Amy's and shook his head unconvincingly. "Not really. But just look at it! You don't have to know anything about it to appreciate how fine it is. Look at all that brass! Nobody's polished her in a long, long time." These last words were tinged with unmistakable sorrow.

"*You* don't seem to be afraid of heights," Amy commented, as Case stared out at the massive expanse of the Pacific Ocean.

"Didn't say I was. Looks like there have been more than a few murres roosting up here. Oh, where did you want that phone?"

Amy smiled. She had grown up loving puzzles, and here was a life-sized puzzle for her to work. "Right *here*," she said, pointing to the middle of a glass pane in jest.

"Whatever you want, lady. I'll just go get my drill."

"I wonder how you turn it on?" Amy mused, admiring the enormous light fixture.

"There are switches behind that panel there, and another set of switches in a box at the bottom of the steps."

Amy turned a quizzical face up to Case. "And just how do you know that?"

"I saw them. It makes sense, doesn't it, that a switch box at the bottom of a lighthouse tower might work the light?"

Amy smirked. "Okay, wise guy, why don't you just turn it on?"

"Can't. There's a law against turning on the light during the day. I think." Case had moved to stand in the small space behind her. When she turned to tell him he'd better come up with a better excuse, she found her face surprisingly close, her lips dangerously close...to his. She had already opened those lips to chastise him, but closed them in view of his serious expression.

"So do you want to go out, or what?" he asked softly.

126

Suddenly weak, Amy leaned back against the handrail. "Out?" she whispered, her face now so close she could feel the warmth of his, feel the words he spoke against her forehead.

"Yeah, outside. I'll take you out on the gallery if you want."

"Oh. N–No, that's not necessary. Maybe next trip."

"C'mon. It's okay, really. The fresh air is good."

She let him. When did he take her hand? The feel of his fingers laced with hers was natural, easy, warm. Gently tugging, he slowly led her through the door. Amy's senses were heightened, at least as much by his touch as by the rush of being so high, so exposed to the world.

He was right, the cool air felt good against her cheeks. Maybe she could get used to it, this high altitude thing. Especially with Case McKenna beside her. She ventured a look down at the small, faintly green lawn that spread in patches to the edge of the cliff. And saw *him* again. The man in the grey shirt.

"Do you see that guy?" she asked, grasping Case's sleeve with her free hand. "Look. Over there. What's he doing?"

Case squinted, looked down. Tilting his head slightly, his parted lips told of his surprise. "That's the guy I saw from my sloop! The guy that fell. He was standing just like that, only facing the lighthouse last time."

Amy turned to look up into Case's eyes. "When was this?"

"When I came into Newburg harbor. I saw this guy fall...but..." Turning to look back toward the cliff, he paused. The man was gone.

Amy pressed her hand to her mouth. "It's the same guy I saw the day you came up here to help. He...he disappeared then, too." She stared hard at Case's face, trying to read his take on their similar sightings. "I don't...I don't get it. What...Who is he?"

Case let go of her hand and slipped an arm around her shoulders. "You're looking a little pale. Let's go back downstairs."

"Yeah, okay." Amy was both disappointed and relieved when Case moved away from her and squatted to pull open the trapdoor. After taking a few steps down ahead of her, he turned and extended his hand.

"I guess I'm the one who needs hand-holding," she muttered, grasping his hand solidly and relishing the warmth that spread throughout her body as a result.

Back in the kitchen, she dropped the key back into the drawer next to the sink.

"What do you make of that?" she asked, her heart still thumping hard in her chest.

"Weird. I thought it was just me. I'd been asleep, I guess. But this time, we both saw him. It's gotta be some guy playing a prank."

"You think?"

"Well I sure as hell don't believe in ghosts."

Amy sat at the table, still shaken, as much from Case's touch as from their sighting. She debated whether to share what little she knew of the lighthouse's unusual history.

"I'm not really afraid of heights either," she began.

Case picked a screwdriver out of his open toolbox and began fiddling with the bottom hinge on a broken cabinet door.

"Riley told me an interesting story about the man who used to live here. *Riley* didn't live in Newburg then, but he says the story goes that the keeper got drunk one night and fell down those stairs and died."

His face solemn, Case moved to the upper hinge on the cabinet. Amy continued.

"Miss Hastings said that the keeper's wife had left him for another man, and that's probably why he drank so much. Isn't that awful?"

"Sounds like a bunch of small town gossip to me." The cabinet door came away with the snap of aged, cracking paint and Case put it on the floor. "You'd probably do well not to listen to that kind of crap."

Amy frowned. "Well, unlike you, I am interested in the local history of this place. That's why I think the journal might be good to read. And if it will make you feel better, I don't plan to share what it says with anyone, except maybe Brian, since it's really his lighthouse."

"Suit yourself."

Amy was disappointed that Case didn't share her craving for the whole story. But she refused to let it discolor her opinion of him. He was the first man she'd met in many years who wasn't afraid to speak his mind about his scruples. Perhaps the first to *have* scruples.

They worked until an hour past sundown, when Amy tapped Case on the shoulder from where he worked at digging out the fireplace grate.

"Come on. Let's go home."

"Home?"

"Yes. Maybe Miss Hastings has some leftover something-or-other she could heat up for us."

"Hastings? Do you–?"

Amy nodded and uttered a girlish giggle while putting on her jacket. "Sorry about the bra," she said, brushing past him out the door, leaving Case his turn to blush.

Chapter Nine

Dr. Hammill's office was pleasant, with an oversized aquarium in the center of the waiting room. Each of the other women in the room was pregnant, all of them noticeably so. Uncomfortable, Amy suddenly wished she hadn't come.

Thumbing quickly through a magazine, she realized the pages were all about babies and mothers–and fathers. Looking around, she wondered sourly if any of the other expectant mothers were single parents too.

Parent. The word sounded entirely foreign in any grouping meant to describe her life. Even the term 'mother' gave her pause. Her own mother had left her so young, without imparting the advice or training essential to becoming one herself. Despite her humorous suggestion to Riley that she had raised her brother, Amy felt like a loose sail in the wind when it came to children.

She crossed and uncrossed her legs, then crossed them again. Another woman smiled over the top of her magazine, and Amy uncrossed her legs once more.

"Miss Winslow?" the nurse called, and Amy nearly left her skin behind. "Come with me."

She was led to an exam room and handed a paper garment. "Open in the front, then drape the sheet across your lap. Is the father coming?"

"No."

The nurse considered her for a moment and then made a notation on her chart. "Doctor will be in shortly."

Shivering in the paper gown, Amy felt vulnerable and alone. Here, in the bright, fluorescent, sterile world of Exam Room No. 9, reality smacked her hard across the face. She couldn't think about her father or her brother, or any person with integrity. She was filled with shame and regret, sadness and fear. She did not dare allow her thoughts to include Case, either, for the very reason she was here precluded any kind of happiness with him. Once he found out about her pregnancy, it would be over, before it even began.

No. She could only focus on Drew, and his part in what was happening to her. She tried to remember feelings of love, tried to recall the times she'd admired his virtues, craved his touch, respected his opinion. All those feelings had evaporated with the knowledge of his affair, leaving only bitterness and anger.

The anger wasn't only about Drew, either. She was mad at herself, for in reality, she could have, *should have* taken precautions. She had been lax, secure in his supposed love and their future together.

If only she hadn't gotten pregnant. If only–

"Amy Winslow? I'm Jeremy Hammill."

He was probably a good doctor, but Amy felt nothing either way for the young obstetrician who examined her, then performed a preliminary ultrasound.

"Two months, give or take a few days. That would make you due...around mid-January. I want you to start the pre-natals immediately, and I'll see you back in two months, unless you experience any unusual occurrences or discomfort."

Amy nodded, making only cursory eye contact.

"I'm sorry, I need to clarify, you are unmarried, correct?"

"Yes."

"You do know who the father is?"

Amy stiffened, ventured a look at the doctor's face. *Don't be offended. He's only doing his job.* "Yes. I do. He's…away right now."

Dr. Hammill looked relieved. "Okay. Great. Well if either of you have any questions, please call me. First pregnancies can be a laugh a minute."

"Got that right," Amy murmured.

Amy wondered if she'd thanked the doctor as she drove to Brian's apartment. There would be mail to pick up, messages to hear. Once inside, she roamed about the flat in a fog, not really seeing anything but the past.

Two months, the doctor had said. May 15th? Sure enough. Drew's birthday, and they had celebrated with an intimate party of fifty or so 'close' friends. That night, they had celebrated privately. She had been drinking, and tired, and had tried to put him off.

"It's my *birthday*, Aims. Come on."

Amy looked again at the large bottle of prenatal vitamins in her bag and began to cry. *I hate you, Drew Richards. I HATE you!* Falling onto Brian's bed, she cried for nearly thirty minutes before falling asleep.

* * *

Case was working on the garage today. On a ladder, scraping the peeling paint from the weathered siding, he decided the structure would be better torn down and rebuilt; the boards and roof were showing signs of major rot. The decision would be Amy's, of course. He'd ask her when she joined him.

When the noon hour came and went without Amy's arrival, Case wondered if she had, perhaps, mentioned that she wouldn't be coming today. She left the inn early, according to Miss Hastings, but said nothing about her destination nor when she would return.

Unable to work, Case wandered about the grounds, his thoughts recounting the day in the tower with Amy. The day they'd both seen the man on the cliff. The false bravado he'd put on bothered him. For try as he might, he could not figure out how the man got there or how he disappeared. He and Amy had each seen him once before.

He walked the length of the cliff behind the lighthouse, cautiously leaning out over the edge. No paths. No footholds. No way for a man to get down without...without falling.

With the sun hanging just above the watery horizon, Case found a spot to sit and watch the sunset do its magic. With the sound of each approaching car on the highway, he turned expectantly, but was disappointed each time.

Finally, at 7 P.M., he locked up the house and trekked back to Newburg. He stopped in at Riley's to see if perhaps Amy was there, but no one had seen her since she'd said goodnight on Wednesday evening.

Irena Hastings sat in her bentwood rocking chair,

watching television in the downstairs parlor as Case strode in.

"Hello Mr. McKenna. Did you have a good day?"

"Fair day, Miss Hastings. Is Miss Winslow in yet?"

"No, I haven't seen her. She isn't at the lighthouse?"

"No."

Case went upstairs, showered, and changed, then came back downstairs. The night was cool and clear, with no hint of the fog that would creep in during the wee hours. He made himself comfortable on the wide, cushioned porch swing and closed his eyes.

As much as he hated to admit it, even to himself, he was worried about Amy. He thought about Jack, back home, and began to chuckle. *Jack would be laughing his proverbial ass off if he knew. Case McKenna, self-proclaimed loner, worried about a woman? A woman he'd known barely two weeks?*

His laughter faded away. He wished she would just show up so he would at least know she was okay.

"This is crazy." *I can't just sit here.*

Case got out of the swing and trotted down the wide porch steps to the sidewalk. He began walking in the direction of the harbor, where his all-but-ignored sailboat was docked. He hadn't heard from Davis yet, so assumed the work was still in process. But now, he wasn't in any hurry to raise the mainsail.

He had walked only a block when he saw headlights approaching from behind him. Turning around, he watched with interest as Amy Winslow got out of her car and hurried up the steps to Hastings House. She had not seen him, and for this he was grateful. He would wait outside until her bedroom light went out.

Amy tapped lightly on the door labeled 'Morgan's Room,' then listened for a response. She thought Case might be curious, possibly a little concerned, about why she hadn't shown up today at the lighthouse. There was no response.

She was tired, but not able to sleep after her unplanned nap in the city. Lying in bed, she longed for something to take her away from her problems. She needed a diversion. For the first time since leaving Carmel, she missed her television and CD player. Perhaps Miss Hastings kept books in the parlor?

Before Amy reached the door to her room, she remembered the journal, still in her purse. Retrieving it, she turned off the ceiling light, turned on the bedside lamp, and climbed into bed.

With a deep breath, she opened the book and began to read.

Point Surrender, California, June 22, 1968
   We are here. What an incredible place, better than we even dreamed. I will write more when I am not so bone-tired.
William R. Jenner, Keeper

Point Surrender, California, July 10, 1968
   The house part isn't as big as we had imagined. We sold Leta's piano and got a

smaller bed, but overall I love this place. There is so much to learn. There's a 3rd order Fresnel lens up there – what a beauty! The foghorn is a little annoying, Leta hates it of course, but it's a necessity. The point is fogged in much of the year, I'm told, and the light isn't much good then.

The murres are everywhere. Not much like the sea birds we had in Seattle. Yesterday one of them crashed right into the lantern.

The garage is higher on the bluff and Leta counted 52 steps to get up there. Not bad in the summer, but not looking forward to climbing them in the rain.
William R. Jenner, Keeper

A sound in the hall interrupted her reading; Case's bedroom door opened and closed. Amy suddenly felt guilty and closed the book, sliding it into her nightstand drawer. She would read more another night.

In the dark, Amy tried to imagine William and Leta Jenner and their first days at Point Surrender.

Her eyes still looked puffy the next morning, but Amy couldn't afford to sleep in. She was already a little late, and hurriedly drove to Riley's, getting there by 9:05 A.M.

"Sorry I'm late," she breathed, shoving her purse into the unlocked safe in the back.

"Late? I didn't notice," Riley said, his arms crossed on his chest while tapping his foot.

Amy ignored his comic stance and went around the room collecting sugar shakers. The fact that they had not been refilled the night before at closing told her that Wendy wasn't up to speed.

Riley met her at the counter to lift the heavy sugar canister from the cabinet.

"Nice day off?"

"Not really. I had a doctor's appointment."

"Well, your building buddy came by last night looking for you."

"Case stopped by? What time?"

"It was around 7 P.M., maybe 7:30. Hey, watch it!" Riley reached out to tilt back the canister in Amy's hand as sugar poured out onto the counter from the over-full shaker.

"Sorry." Amy colored at her blunder. "He probably wonders what the heck happened to me," Amy said, more to herself than to her easygoing boss.

"He did seem a little...concerned," Riley agreed.

"Did he?"

Riley took Amy by the wrist and led her to a booth near the counter. "Look. You haven't known me long, but I feel like I've known you forever. Know what I mean?"

Amy nodded. There was a solemnity in Riley's eyes she rarely saw.

"Now I wouldn't lead you wrong, girl. Unless I miss my mark, and I usually don't, this guy is smitten."

"Smitten?"

"You know, bit by the bug. On the hook. Shot by the arrow. He's going down fast."

Amy waved her arm, dismissing the idea. "And anyway, even if he is, he'll run like a rabbit when he finds out."

"What, that you've got more than biscuits in the oven? If I had to bet, not that I'm a bettin' man, I'd wager that he'll take the both of you, no questions asked."

"I'd like to think there are men out there like that, but the fact of the matter is, it's not very likely." Reality once again beginning to ruin her day, Amy stood up, determined not to get depressed. She had resigned herself, this morning in the shower, that she didn't need them. Not Drew, not Case, not anyone. But she did like having Riley as a friend.

"Thanks for the advice, Ri. I wish you were right." With that she went back to refilling shakers, trying to remember a song to hum.

As with many days before, Case was working away when Amy stopped by during her afternoon break.

"Hi," she called from the steps leading down the bluff. "Anybody home?"

Case was on his back beneath the kitchen sink, a small flashlight clenched in his teeth as he tightened a new 'U' pipe into place. Hearing Amy's entrance, he crawled out and sat up.

"Did you know there are fifty-two steps out there?"

"No, I didn't." He sat staring at her until she put the paper bag she carried onto the table.

"Phone guy show up yet?"

"He was here yesterday. He needs to talk to you. I

suggested he come back tomorrow."

"Oh. Right. Well, I stopped at Holiday Hardware and picked up that sandpaper you needed, and some more of that wood stain."

"Great."

"I, uh, also got a couple of subs from the Dilly Deli, if you're hungry. Thought you might be getting a little tired of fried chicken and turkey sandwiches."

Case got to his feet and turned to wash his hands. "So, where were you yesterday, anyway?"

"Had some errands to run in the city, and I ran later than I thought."

Case nodded, digging into the delicatessen bag for a sandwich. Amy watched him, knowing he was annoyed and wishing she could tell him the truth. She opted for part of the truth.

"Well, actually, I stopped at Brian's apartment. I laid down for a few minutes, you know, just to rest a little after driving all over San Francisco, and just like that, I fell asleep. I was so mad when I woke up, it was like 7:30, and I still had to drive all the way back here."

Case lifted his eyebrows, still unwrapping the sub. His eyes demanding honesty, he gazed intently at Amy, whose own eyes widened in response to his stare.

"You fell *asleep*?"

Entranced, Amy nodded. "Yeah. I, uh, haven't been sleeping very well at night." She got up and turned away, looking out the kitchen window. "I try not to mention it too much, but I'm really worried about Brian. I lay awake at night, wondering if–if he'll ever…"

Case put the sandwich down and went to stand behind her, placed his hands on her shoulders and gently kneaded them.

I must be dreaming. Amy closed her eyes and absorbed the comforting feel of the brief massage.

"I stopped by the hospital yesterday myself. The doctors are still optimistic." Speaking close to her ear, Case's tone was almost intimate.

Just as she had in the tower, Amy suddenly felt weak and leaned back against Case's chest. His hands slid down her arms in an effort to steady her.

"Maybe you'd better sit down," he said softly.

"I'm okay." *Just hold me a little longer.*

"I knew a guy once who lapsed into a coma for six months. The day he woke up, it was like nothing had happened at all."

Amy nodded slowly, not sure if she should believe Case or if it even mattered. Still, she appreciated his effort, and she squeezed her eyes tightly shut trying to prevent the tears that threatened.

At last she pulled away, took a deep breath, and reached for the bag on the table. "We'd better eat these before they get warm."

They ate companionably, chatting about the party on the weekend, and how they would handle it.

Soon Amy walked to the door. "I'm late again. It's a wonder Riley puts up with me."

"No it isn't."

"Bye..." Amy hurried to the base of the fifty-two steps leading up the bluff.

"Hey! Did you count them, or what?"

"It was in the journal!" she called back.

Case crossed his arms and leaned against the doorframe, shaking his head as she disappeared over the top.

Chapter Ten

Saturday morning Riley posted a sign in the window of his locked restaurant: "JOIN US AT POINT SURRENDER - ALL YOU CAN EAT BUFFET—PROCEEDS WILL HELP LIGHT THE LIGHT!"

Amy and Judy had painstakingly hung red and blue streamers from every spot attachable, and Riley had set up two long folding tables in the lighthouse's tiny yard area just outside the side kitchen door. He also brought a large gas outdoor grill and was hard at work barbecuing chicken and ribs by eleven.

The turnout was disappointing.

Irena Hastings sat in a lawn chair in the shade, watching two-dozen or so people mill about with half-eaten ribs in one-hand and paper plates in the other. Amy sat on the porch steps, squinting in the sunlight and half-heartedly keeping an eye on the upper bluff, hoping for more takers.

Judy dished out potato salad and poured lemonade. She, too, watched for newcomers, glancing periodically at Amy with a smile. She had spent the previous night at Hastings House, anxious to help out any way she could.

"Where's Case?" Riley called to Amy, wiping his brow with a small towel.

Amy shrugged. "Beats me. Maybe down at the harbor. He said he would be here."

No sooner had Amy spoken than two men descended the hillside steps. Following Case down was a shorter man with a full gray beard and long, steel-wool hair pulled into a ponytail beneath a rotting Giant's baseball cap. His face was as weathered as the wooden porch planks upon which Amy sat.

Case stood before Amy, his hands dipping into his back pockets. "Amy Winslow, Emery Davis. Local boat doctor."

"Pleasure to meet you, ma'am." The aged mariner tugged on the brim of his cap.

Amy nodded. "Please help yourself to some lunch, Mr. Davis."

"Don't mind if I do," he said, again tipping his hat before moving toward the luncheon feast.

"How's it going?" Case asked, settling himself on the steps beside Amy, who only shrugged in response.

"Don't be discouraged. Something good'll come of it."

"I feel bad for Riley. He really worked hard on this."

Before Case could respond, his attention was diverted by more people on the bluff. A man and a woman, both decidedly 'business class,' their eyes darting about with great interest, picked their way down the steps. Both Amy and Case got quickly to their feet.

"Is this Point Surrender?" the man asked, adjusting his horn-rimmed glasses and peering up at the monolithic tower.

"Sure is. Thanks for joining us." Amy held out her hand. "I'm Amy Winslow."

"Hank Avery, San Francisco Chronicle. This is Meredith Holmes, my assistant."

"Please, help yourself to some lunch," Amy offered, sweeping her arm toward the barbecue and the few card tables set up around the yard.

Avery ignored her offer and wandered toward the edge of the bluff, then turned again to look at the lighthouse and the water. Abruptly he returned.

"You own this place?"

"My brother and his fiancée own it. We're in the process of refurbishing it, and are hoping to interest the public in participating a little."

"I see. Merry, you got my PDA?"

"Right here. You want some notes?"

"On second thought, you got my recorder?"

Hank Avery spoke fluidly into the mini-recorder as Judy gave him a tour of the lighthouse, pointing out the work completed and that still undone.

After pocketing the recorder and dishing out healthy portions of potato salad, chicken, and beans, Avery sat down at a card table and hastily chowed down.

"How did you hear about us?" Amy asked.

"Stopped by the café, saw the sign. We're just on our way back from doing a story in Monterey."

Amy nodded, too afraid to ask what the reporter would do with the information on Point Surrender. She could only hope he was planning a feature.

Case was not so hesitant. "So you gonna plead our case to the good folks of San Francisco?"

Avery sighed, pushed his glasses again up the bridge

of his nose. "Possibly. Could make a good Sunday Lifestyle item. No promises though."

"Of course," Amy murmured, her fingers crossed tightly behind her back. "Any publicity we can get would be great."

"Thanks for lunch," Avery muttered, leaving his not-quite-cleaned paper plate on the table, he hastened toward the cliff, his assistant hustling behind him.

Emery Davis had a not-so-bad short wave radio he wasn't using. Newburg's mayoral office coughed up the funds to rebuild the decaying garage. Roth General Hospital donated an emergency medical kit, a fire extinguisher, and a check for $500.00. Seacoast Landscape offered to clear the brush surrounding the lot and plant new grass and evergreens.

Irena Hastings searched through her attic and produced curtains and mismatched china pieces, and an odd assortment of knick-knacks for Judy to pick from.

Amy sat back against the stiff settee in the parlor at Hastings House. Judy collapsed into the rocker while Irena mixed iced tea in the kitchen.

"Riley knocked himself out," Case said, making himself comfortable on the small couch beside Amy.

"I thought we would get more people. Riley even put a small ad in the Newburg Signal. We took in about $130.00 in cash donations for the lunch."

"Disappointed?" Case asked.

"I don't know. Everything is...I don't know. If only Brian would come around, I think we'd all feel better."

"They're moving him to a regular room today," Judy said.

Before Amy could comment on this new development, they heard the sound of breaking glass in the kitchen. Judy was on her feet first.

"It's okay," Miss Hastings called. "Just a little tumbler."

Judy went to the kitchen anyway, leaving Case and Amy alone.

"Well I think that Chronicle guy will write something up," Case said, turning to face Amy.

"That would be so cool."

"Speaking of San Francisco," Case said, adjusting his legs for a more comfortable position. "I need to head into the city this evening to pick up a part for the boat. You want to ride along? Maybe grab some dinner?"

Amy stared at Case, a bewildered smile gracing her face. "You...have a car?"

Case smiled, revealing a charm he rarely shared with anyone. "Nope." He rubbed his chin, still grinning. "Not here, anyway."

"Oh. Well in that case, I'd love to ride along." Amy smiled back, momentarily forgetting her long list of troubles.

With the new rudder bracket stashed in the trunk of Amy's car, Case started the engine and turned to her. "Any thoughts on where you'd like to eat?"

"Something simple. Something other than burgers, chicken, ribs, pizza..." she broke into a giggle, realizing she wasn't leaving many 'simple' choices.

"You love Chinese, right?"

Amy brightened. "How did you know?"

Case only grinned, shrugged.

Later, while marveling at Case's chopstick dexterity, Amy sighed.

"What was that for?" he asked.

"Oh, just enjoying the meal. You're pretty good at that."

"Took me years to learn. You're not so bad."

"Are you kidding? I might as well be using knitting needles!"

"So tell me about where you grew up. You said something about Ventura?"

Amy described her upbringing, skimming over her mother's death and focusing on the trials of growing up in an all-male household. "Dad owned a small orange grove. He sold it about ten years ago. Now he lives in Gentry Village. It's a senior retirement community."

"I'll bet he's pretty upset about Brian."

Amy looked away, then down at her lap. "I haven't told him yet."

Case tilted his head in question, and Amy felt compelled to explain.

"He's getting on in years. I was just waiting until Brian got better—or worse—before I told him. I know I should do it, in person, you know? But with everything that's going on, I keep putting it off."

Case nodded. "So, you been waitressing for a long time?"

"Goodness, no!" Amy giggled. "I'm a teacher. I'm just...just on summer vacation!"

"A teacher? Wow. Grammar school or what?"

Amy laughed again. "*Grammar* school? I haven't heard that term in awhile. I teach second grade. I love kids at that age. They're so...fresh and full of ideas and wonder."

Case lifted his eyebrows slightly, his expression skeptical.

"I take it you don't agree," Amy said, watching with chagrin as an egg roll slipped from her chopsticks a third time.

Case shrugged. "I haven't been around kids much, don't have much use for them. They're a necessary evil, I guess, for some people."

Amy stabbed and impaled the egg roll. "That's too bad," she muttered, biting into the roll and chewing it brusquely. "So what do you do when you're not hanging around lighthouses?"

"I work in oceanographic research. I specialize in marine mammals."

"No kidding? I never would have thought..."

Her disappointment temporarily pushed aside, Amy was newly intrigued. "You study whales and such?"

"I fix them, when I can. We get a lot of animals in that have been injured by boats, oil slicks, fishing nets, hooks, debris. You know, the kind of stuff you see on *Animal Planet.*"

"So you're really a veterinarian."

"Yup. I don't usually say that because people often

conjure up a picture of James Herriot on the farm with his arm and fist up inside a foaling horse."

Amy laughed out loud. "You're right!" Laughter subsiding, Amy formulated her next question. "So where did *you* grow up? Was it Idaho?"

"Different places. Mostly Idaho, yeah. Lived in Florida for a while, knocked around, then settled up at Grogan's Head. Just south of the Oregon border, north of Crescent City."

"Did you like Idaho? Does your family still live there?"

"My uncle does. My aunt died awhile back. Coeur d'Alene's an okay place, 'bout as good as anywhere."

"So you're on vacation too?"

"Kind of. I was heading down to San Diego when I ran over a bump in the water."

Amy nodded. "And you'll be going back soon."

"Actually, I'm due back on Monday."

Startled, Amy paled. "Oh," she said softly, hoping her face did not broadcast her disappointment.

"Well, I'm thinking about taking a couple more weeks. I should be able to–unless there's some kind of emergency. It's not like I couldn't be back there in a day if necessary. The boat's virtually done."

Case was less chatty on the drive back to Newburg. Satisfied with the quiet, Amy's own thoughts were in turmoil from their discussion and her growing feelings for Case.

In the hall outside their opposing doors, Case held up

her keys. "Thanks for the transportation."

"Thanks for the dinner." She looked past him to the inscribed brass plaque. "Did Miss Hastings tell you the story about Morgan and Jacelyn?"

"I think she tried to," Case said quietly. "I was half-asleep at the time."

"I understand they actually named Point Surrender. Morgan Hastings was…a pirate, of sorts. They jumped from the cliff. Their bodies were never found."

"She didn't tell me *that*."

"I read it–"

"In the journal, right?"

Amy nodded, embarrassed by her enthusiasm. She turned and unlocked her door, and Case unlocked his.

"Would you like to see the pirate's room then?" he asked, swinging the door open before her.

"Well, why not?" Amy slipped her keys into her pocket and walked in as Case turned on the small bedside lamp. Decorated in maritime artifacts, the room was definitely male in character. Amy went immediately to the window. "You have a wonderful view."

The fog was tumbling in over the water, the meager light of a half-moon slowly dissipating in the mist. Case moved in behind her to peer over her shoulder.

"Yeah. I think I may have looked out this window once before."

Amy turned to face him, to see his smile, feel his gaze, watch his lips form the words. She fixed on those lips for just a moment, deciding they looked sensuous.

Sensuous? A word she had never in her life used to

describe anything about a man.

"What?" he asked softly, obviously confused by her stillness.

"N-nothing. I– "Amy started to turn, to hide her obvious fluster, but Case suddenly grasped her shoulders, preventing her escape.

"Amy."

Those lips had spoken her name. Expectantly, she looked into his eyes, his bluer-than-blue eyes that were searching for something in hers.

"I really enjoyed tonight," he began, now slowly bringing his fingers to her hair and carefully sliding them into the tresses.

Amy went rigid with fear. A man, a man other than Drew Richards was touching her. *This can't be happening...it feels too good.*

Like an out-of-synch movie soundtrack, she heard Case's words belatedly and began to nod. Her arms hung heavily at her sides as her purse slipped from her shoulder and onto the bed.

"It's been a long time," he continued, now cupping the back of her head with his long fingers. His other hand slipped around her waist and drew her nearer.

Stumbling in her fixation, Amy finally lifted her hesitant hands to rest against his chest.

It's been a long time, her mind repeated in agreement. *It certainly has. A long time since anything felt this real.*

Additional words unnecessary, Case's lips were upon hers, ending a torturous anticipation, and drinking in the warmth they both knew they would find. Amy nearly collapsed in relief against his firmness, his stability and strength, drawing in his kiss with unexpected passion.

Pausing only for a minimum of air, Case initiated one kiss after another, bending lower to enable Amy's arms to capture him about the neck. Her embrace bordered on desperate; dizzy with emotion, weak with yearning. Sweet, liquid warmth flooded her body. A new sensation, unlike anything she'd ever felt before. Surprisingly new, and that very newness changed her somehow. Changed her forever.

She kissed him back. Lips, tongue, teeth; fingers, muscle, flesh. Kiss for kiss, Amy let go. If only for a moment in time, the restraint she'd been so careful to employ lifted away, there in the dim light of the pirate captain's room. The hours and days she'd spent working beside him, watching his eyes, his lips, his hands, had at last culminated in the inevitable. And it was every bit as electrifying as she'd always known it would be. When she felt herself spinning, she pulled away, her fingers quivering as she touched her tingling lips.

"I–uh–should get...going–"

Case took a heated breath, leaned back against the highboy and raked his hand through his own hair. "Should?"

Amy *needed* to go. Because she needed to sit down, breathe, center herself. She felt the edge of Case's bed against her calves. Tempting. Easy. That look in his eye, the look that said, *I could take you where you've never been before. Come with me.*

Seconds passed. Amy stood caught within her own

web, an impossible conflict between reason and desire. Case reached for her again, and she edged away, nearly stumbling backwards onto the bed.

"I'm really tired," she said, knowing her words were flat and unconvincing. She hated the sounds they made, the sounds of a lame excuse from a woman too scared to tell the truth.

Case said nothing. Lifting his hand to his throat, he slowly loosened the top button of his corduroy shirt, his gaze upon Amy unbroken.

"So...thanks for tonight. For everything. I had a good time, too," Amy managed, still unable to break free of Case's intense pull upon her. Taking a ragged breath, she forced her eyes closed and turned away, only to look back once more from the doorway.

"Sure. My pleasure." Then he smiled, watching Amy tottering into the hallway. "Let's do it again soon."

"Right," she said, lowering her chin with a coy smile before fleeing to her room.

Amy knelt at her window and stared out. The amber streetlight was ringed within the fog, but she didn't see the postcard scene.

She stood and climbed back into bed, but her eyes would not close. Case, and his dizzying kiss, saturated her thoughts. Her seesawing emotions worsened her already upset stomach.

On the upside, *euphoria*. Case cared about her, showed interest in her. It was more than just a stand-up make-out session with a man she barely knew. She felt real affection in his touch. Tenderness in his words. He was smart, sometimes boyishly charming. He listened, cared about her opinions. And he was single.

On the down, he hated kids. And like it or not, Amy had no business linking up with a man who didn't want to accept her child. For that matter, even Drew would be a better choice. At least Drew wanted to have children.

Did Case *say* he hated kids? *Not really*. Yet he made it clear he had no place for them in his life. Worse, the baby she carried was fathered by another man, another lover. While she didn't know Case well, she felt it likely that he would not easily entertain that kind of scenario. He would probably be jealous as hell.

Her mood decaying, Amy made an unhappy resolution. She would make it clear to Case that she was not a candidate for the next woman in his life. It was the right thing to do, but walking away from those mind-numbing kisses would be a challenge she could easily lose.

Case looked down at the water rushing over his hands in the bathroom sink. Her hair had felt like silk, sliding over the backs of his fingers as they caressed her head.

He stared into the mirror, seeing Amy's face, her frightened kitten look when he had pulled her close, her knowing sensitivity when they had parted.

Could it be possible that he had at last found someone worth pursuing? Capable, witty, and intelligent. She seemed to know where she was going, and while a little hesitant, unafraid of the future.

And on top of everything else, she was alluring. Dare he think it? Sexy.

After his last miserable attempt at intimacy, Case had all but stopped trying. Oh, he had little trouble meeting and attracting women, no trouble relating physically to their mutual sexual needs. But emotional intimacy was another animal. The potential for pain was just too great.

Why was Amy different?

On the not-quite-long-enough brass bed, Case stretched his legs and turned onto his side. He would have to get some sleep one of these nights. Pulling the blankets up over his hip, Case started as some object fell from the foot of the bed and softly thudded to the floor.

He turned on the light and retrieved Amy's small leather purse from the rug. Its top zipper was open, and he carefully zipped it closed. With a sigh, he placed the bag on top of the highboy dresser, and then fell back into bed. He chuckled, folded his arms behind his head. *She did seem a bit distracted when she left.*

Amy. She had proved even more enticing at dinner. A school teacher! It fit. She was patient, even-tempered. And to think he'd thought her a married waitress from a tiny seaport town forgotten by time. He recalled with irritation the realization that his vacation was technically over. He would have to decide to either stay longer or head home.

Another sleepless night lay ahead.

"Personally, I thought Irena would come through with something more than chipped teacups," Judy murmured while unpacking a heavily mildewed pasteboard box at the kitchen table.

Amy shrugged. "She's probably not as well-to-do as she looks. She sure doesn't charge much for her rooms."

"I know, but she just has this weird attitude about the lighthouse. I can't figure out what it is."

"I haven't noticed. Can you hand me that curtain rod?"

Judy looked up to see Amy, on her knees, perched on the kitchen counter. "Hey! You be careful up there!"

"Now that I think about it, she's never ventured over here to see the place." After sliding the new curtain rod into place, Amy adjusted the fabric attractively over the kitchen window. "There. Now I've got to get to work."

"Not before you tell me about last night," Judy said. She took Amy's hand, to steady her, as she stepped down the ladder.

"What about it? We had a nice dinner in town. Talked about this place, about the boat, you know."

"That's it?" Judy stood back, hands on her hips. "Yeah, right. And you bruised your neck with a hairbrush."

Amy felt herself blush. "No! Really?"

Judy followed Amy to the bathroom where she leaned close to mirror, examined the small purple mark on her neck below her earlobe.

"I haven't seen a hickey like that since–"

"Okay." Amy bit back a giggle. "Case can be…quite charming. I like him." She paused to stare into her own eyes in the mirror, the memory of the night before seeping slowly into her mind. *No. Stop.* "He's got a lot going for him. But you know I'm not looking for any entanglements right now. I've got more than enough on my plate, don't you think?"

"I wouldn't close that door if I were you," Judy advised with a smile. "Why don't you just tell him about the baby and see what he says?"

"He doesn't like kids, Judy. He said as much last night." Amy hurriedly washed and dried her hands, then looked around for her purse. "I'm running lunch this afternoon. Riley burned his hand on the barbecue yesterday and he's getting it looked at today. Have you seen my bag?"

"I don't remember you having it when you walked in this morning," Judy bent to look under the kitchen table. "Not here."

"I've gotta git. If you find it, could you drop it off at the diner?"

Judy nodded as Amy swept past her and out the door.

"Sorry about yesterday," Riley said. He pulled his apron off over his head and hung it on the hook beside the swinging kitchen door. "I'd hoped for better."

"Don't be silly. You did a wonderful job. You just get that hand taken care of. We'll handle everything. Wendy can fill coffees and Raoul can flip the burgers."

Riley smiled in gratitude, and left Amy unlocking the cash register.

The after-church lunch crowd had not yet arrived, but Amy flitted about making sure everything was ready. She was filling the coffee machine when the phone rang.

"I'd like two troughs and sixteen milk shakes, to go please," the caller asked. Momentarily confused, Amy paused, but the smile in his voice tipped her off.

"Only if you come down here and make them yourself," she replied, bracing the receiver against her ear with her shoulder as she poured water into the coffeemaker.

"I'm on my way."

Stunned, Amy stared at the phone in wonder for a few moments, then reached back to the bar to hang it up. Did he mean that?

I don't need this. Jitters set in big time, and Amy struggled to maintain her composure. Cars seemed to be pouring into the parking lot.

Soon, she was too busy to think about Case McKenna or anything else, for that matter. Wendy made the rounds with the coffee pot, and the part time cook rushed around the kitchen popping pizza into the oven and chicken into the fry pot. Amy met herself coming and going as she took orders and filled them.

"If one more person asks me where Riley is, I'll scream," she confided in Wendy at the counter. Wendy only smiled and Amy turned for another trip to the kitchen. Her task was impeded, however, by Case, as he pulled Riley's apron over his head.

"Reporting for duty, Ma'am. What can I do?"

Amy stared up at Case's imposing figure, her face hot and her mouth open in surprise. They were nearly touching, as close as the night before, when he had taken her into his arms. Amy let out the breath she'd been holding and forced a smile.

"Raoul could really use some help in the kitchen. Can you do eggs?"

"My specialty," he said with a grin and started to turn away, adding, "after instant coffee. By the way, I put your purse in the back."

"My…" Amy focused on his back as he disappeared into the kitchen, taking a moment to absorb the meaning of his words.

Chapter Eleven

"Wow, now I can appreciate how hard this business really is," Case said with a grin as he held the door open for Amy. "Riley makes it look so much easier."

"I'm so glad the burn wasn't too bad. I guess the bandages will only be on for a week." Amy unlocked the passenger side door first, then hurried around to get behind the wheel. "Good thing you knew what to do when it happened. I would have panicked. What should we do for dinner?"

"Don't know 'bout you, but I'm going down to the marina. Gonna install those new parts. You can come watch if you want," Case offered.

"Sounds like fun."

They worked the rest of the afternoon on the *Fancy Dream*. Amy forced herself to remain casual and easy-going. The last thing she wanted was another intimate encounter. Or was it?

"Who named this boat, anyway?"

"Oh, Jack's kid. It's a long, goofy story."

"How old is he?"

Case looked up from where he squatted on the deck. "Seven, now, I believe."

"Is he...a good kid?" Amy ventured, hoping for a positive word about the child.

"I guess. A bit of a pest sometimes. Jack's not near

strict enough with those heathens of his."

Amy crossed her arms across her chest. "Really," she murmured, turning to face the sun, now hanging low over Newburg Bay. "We probably should go soon, right?"

"Go? Where? I was thinking we'd take her out for a spin around the harbor. Make sure she don't sink, you know?"

Amy turned back around. "Are you serious? *Now*?"

"Sure, why not? It'll be fun. Have you ever sailed?"

"Yeah, a couple of times." Did Drew's father's yacht count?

"Here. Help me." Standing, Case took Amy by the wrist and led her to the helm. "I'll untie her, you steer."

"Me? I don't think…"

Case chuckled, and Amy relaxed a little. She liked the sound of his laugh, and she loved the feel of his hand grasping her arm. She forgot, for a time, the baby and her fears about caring for Case McKenna.

They cruised under power to the point, then Case killed the engine. The quiet was sudden and startling.

"Do you…do you drop the anchor?" Amy asked. "I mean, I don't want to sound dumb…"

"It's not dumb at all. I do, sometimes. Water's pretty calm…but I probably should. I don't need to connect with any more rocks."

So they would not just drift. Amy sat down on the maroon striped cushions, her arms still crossed. Soon, Case joined her.

"Cold?"

"No, not really. Just…"

"Nervous?"

Amy felt herself blush. Yes, she was nervous. Case sat close beside her, the length of his thigh warm against hers, his arm draped casually behind her back. "I'm fine," she said softly.

"Good. I've got some wine and crackers below if you'd like." Case got back to his feet, not waiting for her answer as he disappeared through the companionway to the galley. "White okay?"

"Uh, sure," Amy called back, wishing she could really have a glass of Chardonnay. She'd only take a sip or two. Nothing more. And lots of crackers.

He returned shortly with a small silver platter laden with wheat crackers, cheese sticks and two plastic tumblers filled with wine. "The tray came with the boat. No cracks about the glasses," he warned with a brief grin.

"Wouldn't think of it," Amy answered, taking a cracker in one hand and the wine in the other.

"Check out the sunset," Case said, re-settling onto the cushion beside her. He arranged the tray atop a nearby crate, took a sip of wine and again threw his right arm loosely around her back.

"Gorgeous," Amy murmured. She took the tiniest taste of the wine and nodded. "It's really peaceful out here."

"Usually. This is about where I was when I heard the boats."

Amy stiffened slightly. Case leaned back and tilted his head toward the sky. "I'm sorry. Not a pleasant thought."

"It's okay," Amy said, making a point to look into Case's eyes. "It actually helps, I think, for me to know. To see where it happened, I mean."

Case said nothing, only looked back into Amy's eyes solemnly.

Amy smiled and looked away. "You thought we were married, didn't you?"

Now Case smiled also, a whimsical, sentimental smile that charmed Amy. "Well...yeah. I assumed so when we met in the hospital. Never occurred to me that you were anything but a couple. I don't have a sister myself, so..."

"Any brothers?"

"Nope. Some cousins I didn't meet until I was in high school, all boys. Always kinda wondered what it would be like to have a big family. Jack says it's no great shakes."

"Oh, you mentioned he has a son, right. And other kids."

Case took another draught of wine. "Yup. Todd–his stepson–he's gotta be sixteen by now. Davey's about seven, and Mae is just a wee bit. Almost three?"

"Wow. They are really spread out."

"Handfuls, all of them." Case faked a shudder and Amy stifled a wince. "I'm always thankful for the quiet when I get home from their house."

"You'd *love* my job," Amy muttered, this time taking a full mouthful of the Chardonnay. She placed the tumbler on the tray.

"No thanks, lady."

Amy turned her face toward the disappearing sunset. Case leaned closer, his voice vaguely apologetic. "Didn't mean that the way it sounded. I just don't do well around all that...activity."

"No apology necessary. Kids aren't for everyone."

They were quiet for a time, Amy trying to ignore the comfort of Case's hand as he stroked her arm in a gentle embrace.

"Let's go below for a bit. It's getting chilly up here," he said, standing and offering her his hand. "Watch your head on the hatch."

Amy stepped carefully through the companionway and down the ladder-like steps into the salon. Despite her melancholy, the cabin captivated her and she brightened.

"I just love this," she said softly. "It's so cozy in here."

"I like it. I lived in here last summer while I re-roofed my house. It was kind of cool."

Amy moved around the tiny cabin, peering at the few photos firmly nailed to the paneled walls. "Who's this?"

"Me 'n Jack. Taken when he still lived in L.A. He used to work for the studios. He talked me into going to a stupid party down there."

"He's good-looking."

Case chuckled. "Please don't ever tell him. He already spends way too much time looking in the mirror." He gestured toward another photo. "That one is my Uncle Steve. Man. I have to go up and see him soon."

"What's stopping you?" Amy asked.

"Laziness. Pure and simple."

Amy turned away from the photos and sat down on the small corduroy-covered couch. "This is comfy."

"I think so," Case answered, sitting beside her. He pulled her gently against him. "I wanted to tell you..." he began, his cheek so close to Amy's that she could feel its heat against hers, "I had a great time last night. It's been a long time since I've enjoyed a woman's company so much."

Amy licked her lips. She felt the same, but wished she didn't. Wished she wasn't melting. Wished she wasn't falling for a guy who would not, could not love her baby. Yet for all her wishing, Case was only getting closer, and Amy's resolve of the night before flew right out the porthole.

She didn't consciously know exactly when or how it happened, but Amy found herself reclining on the sofa-cum-sleeper with Case drawing her into his arms. With the soft cabin lights only partially illuminating his features, he stroked her hair back as his eyes examined every part of her face. "It was all I could do not to come to your room last night," he murmured, his thumb now gently stroking her lower lip.

Amy surprised herself by smiling. "And you think I would have unlocked my door for you?"

"Yes, I do."

Amy lifted her eyebrows and gave him an affectionate, hopefully quizzical look. "I see. Pretty sure of yourself, aren't you?"

Case gave her a slight shrug. "Well, I guess I could have been mistaken...let's just see." With those softly spoken words, he pressed forward, his lips at first planting only a brief, gentle kiss upon hers, then returning for the real thing. Amy felt her insides begin to quiver with anticipation and delight as the kiss deepened, igniting a passion that both scared and excited her. Her arms wrapped around him, her fingers sliding into his dark, disheveled mane while her lips fought for more of his. Kiss after thrilling kiss made her giddy with a growing craziness from which Amy thought she would never return.

"Well, what do you think? Should I have come to your door?"

Amy was all but panting, unable to answer. Case chuckled and launched a fresh attack on her mouth, then dragged his lips to her ear, her neck, her throat. Reaching the neckline of her blouse, he paused to unbutton the first few buttons before resuming his quest. Amy felt herself falling deeper, a wave a desire rushing over her like the waters of a hot spring. Case's tender yet passionate touch evoked a satisfaction she did not know was possible.

Reality, be damned. Until that reality reared up in a painful way, as her would-be lover found and nuzzled her breast and a horrific message slammed into her brain. The soreness surrounding her nipples was normal, the obstetrician had assured her, and would subside in the coming months. The fact that she was pregnant would not, and she had made a serious mistake in letting Case get so close. His intentions were clear, and she knew she'd encouraged those intentions. She wanted Case to make love to her, wanted it so badly she had momentarily forgotten the baby and the bleakness of her future. Things were happening too fast, and panic lights began to flash.

"I can't–" she began, struggling to ease away from Case's plundering mouth and sit up.

"What?"

"I can't do this. I'm–I'm sorry." Hastily she began buttoning her blouse as Case sat up and pushed hair away from his flushed face.

"*You're* sorry. Wow." He cleared his throat and stood up, his frustration apparent. Turning his back, he took a moment to straighten out his own clothing before turning back to her. "I could have sworn you were into this. Did I misread–"

Amy wet her lips and could not meet his eyes. "I–I don't know. It's just…too fast."

"Is there someone else?"

Amy issued a shaky sigh. Yes, and he or she was there with them right now. Tiny, growing, needing her.

"No," she said, finally lifting her eyes to peer at Case in the dimly lit cabin. "Not anymore. I'm just not ready to start a relationship right now. I'm sorry if I acted otherwise."

Case nodded slowly, then sat back down beside her. He grasped her hand and offered a nervous smile. "That's cool. No sweat. That's, uh, pretty much where I'm at too. Still friends?"

Amy again sighed, this time with relief. "Sure. Friends."

He didn't know how he piloted the boat back to the marina, but hours later Case lay awake in his room, still pondering Amy's abrupt about-face. Maybe it was just as she said. Still messed up from a bad relationship and just wary.

Oh, but she was sweet! He'd never understood what people meant by chemistry, but now he thought perhaps this was it. He could think of no other reason for the wild attraction, the depth of the emotion she evoked, or the flutter of excitement he felt when he laid eyes on her.

Bad past or not, this girl could not tell him she hadn't been into him. And given that fact, there was a chance. A chance he intended to pursue.

Amy, too, lay awake. Confused almost to tears, she held a hand to her forehead.

What have I done? What did I almost do?
And why did I stop?

Indeed. What was the real reason she'd pulled away from the most thrilling night of her life? Was it really the baby? Her face filled with heat as she remembered the obstetrician's unsolicited advice. It was fine to have sex, he quipped, while pregnant. At least you couldn't get any more pregnant than you were.

Was it fear of history repeating itself, an enormous need to protect her heart at all costs? She barely knew Case McKenna, and he knew almost nothing about her. Yet he was willing to succumb to the joys of the flesh with a near stranger. For what? A frolic in the sack? It would make him no different than Drew.

Except that...Case, to her knowledge, wasn't engaged to someone else.

Amy turned onto her side and huffed out a sigh. What was she thinking? Case behaved nothing like Drew. It embarrassed her to admit, even to herself, that she'd never seen in Drew's eyes the compassion and truth conveyed in Case's. She'd never felt him looking inside her, never felt so special in his arms. In fact, she now doubted she'd ever loved Drew Richards at all. That deepened her humiliation several degrees. To never have loved the father of your child was inexcusable. What a fool she'd been.

Monday proved a nothing sort of day, with Amy ruminating off and on about her troubles and Riley reminding her time and again that *he* was the injured party, holding up his bandaged hand. Tuesday morning found Amy watching a summer rain from the porch swing. She had laundry to do, letters to write, and she was in dire need of a manicure. Still, she swayed gently, watching the steady drizzle wash down the street while the gulls flew through the falling droplets in apparent glee.

He found her, of course, expecting her to drive them both to the lighthouse for a day of finish work. Shaking her head, she dug her car keys out of the pocket of her jeans and held them out. "Not going today," she explained with a weak smile. "You go on ahead. I won't need the car."

Case took the keys but did not move. "You got a minute?" he asked, his eyes mirroring the light grey of the sky.

No. Please. I just want to be alone.

"Okay." Amy moved over to make room, and Case sat beside her, soon joining the rhythm of her movement of the swing.

"About the other night."

"And where have I heard that line before," Amy muttered, looking down at her lap.

Case couldn't help a smile. "You're right, it's a pretty lame opener." He took her hand and squeezed it. "I just want to say, I'm sorry. I…hmm. I don't know what happened. I don't usually come on…so strong. I hope you don't think–"

"I don't think anything," Amy said, still not looking at his face. "I don't. I'm sorry, too. Let's just leave it at that. You did nothing wrong."

"Well, I'm not so sure about that."

The swing continued to rock, the rain continued to fall, and Amy began to wish.

What would it be like, she wondered, if this was really real? *Like we were a real couple and the baby was Case's instead of…his…and I could just lay my head on Case's shoulder right now…*

He let loose of her hand, then wrapped his arm around her shoulders, gently urging her against him. She hated herself for being so wooden. So empty.

"Amy, I don't have a clue about what kind of crap you've been through. I know I've had more than my share. But I meant what I said last night about being friends. I'm sure as hell not looking for any big hairy commitment."

Did she stiffen even more? She must have, for Case

squeezed her shoulder and leaned his head closer to hers. "Sometimes...sometimes just a little physical contact is good for the soul. Especially if you've been shot down or stepped on."

Finally, Amy lifted her head to look for his sincerity. It was there, just as she'd known it would be. She knew this man had secrets, but his attraction to her wasn't one of them. It sounded like he was offering her another chance.

Her train of thought snapped like a fishing line as Miss Hastings slammed out the front door. "I'm heading over t'Betty Franzman's for bridge. You two takin' the day off?"

"Looks that way," Case said, leaving his arm snugged around Amy despite her abrupt rigidity. "Have fun."

They watched in silence as Miss Hasting's car sloshed down the street, windshield wipers flapping.

"There's something odd about that woman," Amy murmured, relaxing back into the swing.

"Oh, yes indeed. Definitely."

The quiet returned. Except for the soft rain and the tiny squeak of the porch swing, there was no sound to distract them from their thoughts. Amy closed her eyes. Although she knew she shouldn't do it, she began to relax. She liked the feel of his flannel shirt against her cheek, the smell of the rain in the air, the warmth of his arm around her.

She thought about his words, his proclamation of friendship, his advice about physical contact. It sounded like exactly what she needed right now. A friend and a lover who asked for nothing more.

Amy opened her eyes and tilted her head to look into Case's face. She parted her lips, but no words would come. *Can he tell what I am thinking? Will he know what to do?*

With his free hand, he lifted her palm to his lips, and Amy's question was answered.

Case stood up then, and waited for Amy to join him. Fixing her eyes on his momentarily, Amy made a decision, one she desperately hoped she would not regret.

They chose his bed. Even though Irena Hastings wasn't due back for hours, they locked the door and pulled the shade. And soon, they found themsleves exactly where they'd left off the night before. Only this time, Amy was determined to grab some happiness for herself, no matter how brief. She was due.

There was wonder in his touch. Joy in his kiss. Tenderness, and control, in his hands. Having made up her mind to go through with it, Amy could not get enough of his mouth, his tongue, his neck. He was built differently than Drew, and used his body in ways Amy was quite certain would have made Andrew Richards blush.

"Oh, God..."Amy heard herself moan. It had to be the extra hormones, right? It couldn't be just the way Case caressed her, kissed her, coaxed her hot spots into fiery frenzy. It couldn't be just an exquisitely perfect pairing of bodies and souls. It couldn't be anything close to true love.

The hormones, she reminded herself, when she could think past the thrill of the moment. The occasional glimpse into those summer sky eyes, eyes that knew everything important about her right now. The hint of a smile that told her she was going *first* because he wanted it that way. Then the heated abandonment of all conscious thought as she let go, allowed him to finish the magic, and thrust her senses into another dimension.

She was still navigating that dimension when she heard his groan, felt him stiffen and then gradually relax against her. Hearts hammering away, chests heaving, sweat gluing them together; Amy had never known such 'physical contact' existed. And yes, it *was* good for the soul.

When they were at last able to breathe normally, there was only the sound of the rain, heavier now, on the window. Case reached for his discarded t-shirt and slowly ran it down the length of her as she lay on her back. Then he put up the window shade and lay back down behind her.

Watching the rain fall, they didn't leave the room until dusk, when they ventured into Newburg for a quiet dinner alone. When they returned, she went to her room and he to his.

Amy felt truly alive for the first time in weeks. Case McKenna was the real deal. No man had ever touched her with such passion and yet such caring. There was a glimmer of hope. Certainly, Case cared about her. And if he did, he would take her the way she was, right? Baby and all. All she had to do was summon the courage to tell him.

She would. Tomorrow.

* * *

Tomorrow came quickly for Case, who woke feeling wired, unable to sleep past 6 A.M. He was afraid, he realized. Afraid to believe that he had finally found a woman worthy of his affection. Worthy of his caring. Worthy of his... *Stop! Don't even think it.*

Careful, McKenna. Be very careful. Anxiety niggled at his brain. He had no experience with the feelings that were clouding his head. No understanding of the compulsion he felt, the almost obsessive need to see her again. He was excited, terrified, worried.

Worried. What was there to worry about? Here, finally, was a woman without serious defects. All assets, no liabilities. Granted, he hadn't known her long, but it didn't seem to matter. She filled him. Completed him. Her smile turned his insides to jelly.

She'd come to him of her own free will. Modestly hesitant at first. He liked that about her. As frustrating as it had been when she'd turned tail on the boat, he respected her decision to withdraw.

Now, it killed him that she was across the hall. He wanted her here. Beside him.

Perhaps a walk would do him good. He got up and pulled on a pair of jeans and a sweatshirt, then felt around under the edge of his bed for his shoes. Finding only one, he got onto all fours and peeked beneath the bed-skirt, spied the missing shoe. With a sigh he dragged the shoe out and was surprised by a rattling sound as the shoe emerged. Bending, he again looked under the bed. There! A small amber bottle just inches from the edge had rolled out with the shoe. A prescription bottle.

Thinking it may have been left by a previous guest, Case took it to the bedside lamp and examined the label. His gaze stumbled over the first typed word. Quickly he scanned the rest of the label for a patient's name, a doctor, and the date.

With a vicious knot forming in the pit of his stomach, Case placed the bottle on the nightstand. It must have fallen from her purse before, the night they had first kissed. There could be only one reason why Amy would be taking prenatal vitamins. Apparently, she didn't think he was important enough to tell.

"He said to tell you he'd be in touch," Irena Hastings was saying as she turned the key in the lock on Morgan's room to let Amy in. "He left something for you in here."

The room looked so different in the light of day. Amy walked in and glanced around the room. It did not take long to notice the vitamins on the nightstand.

Despair forced a small sigh. She did not immediately retrieve the bottle. Instead, she walked to the window facing the sea, standing almost exactly where she had the night Case had first kissed her. Kissed the living daylights out of her. Kissed her like his life depended upon it.

Despite her repeated vows to avoid entanglement, Amy watched woefully as the mainsail of the *Fancy Dream* rounded the north point and disappeared.

She cleared her throat and picked up the bottle. She hadn't yet noticed it missing from her purse. "Thanks, Miss Hastings."

"None of my business, but he seemed a bit troubled about something. You two have a disagreement?"

"No," Amy said softly. "Not at all."

"Anything I can do, dear?"

Amy offered a sad smile. "Nope. I'm off to work in a little while. I'll see you later."

Riley watched as Amy went about her work later in the day. As usual, she took great care with the patrons, chatting and efficiently serving their meals with good cheer. Yet something was amiss, and Riley took her aside at closing time.

"Okay, what's up Bo Peep?"

She started to protest, to deny that anything was other than normal. Instead, Amy sat down on a barstool and folded her hands on the counter.

"I need to be gone a few days, Ri. I hope you can handle things while I'm gone. If you need to hire someone else, I'll understand."

"Gone? Where the heck you goin'?"

"Home. To see my dad."

Riley nodded solemnly.

"It's time I told him about Brian. And maybe I just need to take a break myself. I have a lot of stuff to sort out."

"Whatever you want to do is fine. Wendy and I will manage here until you get back. Maybe I can get Judy to pass out peanuts and soft drinks?"

Amy smiled. Riley was an unexpected treasure of a friend.

"I'll leave my dad's phone number with you just in case."

Chapter Twelve

The snapping flutter of the jib was comforting to Case as he piloted the *Fancy Dream* safely around the northern point of Newburg harbor. Sailing his boat was something he knew about–the possible pitfalls, the dangers clear. No hidden factors. *The Dream* had no personal agenda, no secrets. Nothing to guess about.

Although he tried to divert his thoughts, Case continued to think about Amy and the deception that had almost cost him his heart. He'd been nearly convinced that there might be potential in her. Might be something real and even special in those chocolaty eyes, that sunny smile, those enticing lips.

Case drew in a deep breath of salty air. *Focus, Case. Focus on the water. On the horizon. We're going home. Away from Newburg, away from Amy Winslow, away from Point Surrender.*

If only it were that easy. There was a part of him torn apart, part of him that clung desperately to his feelings for Amy and the retreating coastline.

If only she had told him!

What if she had? Would he still want her, *did* he still want her, knowing she carried another man's child? Confusion clouded his mind, amplifying the headache he already battled.

Stubbornly, he lifted his chin and faced the wind. It

was irrelevant, right? She had deceived him. Made him want her when she was not truly available. Enticed him with her sweetness, ignoring the obviously huge obstacle between them. *I should have known better. Me, of all people.* The thought made him grind his teeth. *I do know better.*

Suddenly, he couldn't wait to get back to Grogan's Head and his dolphins.

Highway 126 was a welcome sight to Amy's tired eyes when she finally reached the Heritage Valley. A sleepy agricultural town, Santa Paula was not too far from the coast and filled with citrus orchards. She breezed past the gate at Gentry Village, holding up her electronic passkey to the reader box.

"You're just in time for supper, girl," Tom Winslow said, a twinkle in his eye as he held open the screen door. "Nola picked up the best danged ribs you will ever taste."

"Ribs? Yum," Amy said, with a secret grimace.

Nola Brannigan was wiping her hands on her apron. "We're so thrilled to see you, honey. I'll bet you're exhausted from that drive."

Amy nodded, grateful for the acknowledgement.

"Go ahead and freshen up. Dinner won't be ready for a little bit yet. You can use our bathroom."

Our *bathroom? Boy, life is becoming a laugh a minute.*

After washing her face and using the bathroom, Amy lay down on her father's king-sized bed and closed her eyes. Even though it wasn't the little farmhouse down the road, it was still 'home,' still her father's house, and she felt protected, for the moment anyway. Rolling onto her side, she wrapped an arm around her soft belly, pretending to hold the baby within.

"I'm sorry things are so messed up for us. We'll get through it, though. I promise you," she whispered. "I do love you. You and I, well, we're just about all each other's got."

Just about all. She'd come close, so close, to having so much more.

"Hey little girl, time for some eats," her father said, from the doorway. "Unless you'd rather rest," he added, just a touch of disappointment coloring his words.

"I'm coming," Amy said, forcing a smile. "I just needed five minutes. I'm fine."

They got all the way through dinner without anyone mentioning Brian or Drew. Amy was thankful to have filled her stomach before having to drop the big news.

The three settled in the living room. Amy noticed the TV in the corner blared on, and had since she arrived.

"Do you mind if we turn that off?"

Her father looked concerned. "Must be important. What's up, Amy Lynne?"

Amy cleared her throat and smoothed her palms along her trousers and over her knees.

"Well, there are a couple of things. The most important thing is, and I don't want you to get too upset about this, Brian had an accident. He's in the hospital recovering."

"An accident! What kind of accident?"

"His patrol boat...collided with a ski boat up near Newburg. He got banged on the head, pretty hard," Amy paused to swallow. "He's gonna be fine, though, so don't worry."

"Should we go up there?" Nola asked, her face a network of worry lines.

"It's not really necessary. He'd like it if you'd wait until he's feeling a little more like having company."

"Why hasn't he called?"

Amy smiled brightly at her father, hating herself with every word for lying. "Well, he's had to have some pain medication, and he says he sounds too dopey. He wanted me to talk to you for him."

"Humph. Fool kid. Maybe we should just go up there."

"Dad, really. I've been there all along, there's no need. And Judy's there too. Everything will be fine."

"So what's the other news? Something to do with that flaky boyfriend of yours?"

"Dad! Andrew is not..." Amy paused. Maybe her father was more astute than she gave him credit for. "We've separated. I guess you aren't too disappointed about that."

"Hallelujah and Hershey bars! That's the best news I've had all day. Hell, all year! It's about time you came to your senses, girl. That guy isn't worthy of you. End of conversation."

Well, that part was easy. Amy adjusted her position, looking for a change in subject.

"So how long you gonna stay?" Nola wanted to

know.

Amy glanced around. Had she known her father had a *roommate* she would have made better plans.

"Just a day or two. I have some friends down here to visit."

Her father and his live-in complained graciously about the brevity of her stay and then suggested they have dessert. After they had devoured healthy portions of cherry pie and ice cream, Nola brought out the board games. They played Scrabble until nearly midnight. Amy fell asleep on the living room hide-a-bed as soon as she closed her eyes.

Case slept well beyond his usual 7 A.M. internal alarm the morning after he sailed into Grogan's Head. After brewing a pot of strong coffee, he sat outside on the wide front deck that offered a brief ocean view through the pine boughs and redwood branches. Cloistered on the forested hillside, Case's modest cabin provided much needed isolation from the outside world.

Propping his feet on the rail, he sipped and reviewed his plan for the day. He needed to stock his refrigerator, wash some clothes, and check in at work. Did he have gas in his car? He wondered, fleetingly, if the vintage Triumph roadster would even start since it had been over four weeks since he left.

Four weeks. More had happened in the past month to alter his way of thinking than had happened in the past four years. The death of the manatee had him questioning his value as a doctor, his skill as a surgeon. Ramming the

Dream into the rocks left him doubting his sailing abilities. Falling in love with Amy Winslow had left him feeling like a damned fool.

This final revelation prompted him to toss the coffee from his mug over the railing and hasten to finish dressing. No sense in dwelling on his bad luck.

Ninety minutes later, Case strode casually through the double glass doors where Jack was seated at Case's desk, talking on the phone. Acknowledging Case with a subtle nod, he continued talking while handing Case a small stack of mail.

Case sat in the chair opposite and thumbed through the envelopes. Finding nothing of interest, he tossed it back onto the desk just as Jack hung up the phone.

"Hey, stranger. Thought you just might have hooked up with a Mexican señorita down there. What's cookin'?" Jack stood and surrendered the chair to Case.

"Not much. Didn't make it to Mexico. Didn't make it much past San Francisco. I met up with an unkind hard place in the water."

"You *didn't* run aground."

"I might have."

"So where *have* you been?"

"Newburg."

Jack stared at Case, his face frozen in disbelief. "Newburg? As in, Point Surrender-Newburg? *Man.* When you said, 'unkind hard place', I thought you meant a rock or something."

"I did. Look, let's talk about what's going on here. Who was that on the phone?"

"North Africa is sending us 100 oil-soaked penguins."

Case rolled his eyes, chuckling under his breath.

"What's so funny?" Jack wanted to know.

"Nothing. Birds I can handle."

Point Surrender, California, New Year's Eve, 1970

Two and one-half years we've spent here now. I am still in love with this place, but it's been a hard adjustment for Leticia. She misses the parks around Seattle, Pike's Market and the street musicians. She wants to go back for a visit but I don't know how we can afford it. The only thing she looks forward to is teaching piano to some of the local people in Newburg. Goes regularly to the home of Matthew Hastings to give lessons. He seems like a nice enough guy but keeps to himself. Leta says he used to play in a band.

Point Surrender, California, November 15, 1973

So tired but I know if I don't write this tonight I'll forget some of the details of the most important night of my life. At 4:45 am we brought William C Jenner into this world with a hoot and a holler (my hoot, Leta's holler). What a set of lungs this kid has! A head full of dark hair, too. Leta was a real trooper. I felt really bad that we couldn't get out of here for a proper hospital delivery, but a doctor from Newburg came in toward the last and helped out. Through the rain, too...

...Didn't expect the baby this soon, so will have to move Leta's new spinet out of the second bedroom and order up a crib. In the meantime he will sleep with us. Leta says we'll have to turn off the horn. Of course, I just laughed.

William Jenner, USCG Keeper

Point Surrender, California, Christmas, 1976

The storm has been wailing on us for 7 days now. Hard to explain to young Will how Santa will arrive. Last night I was in the tower, just getting the light going and wiping down the lantern windows when I swore the sea was going to wash us right off this bluff we sit on. I couldn't seem to move, watching this huge wave coming at us which eventually struck the tower. I had to re-level the lens this morning...

Of course the storm has taken out what was left of Leta's winter garden. I doubt she'll try to plant another one. Gardening isn't her thing, she insists.

All we see on TV is about Vietnam. I sure wish it was over and those boys could come home. A half a million soldiers are over there now. When I watch Leta teaching Will to sing, I hope he'll never have to be in a war.

William R. Jenner, Keeper

Point Surrender, California, September 15, 1978

Mrs. Jenner broke her ankle this morning while coming down the steps from the garage. Needless to say, she is not happy about this event, and has ceased all activity while she heals. She has again suggested that we move away. I can't imagine not tending the light. She'll feel better soon.

Point Surrender, California, August 29, 1980

CG inspectors spent 2 hours in the tower today, inspecting every bit of the lantern room and the lens, etc. Everything found to be top notch. William followed the ensign around like a puppy, full of questions. Claims he'll one day be the keeper here.

I think the heat is getting to Leta. She spends most of the day walking on the bluff. I bought her one of those new, small tape recorders that takes "cassettes" so she can practice her singing. She still sounds like an angel to me but doesn't sing much lately...

Amy closed the journal and sighed. So William and Leta had a son. And they knew Irena's brother, Matt Hastings.

Sounds like the woman went stir-crazy. Amy packed the book back into her suitcase.

"You leavin' already?" Thomas Winslow watched his

daughter hoist the suitcase into the small trunk of her car and slam it shut.

"I'm going down to L.A. Jessica has invited me to stay with them a day or two. I'll call you later." Amy gave her father a tight hug. "Tell Nola how much I appreciate everything she's done. She's a nice lady, Dad."

"You aren't bothered by her bein' here, are you?"

"Of course not. I like her."

Tom beamed. "You take care, now. Don't forget to call me."

It was less than two hours to Jessica Taylor's home in the Hollywood hills. The directions were easy to follow, and soon Amy stretched her legs on the smooth concrete circle driveway leading past a rambling, single-story ranch style estate.

Before Amy reached the porch, Jessica flew out the front door and rushed her with a sisterly hug.

"Am I glad to see you!" Jessica took Amy by the hand and led her to the front door. "You look great! Oh, I have so much to tell you!"

Amy felt grateful for her friend's exuberance. She needed distraction, needed to be reminded that some fairy tales do come true.

"Mac's not home yet, but he can't wait to meet you. Come, Devon's playing inside."

Amy was delighted to meet Jessica's two-year-old son. With gorgeous brown eyes and a shock of golden hair, he was the image of Jessica's husband.

The home sprawled across a huge expanse of land,

and after a brief tour, Jessica showed Amy to the elegant guestroom.

The visit with her father had lifted Amy's spirits, and it felt good to be around her closest, *dearest* friend again. She took her time bathing and dressing, then scrutinized her appearance in the large, well-lit boudoir mirror. Leaning close, she examined the roots of her hair, noticing that she was way overdue for a touch up.

Wait a minute. I don't have to bleach my hair anymore!

After a few moments of primping, Amy left her room to join her friends.

"I was thrilled to hear about your trip to New Zealand. Any plans to go back?" Amy asked, looking from Jessica to Mac and then back.

"I'd love to go. We're just so busy right now, Mac's working on a western, and Devon's just started preschool. You know how it is."

"Sure. Of course." Amy wiped her mouth on her napkin and trained her eyes on the youngster in the highchair.

"So, getting back to your story about this lighthouse, you say the wife took off, and the husband kept the boy?" Mac asked, pushing aside his empty plate.

Amy nodded, gratified that someone else showed interest in the mystery. "Listen to this," she began, opening the journal on her lap to the bookmarked page.

"April 5, 1984. Let the record show that on this date, Mrs. Leta Jenner removed herself from Point Surrender

188

lighthouse. She left via cab at approximately 9 A.M., having decided that keeping is not compatible with her basic natural instincts of wanting more exciting activities...

"...Mrs. Jenner has left our son William C. in my care. Let the record further also show that William C. did not cry when he woke and his mother was gone. William R. Jenner, Keeper"

"Then, further to April 5th. Mr. Roderick Brown of Newburg has agreed to take Mrs. Jenner's spinet piano and deliver it to Newburg Elementary School.'"

"It would be interesting to find out what happened to her and her son," Jessica said.

"I keep thinking that too. But I wouldn't know where to begin. She moved out quite awhile before the father died. Nobody seems to know where she went. And the last several pages have been torn out of the log."

"If we could find out where she moved, we'd at least have a start."

"That might be easier than you think," Mac said thoughtfully. "Do you know if she ever went by any other names? Like a maiden name?"

"I guess it might be possible to get a marriage record from Washington, if we assume they were married in Seattle or in the same county," Amy said. "I'll write down what I know thus far."

Later in the evening, Amy called Irena Hastings to see if there was any news concerning Brian.

"None that I know of."

"I guess no news is good news, sometimes. By the

way, this may seem like an odd question, but you wouldn't happen to know Leticia Jenner's maiden name, would you?"

"Gracious, no. We didn't know one another, dear. Why do you want to know?"

"Oh, I was going to look her up, and I thought the information might be helpful. It's no big deal."

"I see. Well. Hold the phone. Judy would like to talk to you," Miss Hastings told her before putting Judy on the line.

Judy quickly doused any concerns. "Nothing's wrong. But you got a package here right after you left. It's from that guy at the Chronicle."

"Open it! Tell me what's inside." Amy waited, listening to the sounds of tearing cardboard while Judy ripped open the Federal Express letter package.

"It's some photocopies of...looks like old newspaper articles. Oh! And a clipping from Sunday's Chronicle! He did write a story about Point Surrender."

"What are the other articles about?"

There was a pause while Judy reviewed the clippings.

"'Last Keeper's Light Extinguished', 'Coroner Says Light Tender Was Drunk', uh, 'Fallen Keeper's Wife Silent'...there's a picture of William Jenner...a picture of Leta Jenner."

"Oh man, I can't wait to see those." Amy turned to Jessica and Mac, who stood by in anticipation. "Judy has some old newspaper clippings! She can take them to the library. Do you have a fax machine?"

"You bet. In the office."

Amy couldn't have been more eager as she stood beside the high-speed laser fax machine in Mac's office. She grabbed each page as it emerged, examined it closely. "Wow. Oh, wow. Look at this. All this history." Amy spread the articles out on Jessica's kitchen table and arranged them chronologically. The photos did not survive the facsimile process very well, but Amy was excited nonetheless. "Point Surrender...site of the infamous and mysterious disappearance of Captain Morgan Hastings and his bride-to-be, Jacelyn Dunbar, in 1864..."

"Weird. *1864?*"

"Says here he was being hunted by a posse of police officers for aiding the Confederate States Navy aboard the J.M. CHAPMAN... anchored at Jackson Street Wharf, San Francisco."

"Was he a pirate?" Jessica asked, her eyes wide with interest.

"They call him a privateer in the article. He was commissioned by a group of Confederates who were planning a surprise attack on California. He almost got away, probably would have, it says, had he not gone to meet his lover. They trapped him and Jacelyn, on the cliff, and..." Amy paused to read ahead. "They jumped off. I heard some of this story from the innkeeper. Their bodies were never found."

Amy took a moment to reflect before moving on to the next article.

"Let's see. Leticia Jenner...left the lighthouse in 1984...ah! It says here she moved to Las Vegas."

"Great! There's our lead," Mac said, as he picked up the phone.

Chapter Thirteen

Amy spent the following morning lying beside the pool. Jessica joined her after putting her son down for a nap.

"So I suppose Drew's begging you to come back by now," she said.

"Sort of. He's crazy if he thinks I'll go back to him now." Amy stretched her arms above her head, relaxing on the posh chaise lounge. "I'm really happy for you, Jess. You've got it all. Mac is just such a wonderful guy! I'm so glad he's not an egotistical snob."

"You think I would marry an egotistical snob?"

"I almost did," Amy said.

"What about that guy who's helping you with the lighthouse? You told me he was…interesting. Is he good looking?"

In spite of her chaotic feelings about Case, Amy grinned. "Oh he's that, all right. He's definitely hero-quality. Blue eyes, brown hair, good build–about six feet tall, perpetually needing a shave…"

"Mel Gibson or Brendan Frasier? Maybe Hugh Grant?"

Amy laughed. "Younger than Mel, more serious than Brendan. Sort of reminds me of…that guy in Lord of the Rings. He has those eyes that just see right clear through you. And a wonderful smile."

Jessica pulled her sunglasses down her nose and peered at Amy whimsically. "You really like this guy, don't you?"

Amy dismissed Jessica's comment with a wave, and was about to announce her plans to go on hiatus from the romance scene when Mac emerged from the glass patio door.

"I've got news. Your lighthouse matron is living right here in Los Angeles, Burbank to be exact. Goes by her maiden name. Mansfield now. I've got an address and a phone number."

Amy's stomach felt like it was in her throat as she locked her car and stepped onto the sidewalk outside the Eastside Apartments complex. Glancing around her, she took in the scene with dread. Open windows without screens revealed residents hoping for a breeze, small children battled over a rusted tricycle.

That Leta Jenner had even agreed to talk to her had Amy whirling. The fact that she was going through with it was unbelievable. Bravely clutching her purse to her side, she knocked on the bent screen door at Apartment 12.

The woman who peeked out, then pulled the door open wide, could not have been the same fresh-faced blonde in the newspaper photo. This woman was overweight, with long, wavy gray hair and a worn face bearing squinted eyes. She held the screen open for Amy.

The small apartment was cluttered, not very aesthetic, but clean enough. Two cats lounged on the sofa back and arms, and a canary flitted about in a hanging black cage.

"Get you some ice tea?" Leta asked, pressing her palms together.

"No thank you." Amy gingerly sat down on the edge of the threadbare couch and laced her own fingers tightly together in her lap. Leta sat opposite in a large rocker-recliner.

"So you've just come from Newburg?" she asked. Amy noticed her expression seemed to be one of perpetual worry.

"Yes, a couple of days ago." Amy cleared her throat. "I really appreciate your meeting me like this."

"I'm sorry to hear about your brother. I don't know that I have anything to offer, but I'll try to answer your questions."

Amy again cleared her throat, trying to gather those questions she had compiled in her head the night before. She decided sympathy might be the best angle to get Leta talking.

"You must have felt terribly isolated there after living in Seattle."

The worried look dissipated some.

"I was a lunatic by the time I got out of there. I hated to leave them that way, but I might've killed somebody if I'd stayed," she said with a throaty laugh. "Liam just couldn't understand. He was always a loner–he didn't fit in with the scene in Seattle. He liked his hair short, if you know what I mean. And in the sixties, well..." She shook her head. "I tried. I really did." The lines returned to her forehead.

Amy asked her about day-to-day life at Point

Surrender, about their social activities, about Newburg. Leta soon became more at ease and recounted her few years in Northern California, in a highly animated fashion. But when Amy broached the subject of her son, Leta got up and went to the kitchen. She returned with a can of beer.

"I've only got 'light', but you're welcome to it," she offered, holding up the silver can.

"No, thank you. Look, if you'd rather not talk about William, I certainly understand."

Leta looked into her lap for a moment. Her voice was soft and filled with remorse.

"I will never forgive myself for leaving William, for sending him away when he needed me the most. God has punished me, will keep punishing me for that forever."

After downing more than half the beer, Leta recalled for Amy the day she got the news that Liam had died and her son would be sent out to her in Las Vegas.

"I was pretty messed up at the time. I sang in a couple of places–bars, really–when I could stay straight long enough to get through a set. Cocaine by day, *Quaaludes* by night, pot all the time. I didn't eat, I didn't really sleep, it was no place for a kid. I could have been the poster girl for the 'Just Say No' campaign. I was so loaded when he got there, I didn't even know he was there until a couple of days later."

Amy sat stock still, listening to Leta's dreadful, but fascinating, tale.

"Pathetic situation. I was so pissed off at the world, at Liam for doing himself in, at myself for being such a low-life, even at Will for being so blessed innocent. Go figure!" She laughed again, this time a raspy, unfunny laugh that sent her into a fit of coughing.

"Sorry. My lungs are shot. Quit smoking a couple of years ago, but the damage was done already. Anyway," she continued, gasping a little. She took another draught of beer. "The poor kid couldn't wait to get away from me. So I put him on a Greyhound back to Seattle, to his Aunt Rose's. Liam's sister. She was a good lady, and I knew she'd take him in. Probably spoil him to death."

"Do you ever hear from him now?"

Leta grunted and turned away, blinking several times.

"I tried calling him on his sixteenth birthday, but he wouldn't take the call. I called when he turned twenty-one, but he'd already moved on. Went to med school, I heard. That's all I know. At one point I had this self-righteous thing going, believing I should tell him about his father. His *real* dad, and the reason Liam was so hostile."

"His real dad? You mean..."

"Matthew Hastings. God love him. What a gentle soul."

Amy was hard pressed to keep the shock from her face. She failed.

"Oh honey, I got no reason to keep secrets now. They're all dead, I will be soon enough, and Will... God knows he might as well be dead to me, too."

Leta struggled out of her chair and went to the linen closet in the short hallway adjoining the living room. She withdrew a dilapidated shoebox and brought it to the coffee table.

"This is Matt," she announced, pulling a faded, color, 5 x 7 print from the box. She handed it to Amy. "Cute, huh?"

The photo had been taken on the outdoor stage of a rock n' roll band. The drummer, centered, was the same man from the photo in Irena Hastings' dining room. Amy leaned close to examine the mustached, longhaired youth with the wide grin and the fringed leather vest. And yes, Amy thought, he was attractive.

"We had an affair. Am I sorry? Can't say I feel one way or another about it now, but William was, *is*, his son. Of course Liam flipped out when he found out. He didn't know for a long time, but when Will got older, it got kinda obvious. He was a spittin' image of Matt."

Amy handed the photo back. "Do you have any pictures of your son?"

Wordlessly Leta pawed through the shoebox, picked out three small photos and handed them over. Amy nodded slowly to herself; the boy resembled the one in the Hastings House picture. The one Irena had called 'a neighbor boy.'

She formulated her next question carefully. "If you could say something to William now, what would you say?"

Leta sniffed, coughed, took a sip of beer. She put the can down and with both hands, pulled her long locks away from her face, forming a temporary ponytail, then released them. Finally, she took the photos back and perused them, one by one.

"I s'pose I'd say I'm sorry. Of course I'd say I'm sorry! What the hell kind of person would I be if I didn't regret the way I treated my only child? Damn if I haven't thought about that every day of my sorry life. How I'd like to see him, his wife and kids, hug him and tell him I'm not as bad a person as he surely remembers..." Leta swiped at her cheek and again got out of the chair, carefully replacing the shoebox in the cabinet. With her back to Amy, she laughed. "And I could use a good doctor about now."

"I'm sure he'd forgive you, Leta. I'm sure he wonders about you, too, wherever he is."

"Not likely." The gruff demeanor returned as Leta reseated herself. "Anyway. I wouldn't expect him to understand how it is for a woman, living with a man like Liam, a man so private, so conservative, so...cold."

"Cold? How?"

Leta sighed, then chuckled. "Did you wonder why I am so sure my baby wasn't Liam's? Hard to conceive when you don't have sex but once in a blue moon," she explained. "I tried everything to get that man up, pardon the expression. I finally threw in the towel. I played piano in Matt's house there on Highwater Street, gave lessons to some of the children in town. Matt was more like me, a free spirit, loving, kind."

"Why didn't you divorce Liam and go with Matt?"

"Maybe I should have. He might still be alive. For one thing there was that bitch of a sister he had. *She* was a piece of work. Invited herself to move right in. Took everything over. She was alone, never married, and he said he felt *obligated* to her! But really, at the time, I just wanted…to get away from everything. I didn't want any ties." Leta paused, her gaze adrift, her thoughts many years away. Amy shifted her ankles. She sensed there was more and waited quietly to hear it.

"He was gonna come. Said he'd go out to the Point, pack up William, and drive out to Vegas in that old VW bus of his. I panicked. I looked around at the sinkhole I was livin' in and I went out and…and…there was this guy, used to hang out behind the Silver Slipper casino. I gave him my wedding ring for some acid."

Amy felt as if she couldn't take a breath until Leta continued. The older woman sitting across from her was still reminiscing, her eyes glazed.

"I had somebody else call Matt and tell him not to come. He said he didn't want to live without me." She paused again, letting the memories engulf her as if she were alone with her thoughts.

The sound of a child's playful shriek in the courtyard outside brought her around. Blinking rapidly, Leta snatched up the beer can again and finished it off. "Next thing I knew, Matt had tossed his poor self off the cliff." She shook her head slowly. "Like I said, no ties."

Amy felt her own eyes welling with tears. *Well, you got what you wanted.*

Leta walked her outside, her bright flowered muumuu billowing out in the breeze.

"You think you'll track down my son?"

"Oh, I wasn't planning on it. I hope you didn't mind my questions, Leta. Sometimes I think I'm just too curious for my own good. I didn't mean to be nosey."

"Aw, don't worry about it. It actually felt good to be letting some of that nastiness out. You take care, and I hope your brother and his girl will be real happy at the Point."

From behind the steering wheel, Amy watched as Leta Jenner turned and went back inside.

Empty. Her life is just pure emptiness.

Amy drove back to the MacKendall home in autopilot, her head reeling from Leta's stories. Married to a man who never touched her, living in isolation on the bluff, away from the music and excitement of the big city. Succumbing to desire with a sexy rock n' roll drummer, and having a love child.

She had gone to Leticia Mansfield's apartment expecting to hate the woman for her apparent crimes. Instead, she had come away with pity and helplessness. And a slip of paper bearing Rose Jenner's phone number.

"Are you going to call her?" Jessica asked as Amy packed her bag to go home.

"Liam's sister? Maybe. I have this obsession with finding out everything that happened after Leta left them there. And it's none of my business! It's weird, like I have to find out the whole story."

"I think it's cool," Jessica said. "That old lady was probably glad you came. Gave her a chance to put the past into perspective."

"I felt so sorry for her, Jess. She's sick, she's lonely. She said God was punishing her for what she did." Amy paused for a moment before snapping the suitcase closed. *Maybe He is.*

The drive back to Northern California was uneventful and gave Amy a chance to sort out her thoughts. Besides obsessing over Leta's story, she obsessed over Case McKenna and his abrupt departure from Newburg. She had to shake her head to dispel the heat that warmed her face when she recalled the mind-bending kisses they had shared. Oh, how she could do with a kiss like that right now!

It was, of course, the vitamins and their obvious meaning. What timing! He'd certainly seemed anything but upset the night before. It hurt to think about that night, about how much of herself she'd given. How she'd actually considered going to him about the baby. She had been all ready to come clean about her life, her fears, her future.

Not only had she been too late, her suspicions were correct–the thought of a baby had sent him running. Running hard.

It was good that she found out. With sorrow, she chastised herself for letting it go as long as she had. Had she intentionally led him on?

Alone in her car, it was easy to let the feelings return. Easy to fall back into the abyss of depression that had threatened her the morning Case had left. Yet she could not be too hard on herself. No, she decided, she had not purposely deceived Case McKenna. She had just helplessly succumbed to his charm.

Once again, she affirmed her commitment to her child. There was no room in her life for anyone else.

Irena Hastings was cutting roses in the front garden when Amy came down from her room, refreshed after her long drive.

"How was your trip, dear?"

"Interesting. Need some help?"

"No, I'm just finishing. Did you see your father?"

"Yes. We had a nice visit. Miz Hastings, I was wondering something. Did you ever meet Leta Jenner?"

Miss Hastings didn't pause her activities to answer Amy's query. "Yes, once or twice, why do you ask?"

"Just curious. I guess she was pretty good friends with your brother when he lived here."

"They were acquainted."

"When did you move here?"

Miss Hastings pulled off her heavy cotton gloves and turned to face Amy.

"Why, it was the early eighties, I believe. Leta Jenner had already left town then. But she came to the funeral." Her last words were meant to end the conversation, evidenced by her abrupt movement up the porch steps.

Whose funeral? Liam's? Amy wanted to ask, but held her tongue. There was something evasive about Irena Hastings' manner, and Amy felt warned not to probe.

Unfortunately, the implied warning only served to push Amy on. She waited in her room until she saw Miss Hastings return to her gardening with a fresh glass of iced tea. Then, with exaggerated stealth, she climbed the stairs to the third floor.

It was obvious that these rooms were not meant for guests. A large parlor with a cozy fireplace and television led to a short hallway accessing three bedrooms. Amy opened the first door with caution, finding nothing but a fresh and untouched bedroom ready for a family guest or relative. The second bedroom was clearly Irena's. Her fat Persian cat lay curled up in the center of the bed, asleep. A frilly boudoir table with several bulb-type perfume bottles stood against one wall, and matching winged-back chairs flanked a window on the other. Her standing wardrobe closet gaped open, revealing her many long gowns and shoes.

Quietly closing the door, Amy turned to the final bedroom door and slipped inside. This, surely, was Matthew Hasting's bedroom. Left exactly, she imagined, as it had been the day he'd died.

A large four-poster bed centered against the main wall was covered by a dark, madras cloth bedspread. Posters, now considered vintage and probably valuable, beckoned from the walls, inviting music lovers to experience the 'Summer of Love' with Jimi Hendrix, Big Brother and the Holding Company, and the Byrds. Centered over the bed was the biggest and brightest piece of psychedelic artwork, a concert sign from the Fillmore West in San Francisco. Matt Hastings was featured center, surrounded by band mates, all putting on expressions of drug-induced glee. Amy smiled in spite of herself.

A highboy dresser stood near the corner of the room. Nearly breathless, Amy pulled the top drawer out as silently as she could manage. Men's underclothing still in neat piles filled this drawer. Braver now, Amy opened each drawer in succession until she reached the bottom one. In here, beneath a brilliantly bold tie-dyed shirt was a framed 8 x 10 photograph. Feeling as if she could be discovered at any moment, Amy looked behind her, straining her ears for sounds of anyone approaching. Satisfied that she was still alone, she lifted the photo.

Drawing in a deep breath, Amy examined the picture of Leta Jenner with Matt Hastings. Her arms were around the singer's neck, and she leaned backward so far her head was nearly upside-down as she grinned at the camera. Her feet bare, her full, flowered skirt was just below her knees, her golden hair hanging halfway to the ground. Matt himself was smiling as he held her there, kept her from falling, clearly enjoying their antics on the front lawn of the house...in the summer of love.

Amy exhaled. *What a photo. What shining love. What a terrible shame.*

Chapter Fourteen

"Today, the greatest threat to black-footed penguins comes from oil spills–and the threat grows as tanker traffic increases. Oil robs penguins' feathers of their insulating properties, so oiled penguins succumb to cold. If they preen, they swallow toxic chemicals. In 1968, an oil spill off the coast of South Africa killed an estimated 15,000 penguins…"

Case rubbed his fingers across his mouth as he watched the video in the small public viewing theater, down the hall from his office. The penguin project was going to be a bigger deal than he originally thought.

"Five hundred oil-drenched penguins were flown by helicopter from Bird Island to Perdevlei yesterday and later driven to the SAS Donkin, Port Elizabeth, in a rescue effort to save the birds. Two hundred more were sent off to the United States for treatment as part of the International Bird Rescue Research coalition.

"More than 1,000 birds were stranded on Bird Island, soaked in oil after the freighter *Manachatta* disgorged its cargo after sinking off Port St Johns last week. We have managed to tag and stabilize the majority of those we have, and we hope to start washing them soon.

"The South African National Foundation for the Conservation of Coastal Birds said some 2,200 of the penguins have died, most during the first few days following capture..."

Case grimaced as Jack joined him in the room.

"We've got our work cut out for us. When do they arrive?"

"The little flappers will be here by noon. We've got twenty volunteers set to start scrubbing and feeding."

"Is Mike Fischer here? He does birds, right?"

"Mike's on his way in from Maine. He caught the red-eye."

Case took a deep breath. An operation of this size would surely help keep him occupied. For every moment he wasn't consciously thinking about something else, Amy appeared in his mind.

Amy, with her silken hair and luscious, warm brown eyes. One of those moments descended upon him again, his own eyes unseeing as he remembered her touch, her fingers digging into his hair as they made love in his dimly lit room. The memories aroused him, annoyed him, and saddened him.

Not one to give orders and sit back, Dr. McKenna knelt with the others on the now soapy, wet floor of the main holding arena, blinking as water sprayed off the wildly flapping penguin barely contained in his hands.

"Okay, squirt. I think you're pretty sanitized." He stood and carried the distressed bird to the 'clean' holding area fenced off to the side, then stripped off the heavy rubber gloves and wiped his brow on his forearm.

"That about it?"

Mike Fischer was wielding a small hypodermic

needle, his assistant restraining a small Blackfoot in her arms.

"Think so. You go on home. I'll finish up. These little critters will be ready to ship back out by Saturday."

Case nodded and offered an exhausted wave to his colleague. Home sounded good, and bad.

Once there, he took a short nap, plagued by disturbing dreams he couldn't remember upon waking. He showered, threw a frozen pizza into the oven and turned on the television, but did not sit down to watch it. He walked past the telephone several times, unable to make himself pick it up. What would he say if he called her?

He put away about half the pizza and turned the television off. The silence, normally comforting to him, was overpowering. No longer able to resist, he picked up the cordless and walked out onto his deck.

Miss Hastings answered on the third ring.

"Amy's not here," she informed him. "Left the day after you did. Went down south to visit her father and her friends."

"Did she say when she'd be back?"

"No dear, she didn't."

Case thanked his former landlady and pressed the 'off' button on his phone. For now, his quandary was temporarily abated. He was left to wonder if her sudden departure had anything to do with his.

Unable to answer his own questions, Case decided to go back to work. Maybe this would be a good time to catch up on his paperwork.

* * *

Irena Hastings placed the phone back on its cradle, watched from the window as Amy's taillights disappeared around the corner leading to Coast Highway. She shook her head slowly, then brightened as one of her guests entered the room.

Amy sat in the mahogany chair and stared down at the phone number. The lighthouse was quiet, the windows open and a pleasant breeze blew through, dispelling the odor of fresh paint that had clouded around her upon arrival. She looked at the phone in her hand.

What have I got to lose?

She dialed. A man's voice, an older man, answered the phone. He paused when Amy asked to speak to Rose Jenner.

"I'm a friend of Leta's. She gave me the number."

After another pause, the man spoke. "I'm sorry, but Rose passed away some eighteen months ago. She was...my wife. Can I help you?"

"I am so sorry," Amy croaked, leaning her forehead into her hand. She hadn't anticipated this turn, and felt terribly awkward. "I am trying to reach William, Leta's son. She told me you–Rose–may have a current number for him. But I don't want to be a bother..."

"Is Leta okay?" the man wanted to know.

"She's not well, and..." Amy's mind raced to formulate a reason. "I thought maybe he should know."

"I have a work number for him. I would ask you, though, please respect his privacy if he doesn't want to talk to you. He's not on the best terms with Leta."

"I understand fully. I appreciate this so much."

Amy hurriedly jotted down the phone number and hung up as quickly as possible. She felt horrible for bothering the old man, for invading his grief.

The next call would be easier to make. She could just hang up if she detected animosity from the man. Fingers trembling, she dialed. She frowned as the recording began its message.

"You have reached the Olson Institute. Our office hours are Monday through Friday, 9 A.M to 5 P.M."

Amy sighed and hung up the phone. Grabbing a pencil, she wrote "Olson Institute" on the piece of paper and left it on the desk.

It took Case all of thirty minutes to go through his mail, and approve the reports left for him by his staff. Dimly, in the background, he could hear the penguins squawking and shuffling in their holding pens. He left his office and made the rounds, checking on a newborn harbor seal and its mother, before stopping to exchange grunts with Winchell, the resident walrus.

Walking back out into the cool night air, Case began to itch. It wasn't on his skin, exactly, or any one spot in particular. It was an internal itch, in a place he couldn't quite pinpoint. And with startling surety he realized, the only relief for this itch was somewhere in Southern California.

Forty minutes later he slid onto a barstool at The Rogue's Pub. Beside him, Jack was swirling a highball glass filled with cola.

"You're doomed," Jack proclaimed with a smile.

"Why didn't she tell me?"

"You're asking me? I still don't understand women. I adore my wife, but I'd never profess to figure her out."

Case drew in a deep breath, signaling the bartender. "I could use some advice, Jack. And a margarita."

Jack chuckled. "I've never seen you like this, man. She must be something else."

"She's been so up front about everything else. I can't get past this...deception thing."

"Okay, let's do a quick scenario here. What if she had said, hey McKenna, you're the best thing since sliced bread, and I've got a baby coming who sure could use a neat dad like you! How would that go down, pal?"

Case groaned. Jack was right. Amy was a proud woman, by all accounts. Telling him she was pregnant would be tough. She would have to ease into the topic. Test the water...

"Shit. I blew it!" Case leaned his head back, his eyes roaming across the darkened ceiling of the bar.

"How so?"

"I think I told her I didn't like kids."

"But you love my kids. In fact, Mae is convinced you're going to marry her when she grows up."

Case grinned in spite of his new misery. "And she would be worth waiting for," he affirmed. "I'll only be fifty-three years old when she turns twenty."

Jack offered a subtle smirk. "As if I'd let her marry a slob like you."

"This isn't helping to solve my problem with Amy,"

Case muttered, sucking down the last of his margarita.
"I've got to go back down there and see her."

"You just got back!"

"I *know* I just got back. But I've got to do this, and I
have to do it in person. I can be back in a couple of days."
Case hated begging more time off. He knew Jack would
cover for him in some ways, but Jack wasn't a medic and
Case's absence would put a strain on the other
veterinarians while he was away. Still...

"So what are you going to say? That you know she's
pregnant, that you'd make a dandy father, or maybe you
just want to date her? You gotta think this through, Doc.
Are you thinking long term, here?"

Case stared at Jack, unable to respond. Jack was
right, again; while he didn't want to shut out the
possibility of some kind of future with Amy, he had not
really considered the obvious: Amy was probably not in
the market for a casual relationship. So what *did* he want,
anyway?

"You inherited a son, I could do that if...we
ever...got that close."

"True, but Todd was already twelve years old. You
would have a different opportunity with a baby who
might never know his real father."

Frowning, Case pulled a twenty from his wallet and
tossed it onto the bar.

"I can't believe we are even having this conversation
about a woman I've slept with only once."

Jack chuckled. "You are in serious trouble, pal.
Godspeed."

* * *

On Coast Highway, he pushed the needle to the limit. He hoped she would be back in Newburg by the time he got there. He hoped she would listen to his apology, understand his screwy viewpoints, and forgive his ignorance. He had been thinking about their wonderful dinner together, her laughter and warmth. He'd also remembered his stupid comments about children. She very likely had written him off.

Could he consider a relationship with a pregnant woman?

Not just any woman. Amy Winslow. But where was the father? Were they married? Divorced? Could she really be completely alone?

Pregnant or not, there was something about her, something he liked being next to. And more, she felt the vibrations, the unseen aura of Point Surrender. She felt what he felt.

That took his thoughts in another direction. Amy's deception, he realized, was not any worse than his own. He had secrets too, and maybe the time had come to share them.

He stopped in Eureka for gas and to put the top down on the Triumph. He stood back, eyeing the forest green roadster, trying to figure out how to transport an infant in a two-seater. He shook his head.

The air was invigorating. He liked driving almost as much as he liked sailing. It gave him a chance to think.

Irena Hastings had not offered much information about Amy's whereabouts, but Case knew Amy would not stay away from her brother for very long.

Heading south, he eyed the horizon thoughtfully. The attendant at the gas station had warned of a storm building off the coast.

"I need to take a minute to make a call," Amy told Riley, when their last lunch patron left the restaurant. At Riley's nod, Amy grabbed her cell phone and headed for the parking lot. This time, a live person answered the phone.

"I'm looking for a Dr. Jenner. Dr. William Jenner." Amy stood straight and squared her shoulders.

"I'm sorry, we have no one here by that name. Were you looking for the Olson Institute?"

"Yes, this is the number I was given for Dr. Jenner. Do you have a lot of doctors there?" Amy asked, feeling foolish once again.

"Not really. I'll read you the roster, if you'd like…Dr. Drake, Dr. Fischer, Dr. McKenna, Dr. Talmadge…"

"McKenna?"

"Yes. Casey McKenna. But Dr. McKenna is not here at the moment. Did you want to leave a message?"

Amy felt her face fill with molten heat. She cleared her throat.

"Is this…an aquarium or ocean-type…hospital?"

The receptionist chuckled softly. "We are technically an oceanarium. We do research and rescue of marine wildlife. Our doctors are all qualified–"

"–veterinarians."

"Yes. Is there anything I can do for you, Miss?

Would you like to leave a message?"

"Just one thing…does Dr. McKenna go by any other name that you know of?"

"I'm sorry, Ma'am. I don't know, other than that his first name is listed as 'William' on the staff phone list. Everybody here calls him 'Case'. I do have another line to answer…"

"That's okay. No message. Thanks."

Amy pressed the 'END' key on her phone and turned to lean back against the wall.

William McKenna.

William C. Jenner.

William Casey Jenner?

William Casey McKenna?

Oh my God.

Chapter Fifteen

Leta was dreaming. She knew it had to be a dream because she was flying, and she hadn't touched the hard stuff in years. Yet here she was, sailing through the sky, the golden curls of her youth fluttering behind her.

Oh, but it felt grand! Soaring high above the trees, nearly weightless, and that God-forsaken pain in her chest was gone. She could breathe, she could see, she could feel.

As long as she was dreaming, she might as well go somewhere big. Yes, there was definitely somewhere she needed to visit, to return to. Vegas? Ha! Seattle, maybe? Naw.

She was still trying to decide where to fly when she noticed the question had been answered for her. The lighthouse sure looked different from above. She circled now, flying with the gulls around the lantern, surprised at the enjoyment she felt. She'd never once wanted to return before.

Then she saw him. A man standing in the yard, not far from the edge of the cliff. She felt her face break into a smile.

"Matt! Matt, is that you, honey? Oh, Matt..." He looked up then, and smiled back. What a smile that man had. No wonder he'd charmed the pants off her. Literally. "Come with me!" she called down to him. "Come fly, you can do it. It's my dream, after all!"

But the man on the bluff shook his head. "Can't do it, babe. Not now. Soon, maybe, I'll catch up."

She was hovering, she realized, about thirty feet above the ground. Closing her eyes, she felt the wind lift her and she soared out over the waves. When she looked again, Matt had changed. Had become someone else. Leta felt herself change, too, as she drifted down to the rocky edge of the cliff.

What is happening to me? Where is Matt?

The sun was rapidly disappearing. Joyous, she found herself standing on the bluff beside Matt. Or was it him?

"You are lovelier than ever, my darling Jacelyn. Take my hand, we'll walk together in the moonlight."

Leta looked down at her dress, a sturdy vintage gown she'd never have squeezed into had she been awake. She could feel the stays! Turning back to her companion, she stared in surprise.

"I know you! You're Captain Morgan Hastings!"

Suddenly the Captain's words sank in. She realized that she really had become Jacelyn Dunbar. Yes! She was Jacelyn!

They walked for a bit, pressing against the wind, then she turned around. A storm was brewing. On the craggy cliff behind them, the lighthouse stood, dark and foreboding, amid swaying grasses. Above, on the higher bluff, a posse of mounted policemen held torches and began shouting.

"Morgan, who are those men?" she cried, alarmed. Why would they appear in her dream?

"They are here for me, my love. They're here to take me away."

"No! We can't let them. We've only just found each other again! Please, don't go with them!"

The men came closer, guns drawn. "Surrender, Hastings! You've no choices left. No place to go! Surrender now, Rebel pirate, and pay for your crimes against the United States!" Rain began to fall, evident in the firelights lining the bluff.

"I'd rather die than leave you again." Morgan, with Matt's beautiful face, bent to kiss Leta's cheek. "We will, one day, return. Our love will not die, Jacelyn!"

Leta understood. Taking Morgan's hand, she stepped with him to the edge of the cliff. She turned for a last look at the lighthouse, but the beacon remained shadowed, cold. "It's so dark," she murmured, as she looked down to the swirling water below. The sea was a black abyss with an invisible, powerful roar.

"Salvation is waiting," her lover said, squeezing her hand. He bent to speak directly into her ear. "There's a boat below; if we make it."

More demands were shouted by the approaching lawmen. Morgan straightened, took another step. "They want us to surrender? So be it!"

"How is she?"

"I've increased her morphine as much as I can without risking cardiac arrest."

"She seems fretful."

"Probably hallucinatory dreams."

The nurse agreed and lifted Leta's wrist to check her pulse. Frowning, she adjusted her hold and tried again. "Doctor!"

The doctor had left the room. The nurse hurried to the door, leaned out and called, "I've got a code blue in here!"

Riley pushed open the heavy wood plank door and leaned outside, then pulled the door closed. "Yup. There's a nasty one comin' in. We won't be busy tonight." He returned to the counter and watched as Amy wandered back into the room, absently closing her cell phone, her eyes vacant. "You feeling okay?" Riley asked, concern creasing his forehead.

"I'm fine," she answered, the vagueness of her tone a giveaway that she really wasn't. Nonetheless, she went about her duties, cleaning the last table and loading plates into the dishwasher.

Riley kept an eye on the gathering clouds. As the sun set in an already dark sky, he glanced around the empty restaurant. "Think we'll close up early tonight."

"Fine with me," Amy agreed. She wasted no time in whipping off her apron and getting her purse out of the back room. "See you tomorrow. Say hi to Wendy."

Before Riley could reply, Amy was out the door.

With a referral from the United State Lighthouse Society, Judy had hired an electrician to work on Point Surrender's light in Amy's absence. During testing, it worked intermittently. The contractor said a new, modern, switching device was on order. Amy stopped at the lighthouse on her way to the hospital to check things out.

Once inside, she hesitated, mesmerized. Touring the rooms, she saw them anew. She saw a young, vivacious Leta Jenner pacing the floor, a small, blue-eyed child toddling after her. In the larger bedroom, she saw the bed where Liam Jenner lay with his back to his bride. In the small bedroom, the narrow, iron framed cot where William Jenner had lain at night for eleven years.

Amy recalled the first day Case had worked with her, his hesitation when entering that room. *Of course! He was seeing ghosts.*

He could have told her. Trusted her with his true identity. Why the charade? Why the secrets? He had lied, plain and simple, and it hurt Amy to her very vulnerable core. No wonder he didn't want her to read the journal. It might expose him for the imposter he was.

And worse, he was the son who'd refused to talk to his mother. She thought of the sorrow in Leta Jenner's eyes.

She drove to the hospital, still troubled, her anger growing with the revelation of Case's deceit. The rain began to fall, the droplets increasing in size with each passing moment. She parked as close as she could to the door and hurried inside. A passing orderly stopped her.

"Amy! We've been trying to find you. Brian's condition has changed."

Wordlessly she rushed down the antiseptic halls to Brian's room. Inside, she found him tossing on the bed. His lips moved, the words jumbled.

"Brian! What is it?" Amy leaned close to his mouth,

trying to decipher his words.

"The light," he murmured, twisting his head to one side. "Light. The light. Light...the light."

"Light? What light?" Amy looked around in vain for a lamp, a light fixture that Brian may be referring to.

"The storm...light...Point...Surrender...need to...a boat..."

"He wants me to light the lighthouse!" Amy looked at the attending nurse in horror. "Why is he saying that?"

Brian continued to stir, his requests becoming more and more animated, desperate. Finally he opened his eyes wide.

"A man was here. He had...long hair...he said there's a boat...get the light working!"

"What should I do?" Amy asked as the nurse prepared to take Brian's blood pressure.

"We've called his doctor. He should be here any minute."

"Brian, I don't understand." Amy bit her lower lip, awash with indecision. She turned back to the nurse. "Has anyone been in this room?"

The nurse looked up from the blood pressure cuff and shook her head. But Brian was adamant, reaching out to grasp Amy's arm.

"I saw him! You've got to go, Amy. Go now!"

Amy stared hard at her brother's distressed face. Finally, she turned to go. "Would you call Judy Cashion? She should be at Hastings House, tell her to come down here. Please!" Amy rushed out of the hospital and back to her car.

I'm truly certifiable now. This is pure craziness. She tore out of the parking lot.

The rain was pelting now, the wind becoming fierce. Amy could barely see out the windshield, the wipers nearly useless against the deluge. Once again at Point Surrender, she quickly picked her way down the steps, squinting as the wind battered her face with wet spears.

Inside the house, the radio squealed, a choppy conversation broadcasting. She went to the radio and carefully attempted to tune in the voices. Her hair dripped on the counter, and her fingers were cold and shaking. She was surprised to hear a *May Day* call. A boat in trouble. A boat whose captain thought he might be nearing the rocks at Point Surrender.

"The light," Amy whispered. "Brian…"

She hesitated only a moment before ascending the iron staircase in the tower, not bothering to turn on the lights in the stairwell. At the top, she forced open the heavy trapdoor and climbed up into the lantern room. She looked quickly at the lamp, searching for the switch panel door. Disoriented by the storm, the darkness and her own confusion, she was compelled to look out toward the sea, saw the sky lit with jagged, electric fire. The brief illumination was just enough to reveal two figures standing on the edge of the cliff below.

"It's *them*," she murmured aloud. The crack of thunder startled her, reminded her of Brian's demand. Throwing open the panel door, she stared in awe at the row of small levers and swallowed hard. "Oh God. Now what?"

* * *

Case passed by the darkened windows at Riley's and headed on. He was nearing the turn off to Point Surrender when his headlights illuminated the figure of a man standing in the road ahead. Despite the pouring rain, he seemed unfazed and waved his arms for Case to stop. Case narrowed his eyes, trying to see through the downpour as he pulled to the side of the road. He felt under his seat for the flashlight he kept there.

Carefully training the light's beam on the roadway, Case looked for the man. The man, he now realized, who wore a heavy gray plaid shirt. He knew, without much effort, that he would find the pavement empty and that he'd unintentionally parked his car on the driveway to Point Surrender.

Amazingly, Amy's car was parked, askew, at the top of the steps. Case felt a sense of foreboding. A heavy darkness swelled within him, tightened his chest. He took the steps three at a time, unmindful of the slippery stones set into the hillside. Somehow he got to the front door without falling and burst into the house, calling Amy's name. The partially open door to the tower beckoned him.

Case stopped midway to the door. From the kitchen he could hear the squawking of the short wave, the frenetic call for help blasting through the night air. Competing were the sounds of the crashing surf, the pounding rain. With hands of fear gripping his heart, he flung open the door to the stairway. "Amy! Are you up there?"

The din of the storm was overwhelming in the

stairwell. Lightning streaked from cloud to cloud a short distance away, and the rumblings of thunder grew closer by the minute. Case could hear the frantic flipping of the switches as he hurried up the steps.

"Amy!" he yelled again as he reached the top. "What are you doing?"

"What does it look like I'm doing?" she screamed back, refusing to look him in the face. "There's a boat in trouble!"

"Let me do that!"

"No, I can do this. Just go away. I don't need your help, *Doctor* McKenna, or William Jenner, or whoever the hell you are!"

Case paused momentarily. He edged closer to the switch box, but Amy pushed his arm aside. "I said go away! This isn't your lighthouse anymore, it's Brian's, and he needs me to do this! Find someone else to lie to!"

"Amy, you don't understand...this is tricky..." He reached past her and forced all of the switches in unison. The light began to glow, its gears to turn slowly. Incensed, Amy placed both hands against Case's chest and shoved him away. It took quick reflexes on his part not to fall through the gaping trapdoor behind him.

"Calm down! We need to talk. Let's go downstairs." Case tried to take Amy by the arm, but she struggled.

"Don't touch me. Don't feed me any more lies. I trusted you! Why did you do it? All that time, you knew, knew everything. Were you laughing at me? Why?" Her face stricken, she stared at Case, a picture of misery that tore at his insides.

"Look, I was planning to tell you, I swear!"

"Yeah, right!" She wanted to hurt him, he knew, in return for the emotional pain she was suffering. Well, he'd suffered, too. "What about you! You dropped a hook in front my face, slept with me for Christ's sake, all the while you were pregnant with some other guy's kid! So who was laughing, Amy? *Who?* Not me. Not me!"

His words only swelled the pain in her gut. She lashed out again, with both fists. At that moment, the turning light slowly passed across her face.

"Close your eyes!" Case shouted, but belatedly. Startled by the blinding beam, Amy lost her footing as she lunged toward him and stepped off the edge of the opening to the stairwell. Her cry was muted by an ominous crack of thunder just overhead.

Case gasped and stared in disbelief at the rectangular opening in the floor. Frozen in time, he was again eleven years old and his father, not Amy, had just tumbled down Point Surrender's steep winding staircase to the bottom. A memory, blurred by time, began to run in his head, like an old movie he had seen too many times. His fearful descent down the iron steps; his first glimpse of his father's distorted figure on the floor at the bottom; his own knees hitting the floor nearby as he fell involuntarily upon them, staring in grotesque wonder at his dying father.

"Daddy? Daddy? DADDY!"

Outside, the storm raged on.

Amy's moan brought him back to the moment. Amy had fallen! How long had he hesitated? Case hurried down the steps to find her in the same spot his father had landed; only she was sitting up and rubbing her neck.

"*What are you doing*? Don't try to get up. You may be injured!" Case demanded, instantly squatting by her side.

"Leave me alone! I'm fine. Just a little bruised."

Case ignored her comments and tried to make a quick assessment while she fought him off. "I'm taking you into Roth. You need to be checked out."

"Forget it. I'm fine, I told you." Amy got shakily to her feet. "I'll go by myself. If you want to do something, you can lock up for me." Trying to make a dignified exit, Amy walked purposefully out the door and into the rain.

Case watched her go, then sat down on the last riser at the foot of the stairs. He looked at the place where she'd lain, then back up the curving stairs above him. He expected to feel something, some horrendous, painful sensation brought on by the events of the past few minutes. Instead, he felt nothing, was numb. Here was the place, the very spot where he had watched his father die. The home of his nightmares, the seat of his fears.

Seeing Amy get up and walk away had been a miracle.

By the time Amy maneuvered her car onto the highway, the cramping had begun in earnest. She pulled over, grasping the steering wheel as hard as she could while the searing pain progressed across her abdomen. She was afraid of what the pain meant, afraid to think about what could be happening. She drove on.

Leaving the car at the entrance, she stumbled through the swinging doors at Roth General Hospital and gripped the edge of the admittance counter.

"Amy! We have great news!" The night nurse called from the hallway. "Brian–" Her words were clipped short as Amy's knees began to buckle. She rushed to Amy's side. "What is it? What's happened?"

"I fell. I'm two months pregnant."

They wasted no time getting Amy into a hospital bed. A doctor gave her a shot, after which all the faces around her blended together like watercolors in the rain. She could feel the contractions, but they seemed to be happening to someone else. Consciousness faded into a thick fog.

Brian's nurse mopped Amy's brow, her voice confusingly jumbled with the others in the room.

"Too bad...her brother...the coma...no reason...more children...so much blood..." Muted sounds, and darkness.

Several hours passed before Amy finally came into clear consciousness. She thought she was still dreaming when she looked up into Andrew Richards' concerned face. He shook his head.

"You should have told me, Aim."

Amy struggled to sit up, turned to look at the I.V. drip attached to her arm, the nurse writing on her chart. She refused to look back at Drew.

"What are you doing here?" she rasped. "Can someone get me some water?"

"I came down this afternoon to see Brian. Decided to

wait out the storm before driving back to the city."

"You came to see Brian? Why? Looking for your money?" Gratefully, Amy took a cup of water from the nurse.

"That's not fair. And it's not fair that you didn't tell me about the baby. We could have patched things up. I should have been told."

"Like it would have made a difference," Amy murmured. "I don't need you. We'll be fine, alone. A lot of women raise kids alone."

Drew looked confused. He turned toward the nurse, then Judy, who waited beside the door.

Judy walked over and sat on the edge of the bed. "Hi Amy." She glanced nervously at Drew and then back to Amy. "Guess what? It happened! Brian woke up!"

"Are you serious? That's wonderful! Oh, that's great news…" Amy's smile faded as she detected a trace of pain still on Judy's face, and the ashen look on Drew's.

"There's some not-so-good news, too," Judy began, taking Amy's hand.

Amy felt the blood drain from her own face as realization set in. Instinctively her hand moved to her abdomen and rested there. She had lost the baby.

"I'm not pregnant anymore, am I?" she asked, and Judy shook her head mournfully.

"I'm so sorry, Amy. Nobody knows what happened. You just came in and said you'd fallen."

Amy rushed her hand across her eyes. Her chest heaved with a sob that began deep inside. "My baby," she moaned. "Oh…*my baby*!"

Drew instantly took her into his arms "It's okay, it's gonna be okay," he soothed, rocking her gently in the bed. "We can have more children."

Case watched from just outside the hospital room door. He frowned as Judy emerged from the room, wiping her eyes with a tissue. She looked up in surprise. "You heard what happened?"

"I was there." To Judy's shocked expression, Case shook his head, then looked again at the man cradling Amy. "Who is that guy?"

"Her ex. Drew Richards."

The baby's father. Talking about having more children with Amy.

Case turned and walked slowly out the front door of the hospital. He missed seeing Amy slap Drew's face, didn't hear her demand that he never come near her again.

Chapter Sixteen

Amy stared hard at the kitchen calendar, forcing her mind to focus and determine the date. August was nearly half over, yet she couldn't remember what she had done to fill the days during the past three weeks.

Through the kitchen window she could see Brian and Judy strolling around the yard, talking intimately about their plans. The lighthouse was really too small for private conversations, and Amy felt out of place.

Upon her discharge from Roth, Amy moved her belongings to Point Surrender. Brian came home not long after, and he relinquished his San Francisco apartment. The Coast Guard picked up the tab on his moving expenses. Judy began to plan their wedding.

Much to Amy's relief, the repayment of Drew's loan was handled via electronic transfer. It would be several more weeks before Brian could return to work. Until he did, Judy continued to work but cut her hours significantly so that she could help with Brian's recovery. Amy decided that when Brian resumed his job, she would move out.

Despite the fact that her options were now wide open, Amy remained uninspired. On the outside, she was smiling and witty to those around her. Inside, she wallowed in an abyss of loneliness and sadness. Her relationship over, her baby lost, her future empty.

August. It meant nothing. It could be February, November, or May. She didn't care.

For Brian's sake, Amy carefully pasted on a smile every day. The therapy wasn't easy, especially for an athlete like Brian. Patience was not exactly his forte, either.

"Great. That's ten. Now let's do ten more," she directed, as Brian lay sweating on the exercise mat in the living room. "I promised Judy I'd keep you going while she's in Florida. C'mon, you can do this."

With a groan, Brian resumed his sit-ups, as Amy held his ankles. "What about you? You should be doing this stuff, too."

"I run on the beach every morning. Don't give me grief, Bro. Dad and Nola will be here next week and he'll give you what-for."

Brian paused, pushing himself up to a sitting position. "He's bringing her? I didn't know that. Where will we put them?"

"They'll stay at Hastings." Amy helped Brian to stand up and gave him his cane. "You'll like Nola, don't worry."

"I'm not worried about liking Nola." He was still panting as he sat down on the couch. "It's you I'm worried about."

"Well, don't." Amy crossed her arms. She frowned, then ventured a question she'd been pondering. "Do you remember much about that night you woke up in the hospital?"

Brian closed his eyes and nodded his head with an

embarrassed smile. "Unfortunately, yes."

"You said something about a man coming to your bed. Was it Drew?"

The smile faded and Brian's eyes grew serious. "No. It was someone I'd never seen before. He had long hair. Kinda curly. A mustache. Blue eyes, I think. He told me something about a boat in trouble, near the lighthouse. Something about the boat trying to pick up two swimmers."

"Wearing a gray Pendleton, right?"

"Actually, yeah. Seems like he was. Kinda weird how they let him come in like that. I didn't think about it at the time."

Amy pulled in her lower lip but said nothing more.

"That's it. Nice and easy. You've got it," Case said, his voice purposefully calm as he watched Jack lower the young dolphin into the tank. The moment the sleek, silvery creature touched the water, he was off to the opposite side of the pool, diving and sounding playfully.

"I'm not shaking at all..." Jack said, comically holding up his quivering hands.

"Easy, wasn't it?"

"Oh, sure. Piece of cake. Delivering my daughter was easier!"

Case grinned. "When do you start school?"

"Not soon enough. About ten days, I think. Hey, that reminds me. Maddie has a class tonight and I thought I'd take the brood out for pizza. Wanna come?"

"When have I ever turned down pizza? As long as I

can sit by my future bride."

"In your dreams, pal."

Case squatted down and tapped the side of the tank. "You don't want to know about my dreams," he muttered, then reached into the water to caress the dolphin. The young animal was slender but tough. Healthy. Strong. "This one won't be here much longer." He stood, dried his hands on a towel, and turned to Jack. "I'm ready when you are. You buying?"

It was no small feat, Case decided, balancing a wiggly two-year-old ballerina with one arm and carrying a pitcher of root beer with the other. Especially when the little prima donna stuck her tiny finger into his ear. Back at the table, he gratefully handed the youngster over to her father and put the pitcher down before Jack's two sons. Case slid onto the wooden bench across from Jack.

The pizza parlor was only half filled with patrons, most waiting for the classic rock band to start playing. Case was subtly reminded of the few nights he dined at Riley's, on Newburg's outskirts. He looked around, recognizing familiar faces here and there. Grogan's Head was a very small town. Yet at the table directly behind him, two strangers sat facing one another, sharing a pitcher of beer and watching the country music videos playing on the corner TV.

Ignoring them at first, Case became aware of their conversation when he heard them talking about boats. Being a favorite subject, Case turned his head slightly, eaves-dropping on the two young men.

"You don't think he got a good look at us, do you? I

mean, now that the kid woke up he might be talking," the first voice said.

"Not the kid. Maybe the guy in the dinghy."

"Shit, man, it's been two months. If they were gonna come lookin' for us, they'd have been here by now. I say we go back and get the stuff."

"The flounders have probably gotten to it."

"Hell, you haven't heard any reports about flying fish in Newburg Harbor, have you? And those fish *would* be flying if they got into that supremo stuff. Don't worry. It's sealed up tighter than a can of beans."

"So we just hire a diver?"

"Hell no, we'll go down and get it ourselves. We know about where the damned boat went down, we'll just rent some SCUBA stuff and go after it."

"I don't know. I'm not that good a swimmer. It nearly did me in that day, swimming out to the point."

The voices paused. Case's blood turned cold. Abruptly, Case realized he'd missed a significant part of the conversation at his own table. He looked up to find Jack quizzically staring at him. Beside Case, Mae was waving a straw in his face.

"She wants *you* to poke it into her lid, *Uncle Case*," Jack told him.

"Of course she does." He performed the requested task and tried to appear casual while tuning his hearing back upon the two behind him.

"Maybe we should hire someone. They won't have to know what's in the box. We should get someone from this area. We don't want to have any connections to

Newburg."

Case's mind raced. He was convinced that these men were Brian's assailants. Unbelievably, they had turned up right here in this tiny blip on the California coast. Grogan's Head comprised little more than the Olson Institute, one motel, and a gas station.

He had to think of a way to detain them, identify them, and turn them over to the authorities. But without the boat and some way to connect them to it, the evidence was slim. It sounded as though they were planning to go back to Newburg to retrieve something, possibly drugs, from aboard their sunken ski boat. A plan appeared, full blown, in Case's mind.

He waited until the waitress came by with a booster seat for Mae.

"Hey Sue, how's it shakin'?" he asked, his voice just a shade louder than necessary.

"It's shakin' pretty loose, honey. How's 'bout you?"

"Just wondering if your old man was interested in selling that dive equipment yet. I'm looking for another set of tanks, and I need a second regulator."

"You know he wavers back and forth all the time, but I'll let you know. Keeps sayin' he's getting too old to dive, then he loads up his SCUBA gear and he's gone."

"Never too old," Case admonished. "I'm looking for some good dives if you hear of any," he told her as she walked away.

Case took a slug of root beer and waited. Jack looked puzzled but said nothing. He got up to take his younger son to the rest room. "Keep an eye on Mae for me, will you?"

No sooner had Jack left the dining room than one of the two men stood and sauntered up to Case. "Heard you talking about wanting a good dive. We just might have a job for you."

Jack snapped Mae's safety seat buckle and closed the back door on his SUV. "Are you out of your freakin' mind?" he asked, his eyes wide with unabashed surprise. "Those guys are felons! They'd just as soon kill you as talk to you. Don't be dumb. Call the police."

"That would blow the whole deal. I'll call the police when I'm ready to do the dive. When they take the dope from me, the cops will bust them." Case rolled his shoulders, slipped his thumbs into the front belt loops of his jeans. The parking lot was emptying fast. He was anxious to get home and pack.

"I think you're nuts," Jack said, shaking his head. He rounded the car to get behind the wheel, paused with his hand on the door. "Mae isn't going to like this."

Case looked away. "Do you think I could live with myself if these hoodlums got away? I owe it to Amy. And her brother."

"If you're just trying to get next to the lady, I can think of a lot of safer ways to do that."

Both men climbed into the front, and Jack backed the vehicle out of the parking space. Silence prevailed as Case thought about his friend's suggestion. If called upon to examine the truth, he'd have to admit that he wanted to see Amy again. But it certainly wasn't his motivation for trying to catch her brother's attackers. Not really. *Well, maybe a little.*

"Look, I saw an opportunity to do something right and I'm doing it, that's all. If I happen to see her down there, great. If not, well, great."

"When are you going to notify the police?"

"Just before the deal goes down."

Jack let out an exasperated sigh. "I guess I can't stop you."

"No, I guess you can't."

"You know I can't condone what you're doing," Deputy Carnahan said, the scowl evident in his voice. "I can't even know you're doing it. You really do have that super-hero complex."

"Yeah, I'm a tough guy. The dive will be around four tomorrow afternoon. The guys' names and the details are in the fax I'm putting through right now."

Case hung up the phone before the lawman could object. He laced up his boots and walked outside behind his cabin, glanced up at the majestic redwoods around him. As he walked, he sorted his thoughts.

Tomorrow he would drive south to Newburg and make the dive. If things went as planned, Carnahan and his men would be nearby, watching and waiting. Ready to make the arrest when the deal went down. If things went as planned.

The two men buying his services had seemed pretty harmless up close in the pizza parlor. Carnahan had warned that the crooks had at least one gun. Minutes before the collision, Brian Winslow had reported two vandals taking shots at a harbor buoy, then firing on some unseen object or creature in the water. Now that he was conscious, Brian had added details to his story. Just before the ski boat reached him, one of the men had popped off a round in Brian's direction.

Still walking, Case found himself in a clearing, cut by a small band of renegade loggers several years before. He sat down on one of the foot-wide stumps and again gazed skyward, breathing deeply of the powerful redwood scent that clung to the growing mist.

I'll bet she would love it here.

He recalled Amy's fond description of the wooded valley where she had played as a child, and her distaste for San Francisco's populated streets. *This would be a wonderful setting for her recovery. If only–*

If only things hadn't gone so terribly wrong.

"They didn't see you come here, did they?"

"No. I convinced them it would be too risky for all three of us to come into town together. They're both nursing killer hangovers in a camper van parked in the corner of Riley's lot." As Carnahan began to protest, Case held up his hand. "Riley knows to ignore them."

The deputy shook his head. "You understand the risk you're taking. Why don't you just let us pick them up?"

"You know as well as I do the case will be much stronger with the evidence. Look, I've been diving for years. I'm good at this."

"Alright. We go with your plan. But I don't like it."

* * *

Case checked his regulator a third time before dropping himself over the side of the skiff. It took him all of eight minutes to find his goal. The wreckage was within ten yards of where Douglas Handley had said it would be, about ten fathoms down.

Sixty feet deep. No wonder no one had seen the wreckage yet.

Case circled the remains of the ski boat, then grabbed onto the corner of the windshield and pulled himself into the seating area. In the storage compartment behind the driver's seat was a sealed canister. Case hovered above the sunken boat, retrieved the can, and forced it into the netted bag that hung from his weight belt.

He took a moment to examine the damaged vessel, making certain in his mind that it was the same ski boat he had witnessed screaming into Brian's small patrol boat. Swimming around the hull amid the riotous bubbles escaping from his regulator, Case examined the scrolling gold letters emblazoned against the deep purple paint: *Night Music.* The large outboard was separated from the hull, the damage apparently the result of the impact with Brian's boat.

Drifting back to the front seats, Case wrestled open the small glove box and felt around inside.. He was rewarded by the discovery of a packet of papers sealed into a zip-lock plastic bag.

There was no sign of a gun, but he had what he needed.

Taking one last look around, Case headed for the

surface where his dinghy waited.

Handley and his accomplice had insisted upon meeting him at the dock. They didn't trust Case with their high priced goods, and had originally wanted to accompany him in the small dinghy. Now, they watched his every move from the time he emerged from the water.

Case took his time returning to shore. From a brown paper bag he pulled a sandwich and took a bite while piloting the small boat toward the dock where the two waited. Behind them, Case could see Carnahan and another deputy in civilian threads standing outside the boat rental shack. At the end of the dock, another plain-clothes lawman casually observed the horizon. Case smiled.

Unhurried, he tied up the dinghy and hoisted his tank onto the dock, followed by his knapsack and finally, himself. His 'business partners' nearly stumbled over each other to get to him.

Case handed over the canister. "Man, that's a nice boat. Or I should say, *was* a nice boat. You know the whole stern is gone?"

"I figured as much," Handley lamented. "Too bad. It was my dad's boat. Hey, I'll just buy him a new one!" He and his crony laughed. Case saw Carnahan on the move.

"I looked for the outboard," Case said, shaking his head. "How was she titled?"

Handley grinned. "*Night Music*. Poetic, huh?"

"You a poet?" Case asked, grinning back. The deputy, now within earshot, sauntered down the dock.

"Oh, yeah. That and other things." Handley pulled an

envelope from the inside pocket of his windbreaker, stared at it for a moment in his hands.

Case didn't miss the revolver tucked into the waistband of the felon's jeans. Glancing to the side, he sensed Carnahan had almost reached them.

As if resigned, Handley held out the envelope. "Here you go. Thanks for your help."

"Oh, don't thank me." Case took the envelope and put it with the plastic registration packet before handing them both over to Carnahan, who'd suddenly appeared at his side. "I think that's all you need."

The deputy flashed his badge, and Handley's expression turned grim. He turned quickly to his right, only to find his path blocked by a second deputy.

"We'll relieve you of these, too," the other deputy said, then reached between them to take the gun and the canister.

Handley began to sputter and Case thought the man would swallow his own tongue. "Why you stinking double–" A third deputy began reading their rights as Case walked away from the stunned perpetrators.

"We'll need your statement," Carnahan called after him. "And I don't want this!" He held up the envelope filled with cash.

"Give it to Brian Winslow!" Case called back over his shoulder.

"It was flawless," he told Jack over the telephone. "Those bastards didn't know what hit them."

"You're lucky, man. Things could have gone

sideways real fast."

Case refused to think about what could have happened. He regretted enough things in his past to add anything more.

"When will you be back?"

"I just have to hang around a day or two to make a statement. I'm at Hastings House again if you need me."

Case snapped his cell phone closed. Back in Morgan's room, he lay down on the bed, folded his arms behind his head. His gaze idly traveled around the room, perusing the plaid wallpaper, the antique sextant on the wall, the lamp base shaped like a lighthouse. His mind traveled back to a place he rarely visited, his childhood. Involuntary images appeared, memories of holding his mother's hand as they walked up the wide wooden porch steps and entered Matthew Hastings' living room, then his mother sitting at the piano while he sat in the corner beside the fireplace with a pile of building blocks. Matt Hastings standing behind his mother, his hands on her shoulders while she played.

"Why do you have hair like a girl?" young William had asked. Matt had thrown back his head and laughed.

"What, you think guys should all have butches like your dad?"

"What's a butch?"

When Matt laughed again, William colored and went back to his blocks. His mother continued to play. Soon, Matt joined him on the floor.

"You having some trouble here?" he asked, his voice gentle and patient.

"Can't make my house," the small boy confessed, trying in vain to get the blocks to form a conical tower.

"Not all houses have round sides, kid. My house is pretty straight. Try building this house."

Later that night the younger Jenner had re-created the Hastings House on the kitchen table for his father. Liam Jenner all but ignored it, demanding that William put the blocks away.

"What's a butch, Dad?"

Liam paused at the sink, his eyes narrowing. "You been hanging out with that hippie freak Hastings again? Leta!"

An argument ensued, only one of what seemed like hundreds to the small boy as he quickly retreated to his room, blocks in tow.

Case's memory faded to black when a knock at his door brought him around. He opened it to an elderly gentleman with an apologetic smile.

"You don't happen to have a phone in your room, do you? I need to reach my daughter and I can't find the proprietress. We're just across the hall here..."

"No, I'm sorry," Case said. "Is it urgent? You can use my cell. Or, Miss Hastings has a phone in the kitchen downstairs. I can walk you down there if you'd like."

"Would you mind? I've never quite gotten the hang of those cell things. These stairs are a pain in the rear for me, and my girlfriend's outside somewhere wandering around the grounds."

"Not a problem." Case slowly descended the stairs just ahead of the man, led him to the kitchen phone.

Spying the squinting frown on the man's face, he cleared his throat and picked up the receiver. "Need some help dialing?"

"Can't read the blasted number. Here, if you don't mind."

"Sure thing." Case took the number and dialed, handed the phone to the man and then started away. The man mouthed an exaggerated 'thank you' and then spoke into the handpiece.

"Amy? Is that you, sweetie? It's Dad. Yeah, we just got in a bit ago."

Case stopped at the kitchen door. How in the world could he play this unexpected card?

"Well I guess we're gonna have a little dessert with the proprietress. No, don't worry about that. We can see you in the morning."

Amy's father. He could see the resemblance. Same determined jaw, same soulful brown eyes. Case started as someone tapped him gently on the shoulder.

"Care to join us, Mr. McKenna?" Miss Hastings asked, as she swept past him into the kitchen. "I've just pulled a blueberry strudel out of the oven."

Case stroked an imaginary beard, then accepted. "Guess I'd be a fool not to."

He sat across the table from Tom Winslow. Tom was a warm, likable guy, which didn't surprise Case in the least.

"How long did it take you to get here?" he asked.

"Oh, we took our time, stopped at a coupl'a wineries, I'd say 'bout seven hours. We aren't in any big rush. Come up to see my son, Brian. Just got out of the hospital."

Case nodded as he wrapped his lips around a bite of strudel.

"My daughter's up here, too, now. Amy. She's a schoolteacher."

Swallowing hard, Case again nodded. "How's your son doing?"

"Pretty well, considerin' all he went through. What a great kid."

"They're *both* great kids," Nola added with a sunny grin. "Very devoted to each other."

Standing behind Tom, Miss Hastings was smiling. For a fleeting moment, Case saw something else in that smile, something he didn't like. He found himself staring, considering.

"Mr. McKenna is a marine veterinarian," Miss Hastings said, leaning between her guests to pour coffee. "But he's leaving soon."

"How about you? Staying long?" Case asked, as Miss Hastings walked away, breaking his stare.

"Just a day or two. Gonna tramp around Frisco, then head on up the coast to Oregon. We got ourselves a little motor home."

Miss Hastings sat down at the head of the table. "That sounds like fun."

"Oh, it's the best. We were going to try to convince Amy to come along. Poor dear. She's been through so much," Nola offered.

Case loaded up his fork but paused before bringing it to his mouth. "Were?" he asked.

Tom turned his attention from the strudel to Case's eyes. "Well, she's a bit down. As Nola said, she's been through hell lately, what with her brother's ordeal and all, plus she's had some personal problems, too. There's been some guy she's been moonin' around about, he's the one who–"

"I'm sure that's more than this young man was lookin' to hear, Tommy," Nola interrupted, her grasp firm on Tom's wrist.

Tom smiled and nodded. "I'm sorry. I get carried away when it comes to my baby girl. She's such a sweet soul, deserves so much, just gets dealt the wrong hand all the time. Maybe we'll try again to get her to go with us."

Nola turned back to her own plate. "She's got to find her own way, dear. She'll get her day. Her day in the sun." Lifting her gaze, she stared directly into Case's eyes. "One day soon."

Case found it hard to look away. Nola's eyes crinkled with merriment and love. He put down his fork and grabbed his napkin.

"It was really nice meeting you both. I hope you have a great trip up north." Standing, he pulled his wallet from his hip pocket and withdrew a card. "When you pass though Grogan's Head, give me a call. Maybe you'd like to see our aquarium."

"Oh, fabulous! We will call you," Nola replied, snatching up the card as Tom rose to shake Case's hand.

"I hope things work out for your son and…your daughter," Case murmured, then took his leave.

Chapter Seventeen

Amy sat in an Adirondack chair facing the sea. Case McKenna had come to Newburg and aided the sheriff in bringing the criminals responsible for Brian's injuries to justice. More, he had sent a thousand dollars to Brian, apparently his fee for 'assisting' the hoodlums. Yet he hadn't called, hadn't stopped to meet Brian or say hello to Riley.

It's me, she thought glumly. *He doesn't want to chance running into me.* The night of the storm dominated her thoughts most days, the events leading to the traumatic loss that still hurt.

Glancing upward, her eyes rested on the black iron railing that formed the gallery around the light. She imagined the storm lashing those windows, the lightning cracking, and Case's eyes, so distressed, so pained as she attacked him. The rage of the storm and her emotions had crashed into them both that night.

She knew she could never take back the angry words she had flung into his face. Probably would not be given the chance to apologize. Whatever they were, Case McKenna's reasons for keeping his identity to himself were his business, not hers, or anyone else's, and she had crossed the line.

She had been such a fool.

By his mother's own account, Case had suffered

greatly as a child, and had grown up with secrets he wanted to keep hidden away. He had asked her to leave it alone. She had blundered on ahead.

Judy interrupted her troubled thoughts, a small stack of envelopes in her hand."You got a letter."

Amy stood. *Another letter from Drew?* She hoped not. She had received one short missive from him after the miscarriage, glanced through it, and tossed it into the trash. Amy took the manila envelope and quickly checked the return address. "Phoebe Allen...? Burbank, California."

Judy shrugged. "Rings no bell with me. You want some lunch? I made tuna salad."

"Sure...in a minute." Burbank, California *did* ring a bell. Amy returned to the wooden chair, then carefully tore open the seal. Inside were a letter and two pink, business sized, sealed envelopes.

"Wow. Judy! Listen to this. 'Dear Ms. Winslow, my name is Phoebe Allen. I am Leta Mansfield's neighbor and friend.'" Amy's eyes widened at the site of Leta's name, handwritten so painstakingly in beautiful script. She glanced quickly at Judy, then back to the letter in her hand.

"I'm so sorry to tell you that Leta passed four weeks ago. She was in the hospital for a couple of weeks. The cancer finally got her. She knew she was dying, and she left this envelope for you. She didn't have a phone number for you or I would have called. I would have sent this sooner, but I've been sick myself. I believe you will find that she wants you to handle some arrangements for her, so time is real important and if you don't want to do it you have to let me know immediately."

Here, Phoebe Allen had printed her phone number.

"In either case, I wait to hear from you."

Amy wasted no time in opening the envelope marked with her name. This handwriting was not so neat. She cleared her throat, then resumed reading aloud.

"Hi Amy. Well you might regret having looked up this old flower child when you did. But frankly, you are the nicest person I've met in years, and the first to not judge me for my crimes. It looks like my lungs are just about to cry uncle so I'll be thankfully leaving this world soon. I still think about your visit and wonder if you were able to locate my son. If you did, he must still be pissed off at me for I haven't heard word one.

"Anyway, I am calling upon your kindness. It is my last and only wish that after they burn me up, I be buried in Newburg beside my husband. I realize Liam just might well raise up and move to another part of the cemetery, but that's a risk I can take! Phoebe, bless her heart, is not truly capable of handling this for me, so I was hoping you'd be able to see it through. In the other envelope is my will, and I'd be so grateful if you would gather some folks together and read it..."

Amy shook her head slowly. This was certainly a bizarre request. The letter went on to say that there was money for the transportation and burial expenses, and that Amy should call Phoebe to get it.

"Amazing," Amy whispered past the lump in her throat. Gathering together the letters and envelopes, Amy followed Judy inside to tell Brian.

Even more amazing to Amy was the ease with which she was able to comply with Leta's wishes. The urn bearing her ashes arrived quickly and without incident, and Newburg Cemetery proved gracious in their dealings. The plot beside William R. Jenner was made ready, and a graveside service planned.

"I'd like to have a small reception," Amy said into the telephone, "to read her will and talk about her life. I thought your house would be perfect."

"I don't think so, dear," Irena Hastings said quickly. "It wouldn't be appropriate."

Amy was dumbstruck. She had not expected Miss Hastings to do anything other than endorse her idea, maybe offer to help. Her reluctance, no, *downright refusal*, to host the reception was shocking.

"I see. Well..." Amy looked around Point Surrender's limited space. "We can have it here." She hung up feeling oddly dismayed.

She made a few more phone calls and was able to compile a brief list of invitees. There were two or three people living in town, former piano students, who expressed an interest in attending. She had put the word out. It was the best she could do.

"Are you going to talk to Case?" Judy asked that evening, in the kitchen, as they discussed the plans. "He's still in town, you know. I saw that little green sports car parked in front of the deli."

"No, I didn't know." Amy bit her lower lip, chagrined

that even Judy knew more about Case's activities than she did. She busied herself rinsing the sink. "I guess we should at least tell him."

Judy nodded. "He's most likely staying at Irena's."

"She didn't mention it."

"Does that surprise you? I think she's wacko. She says some pretty strange things sometimes."

"Maybe he doesn't want her telling me he's there."

Judy sighed. "I'm sure that's not true."

"I just don't feel like calling over there again." Amy dried her hands. "Maybe I'll try his cell. Later."

"Well if the funeral's tomorrow, you don't have a lot of time."

Amy went to her room and dressed for work. Sleeping in Case's boyhood bedroom was weird in itself. Now, she had charged herself with the duty of telling him his mother had died. Unreconciled.

"You look good today," Riley commented as Amy breezed past him on her way to the kitchen. "Whaja do to your hair? It looks great!"

Amy paused in the doorway and turned with a smile. "Is it my turn to clean out the garbage can or what?"

"No, really…it's darker or something."

"Judy and I put it back to its right color last night. Thanks for noticing."

"Aw, you always look good, lady. Your hair could be purple."

Amy gave him a sunny look and disappeared into the kitchen.

"You seen Case since he's been back?" Riley called after her.

The still swinging doors flew back open with Amy framed between them. "Not yet. Did you?"

"He was by here yesterday. Said he'd stop by today to say good-bye."

A lump magically grew in Amy's throat, but she forced a smile. "Great," she sang out, then turned back to the kitchen. "Just great." These last words were murmured to herself as she lugged out the hefty bag of coffee beans and dropped it unceremoniously on the counter beside the grinder. Her fingers, clumsy and uncooperative as she fumbled with the tear strip on the new bag, frustrated her. Jitters. That was the only word for it.

She was still edgy as she served scrambled eggs and bacon to the local patrons. More than one piece of toast burned, and a creamer met its demise on the floor behind the counter.

"I knew I shouldn't have mentioned he was coming," Riley murmured as Amy swept past him on her way to the cash register.

"Shut up," she muttered good-naturedly, poking him with her elbow.

Riley's grin broadened as he watched Case McKenna stride casually into the room.

The customer paying his tab whistled as Amy slammed the register drawer shut. "Excuse me?" she asked.

"You just gave me change for a twenty," the man said with a laugh.

"And?" Amy raised her eyebrows, tilted her head.

"I only gave you a ten."

"We aim to please," Amy said softly. Her face felt feverish with embarrassment as she opened the cash drawer and recounted the man's change. "Sorry. And thank you." It was hard to conduct business while trying to ignore Case, which, of course, was impossible. Just seeing him walk through the door had put her entire body on high alert.

She escaped to the kitchen, apron strings flying behind her.

Wendy Paul sat in the back, kneading pie dough on a floured breadboard. At the sight of Amy's flushed complexion and wringing hands, she smiled warmly. "Oh, my. He's here."

Amy poked out her bottom lip and pushed her bangs back from her forehead. "Oh Wen, what am I going to do? I'm flat-out miserable."

Newburg's award-winning pie baker stood from her low stool and brushed flour from her thin hands, then adjusted the scarf covering her nearly bare scalp.

"You mean what would I do?" she asked, wrapping a motherly arm around the younger woman's shoulders. "I know he doesn't look too buff these days, but Riley was a real hunk of meat when I met him. He had a whole wagon full of baggage, too, what with losing his mother so young. I was headstrong, independent. He infuriated me by being such a blockhead sometimes. But I couldn't get past those blue eyes of his. There was so much sincerity there, more than the sum total in the eyes of all my previous suitors. I had to have him. And to do that, I had to help him get over his past."

Amy nodded, then glanced nervously at the swinging doors to the dining room. Wendy leaned close and kissed her forehead. "What have you got to lose?" she whispered.

Her simple question made complete sense. It was true. She had nothing more to lose by trying to reconnect with Case. The attraction had been there, powerful and fulfilling. He had felt it too, she was certain. But unless she did something, he would walk right out of her life and back to his probably lonely existence.

Amy drew in a deep breath and she hugged Wendy as tightly as she dared. Then she went into the tiny bathroom in the back and took an appraising look in the mirror.

"Amy? Yeah, she's here somewhere," Riley said, filling Case's coffee mug. "Be out in a minute. Say, that was some fine police-work you did! Folks have been talking about you all over town."

Case shrugged and turned away, his gaze returning to the stainless steel kitchen doors. "Those crooks would have been caught eventually. Brainless heathens."

"Well, you're Newburg's national hero."

Case offered a reluctant grin. Riley was one in a million, and Case would miss his company.

"Your breakfast will be right up."

"Thanks." Case dug his fingers into his hair, wondering fleetingly when his last haircut had been. It was getting pretty shaggy in the back. He looked at his hands, examining his fingernails. He waited. It was another four minutes, a long four minutes, before Amy emerged from the kitchen.

He wasn't prepared for his own reaction to her appearance. Her hair seemed longer, darker, straighter, and by all accounts, sexier. She busied herself behind the counter, buttering toast and refilling coffee, averting her eyes. Case couldn't help his stare. It took all of his meager willpower to stay in his seat, to not get up and corral her in the corner, not to run his aching fingers down her spine, slide them across that enticing playground in the small of her back.

He blew out a sigh from pursed lips. Recalling his brief conversation with Amy's father, he was even more convinced he'd made a wrong assessment of her life, her character.

Blinking, he swigged the last of his coffee. Case glanced around for Riley, but couldn't locate the gentle giant with the bottomless coffee pot. He wondered if Amy would approach him.

And when she did, what would he say?

Jack's words came back to him, demanding that he decide what he wanted from the woman who dominated his thoughts, wafted in and out of his dreams. Watching her now, flitting about behind the counter, Case knew what he wanted. But first he had to find out if she was still angry, and if she would persist in dwelling on the past.

As if he had willed it, Amy finally made her way to his table and wordlessly filled his mug.

Their eyes met, and Amy set the pot on the table. He

noticed her hands were shaking slightly.

"How are you, Amy?"

"I'm fine, thank you. You're all the news these days."

"Happy to help out*." And doesn't that sound trite?* "I met your dad."

"Thought you might."

"He's a great guy. His lady friend's a kick, too."

Amy nodded, and she picked up the pot as if to go. "Yeah. They're both pretty cool. I think I'll keep them."

"I'm, uh, heading back today."

"So I hear. I'd like to talk to you before you go."

Aha. She wants to talk. He motioned for her to sit.

Riley must have felt the resonance emanating from the corner booth, for at that moment he returned from wherever he had been and nodded to Amy. She slid into the booth opposite Case.

"If this is about that night," Case began, his apology ready to leap from his lips.

Amy swallowed. "No. It's not. It's about your mother."

Case's eyebrows lifted slightly, and he paused to stir some milk into his coffee. *Damn. She's still working on her history project.* "I really don't want to discuss her right now."

Amy wet her lips, her eyes focused on Case's fingers, wrapped around his coffee mug. "Case, I have to tell you this. I'm sorry, really, but I owe it to Leta."

Leta? She owes Leta what? Case set his jaw. Why did this woman insist on invading his dungeon? Now, she was on a first-name basis with his estranged mother!

"Just hear me out, okay?" Amy rubbed her palms together and took a deep breath. When Case did not answer, she went on anyway. "Your mother died last month. I just found out. She asked me to-to bury her ashes here. There's a service tomorrow, and we're having a short reception at the lighthouse. I know she'd love it...w-would have loved knowing that you would be there...if you want to, of course. The choice is yours."

Case felt his face turn to stone. His mother, *dead?* It was a concept that did not immediately register. She had, after all, been gone so long.

Amy raised her eyes to meet Case's, then got to her feet. "I'm sorry," she whispered, then turned to go.

Still unable to fully process the news, Case reached out and grasped her wrist. "Amy, wait."

She stiffened slightly, but did not pull away. Case loosened his grip. "She's...really gone?"

"Cancer," Amy murmured.

"Was she sick for very long?"

"I'm not sure. Seems like it. There's a will. I'll be reading it. You really should come."

"I don't know," Case said quietly. "I have to think about this."

Amy nodded. "Graveside is at two, reception at three. I'll understand if...if you don't....can't..." Gently she pulled her wrist free of his grasp and picked up the coffeepot. "It's good to see you," she added, her voice cracking slightly with emotion.

Case watched her as she made her way back to the coffee maker, his pulse racing. He stood, hoping Riley would understand why he left his breakfast untouched.

Chapter Eighteen

Amy held tightly to Brian's hand as they walked together beside a row of headstones of various sizes and shapes. On Brian's other side, Judy picked her way carefully through the grass.

"The pastor was so nice," Judy murmured as they walked. "Mrs. Jenner would have appreciated the nice things he said."

Amy smiled, keeping her own opinion private, knowing that the embittered Leta Jenner would be laughing at the clergyman's euphemistic portrait of her turbulent life. Before reaching the edge of the cemetery, they came upon a tall statuette marking the last grave. Curious, Brian broke ranks and walked around to read the inscription.

"Hey, look at this. Irena's brother sure got the royal treatment."

Frowning, Amy joined her brother and read for herself. She realized she had never asked about Matthew Hastings' death. She was surprised to see that he passed away just three months prior to Liam Jenner.

"How sad," she commented, quickly calculating. "Only 35 when he died. I wonder what happened?"

"You should ask her."

"Who, Irena? *You* ask her! She's been acting pretty weird to me lately," Amy said with a short laugh.

Brian shrugged. "People get a little strange living alone for twenty-some years."

No, it was more than that. Even Leta had alluded to evilness in Irena Hastings. Amy had passed it off as jealousy when Leta made the comment, but now she began to wonder.

The mourners gathered at Point Surrender. Not particularly somber, most treating the whole affair as a necessary duty. Judy passed around hors d'oeuvres and soft drinks. Amy looked around the room in a mental roll call.

Riley and Wendy sat close together on the couch. Hal Franzman, the owner of Holiday Hardware, stood in one corner, his brother Joe beside him. Emery Davis helped himself to several canapés before settling on the couch beside Riley. Even Irena Hastings was there, making herself comfortable in Brian's easy chair. Brian stood by, anxious for Amy to begin. Only one person was missing.

Amy stood in front of the newly refurbished fireplace and cleared her throat. The letter in her hand fluttered slightly as she perused it for the hundredth time.

"Thank you all for joining us today. Um, we're here because Leticia Jenner asked, before she died, that we assemble to hear her last thoughts and wishes. If anyone is uncomfortable with that, please feel free to go."

No one made a move.

"Okay. Before I begin, does anyone have anything to say?" Again there was no motion in the room. Amy reviewed the faces around her, some openly waiting, others quietly reserved. "I'll begin. I met Leta Jenner, or Leta Mansfield as she called herself, five or six weeks ago in Southern California. I didn't know it at the time, but she was already quite ill with the lung cancer that eventually took her life. She lived in a small apartment with two cats, a bird..." Amy took a breath, paused. "Like you all want to know that. Anyway, she was humble, and saddened by many events in her life that she regretted. Still, I found her to be, uh, warm and friendly. I would like to have known her when she was young, when she first came to Point Surrender. Unfortunately, lighthouse tending was not her...thing, as she put it."

"*Pssh*."

The sound had come from Irena's mouth, Amy was certain, but when she turned to look, the old woman remained silent and looking out the window.

"I just want to say she was always nice to me," Joe Franzman said, smoothing his hair back against his scalp. "I'm embarrassed to say, I never did get the scales down, but she was a good teacher anyway."

A chuckle went around the room and his brother nodded vigorously.

"She was patient and never got mad at us. Once she handed back the lesson money my mom had sent, told me to get myself a root beer float on the way home."

More laughter.

"Anybody else?" Amy asked, looking around. She realized Irena Hastings and Emery Davis were the only others in the room who had known Leta. Both withheld their thoughts.

"Okay then. I'll open her last envelope."

As she slipped her finger beneath the sealed flap, a movement caught her eye and she turned to see Case's lean form framed in the doorway to the kitchen. Coloring, she withdrew the single sheet of paper.

The words were typed, with misspellings and corrections filling the page. Still, the paragraphs were clearly drawn.

"It is my hope," Amy began, pausing to clear her throat, "that Miss Amy Winslow is reading this paper at my funeral, and that she will take steps to make sure all the stuff written here gets done.

"I have already given my car, such that it is, to my good friend Phoebe Allen, who needs it more than anybody who might be listening. She's also taking Jimi and Janis, my fat kitties, and Caruso, the yellow bird, who I would rather set free but she'd probably die in the L.A. smog.

"I have some clothes and furniture ready for the Vietnam Veterans to pick up.

"I have given Phoebe enough money, I hope, to pay for dragging my ashes–" Amy paused to hide a smile. "–my ashes back to Newburg. I know there will be those protesting my burial next to Liam, but we're both dead now so leave us alone."

Amy drew in a deep breath and glanced briefly at Case, who remained leaning against the jamb, his arms folded against his chest.

"The rest of the money in the account should go to my son, William Casey, if he can be located. It's not a lot but I'd rather he have it than any of the vultures trying to collect on my bad years.

"Amy, please take my shoebox full of memories and do what you think is best. Your brother might like to see some of the pix from the early days. And of course Will's baby pix are there too.

"Now, the apologies. To my dear late husband Liam, I am sorry I couldn't make it as a lighthouse keeper's wife. I am sorry I didn't leave you sooner, before you got used to having me around. I know you could have found someone better suited to the life you wanted.

"Irena, I'd be as shocked as hell if you are there listening to this, but I want to say to you, I'm sorry if you're still alive, you misera–" Amy stopped, horror-stricken, to look for Miss Hastings' reaction. "I'm sorry," she finally continued, "that I didn't just hand Liam over to you all those years ago. You were probably even–" *colder in bed than he was.* Again Amy cleared her throat. "Some of this is…blurred."

"My dearest Matthew. It is you I owe the biggest, realist apology to. I should have listened to you. We could have been happy together, and maybe I wouldn't have messed up so bad on my life. Just know that I did love you, probably more than any man in my life. I was shattered when I heard what you did. Believe me, I wasn't worth dying over. But you were never really that strong. I should have come back for you and William. We could have escaped your witch of a sister somehow."

Irena Hastings squirmed in her chair and crossed her legs, her action allowing everyone else in the room a moment to exhale.

"William, I'd be just as surprised if you are there. I can't tell you what made your mother become what she did. I can only beg your forgiveness, and beg you not to ever jump to conclusions about people and things you don't understand. Life doesn't come with a manual, not that I was ever very good at taking instructions!"

Amy wetted her lips, now afraid to look in Case's direction.

"I just want you to know that your father was a wonderful man. Kind, generous to a fault, gentle in spirit. A gifted musician..."

Oh God. She's talking about Matthew, Amy thought, swallowing hard.

"If you don't know your true parentage by now, I'm sorry if this is a shock. He really wanted us all to be together, but I was hooked by then. My drug habit was substantial, to say the least. When Matt killed himself, I went more downhill, if that's possible."

A general gasp went around the room, ending back in Amy's own chest. Irena Hastings got to her feet.

"That's a bold faced lie. Matt would never have killed himself over a trollop like Leta Jenner!"

Her angry words bounced from the walls, eliciting shocked expressions on the faces around her. All except for Case McKenna, who remain stoic, motionless.

Irena sat back down, folded her hands in her lap, and took a calming breath. "It was an accident. Matt fell from the cliff that night. Probably drunk with worry over that worthless adulteress, but he did not commit suicide."

Surprisingly, it was Riley who spoke next. "What did the Sheriff's office determine?"

"Pack of fools," Emery Davis put in, leaning forward to put his empty beer can on the coffee table in front of him. "Those idiots couldn't place a cause of death on a dead possum in the road."

"What cliff?" Brian wanted to know.

"Out yonder. Right here behind the tower."

"Matt Hastings fell from the cliff?" Amy asked, her own morbid curiosity piqued. With startling clarity, she remembered the man she and Case had each seen on the cliff. Matthew Hastings. *Case's real father.* Case refused to meet her eyes when she looked his way.

"You betcha, yes, he did," Emery said. He stood and turned to Miss Hastings. "It wudn't no suicide, but neither was it an accident. Matt got pushed off the cliff that night. Matthew Hastings was *murdered.*"

"Good Lord," Riley blurted out, his eyes wide with excitement. "Somebody get me a beer."

Brian was quick with the brown bottles and distributed them to nearly everyone in the room.

"Hogwash," Irena Hastings asserted. "Nothin' but hearsay."

"I seen it with my own two eyes," Emery said, then guzzled the new beer handed him. "They was arguin' over the boy. Matt wanted to take him and go out to Vegas to be with Leta. I got to chuckling because, quite rightly, she wudn't worth all that quibblin'. I had my turn at her early on."

Amy covered her eyes for a moment. This discussion

was almost more than she could handle.

"You were there, then?" Riley asked. "So who allegedly pushed the man off?"

"Why, it was Liam of course. Liam wudn't about to give up that boy, even though he wudn't his kin. It was the last thing he had with Leta, he said. They was both half crazy out there, tussling near the edge like a couple of kids. Liam'd been into his booze, Matt'd probly had hisself a toke or two on a joint. I seen what was about to happen, but it was too late. Liam gave him a right hook, a bad one at that, and poor ol' Matt just toppled right over the back. He wudn't the type to fight, you know? I felt kinda sorry for Liam. I don't think he really meant to kill Matt. He was damned jealous about the boy, though. Case here, that is. No offense, son. So we agreed in our telling to the Sheriff, that we neither didn't know nothin' 'bout it."

"Nonsense," Irena Hastings shouted. "Liam would never have killed my brother! And how dare you sully my brother's reputation with references to drugs. That's a load of bull from the town drunk."

Emery turned and bowed before Miss Hastings.

"I thank you, dear lady, for your flattering words. You leave me no choice but to tell these good people here how you come to my place lookin' for a tumble or two back then." He turned to others in the room. "Of course I turned her down. Didn't want my jewels to freeze off, if y'all know what I mean."

One of the Franzman brothers snickered.

Amy struggled to take a breath. She looked from Emery Davis to Irena Hastings. Had either recognized

Case as the devastated child sent away all those years ago?

"I think we've all said about enough," Riley said, rising from the couch. "Time we be leavin' these folks alone now."

Amy turned at the sound of the kitchen door slamming shut. Whatever Case's reaction had been to the revelations offered, Amy would not be seeing it today.

"Could you believe those people?" Brian asked at the dinner table that night. "Such nastiness! What a soap opera."

"I feel bad for Case," Judy said softly, looking at Amy, who sat mum. "So much to find out all at once. His mother dead, his father not his father, his real father accused of killing the man he thought *was* his father, or was it the other way around? And then his newly discovered aunt with a sordid past of her own..."

"That would be hard to stomach," Brian agreed.

"And all because of me," Amy muttered. "Because I wouldn't let it alone."

"Oh, come on, Aim. That's not true."

"Sure it is. If I'd never dug around, found Leta, she never would have written all those things. She would have just died quietly, and no one would have been the wiser."

"And Matthew Hasting's death would have gone unsolved. I've never believed in ghosts, Aim. You know me. But something weird's been going on around here and I do believe that things happen for a reason."

Amy ignored her brother's words and continued her

own regrets. "Case could have gone on believing what he'd always believed, what he'd learned to deal with. Now he's got all this other drama to worry about."

"You don't give him much credit, do you?" Brian asked quietly. "What about his rights? His right to know the truth about his parents? I would want to know, no matter how painful."

Amy didn't answer. There was no answer.

Chapter Nineteen

The events of the previous day had taken their toll on all who had attended the reception for the late Leticia Mansfield Jenner. Amy felt hung over and lethargic as she dressed for the day.

"We're heading out. Need anything from the city?" Brian asked from the hall outside Amy's bedroom door.

Amy opened the door. "Going to your therapy appointment?"

"Yeah. We probably won't be back until this evening."

"Have fun. Be careful," Amy said, giving her brother a spontaneous hug. "Love you."

"I love you too. Hey, if you go anywhere, leave me a note?"

"Sure."

Where would she go? Did a walk on the beach count?

It was a picture perfect day. Indeed, the weather had been beautiful, except for the night of the big storm, since her first visit to Point Surrender. She wondered how it would be in the winter. She didn't intend to find out, however.

Too much had happened. Despite the fact that she now knew the probable cause of her uneasiness inside the lighthouse, it didn't change the fact that she didn't want to be there. Brian and Judy seemed unaffected by the disquiet that haunted her. Taking Leta's nicotine-stained shoebox with her, Amy left the house and headed for the beach.

Once outside, her spirits improved. She would have to stop bathing in self-pity and straighten up. It wasn't like Amy Winslow to succumb to depression.

She thought of the children in Carmel, getting ready to go back to school. Would they miss her? Wonder how her summer had been? Perhaps that was the answer. She should go back to work. To teaching.

Amy wandered down the beach, watching the murres flying overhead, and as she turned, she caught a glimpse of the white tower. Was it really looking back? It didn't want her there, she knew too much. *Cared* too much.

Recalling the day she left the hospital, Amy shook her head at the memory. She remembered the skeptical looks she received from the others who claimed the radio in the lighthouse was not on when they returned there that night. That no other radio in the area had picked up a distress call. Even the newer light station just a few miles south had heard no such SOS. And more, no one had seen Point Surrender's light go on.

Could Case have turned off the radio and the light after she had rushed out into the storm? Somehow, she doubted he had. She might never find out. Another loose end she would have to let go.

The fact that Drew was at the hospital when she awoke was another mystery. Why had he come? Was it truly to see Brian? Did it really matter?

She had pretty much resigned herself to the fact that

Matthew Hastings had been dogging her from the first time she'd entered the lighthouse at Point Surrender. Case, and even Brian, had also witnessed his appearances. Was it true that murder victims could not rest until their stories were told?

And what about the couple on the cliff, barely visible through the waterspout that had passed through that night? Was it really the pirate and his lady?

Amy, AMY! It doesn't matter now. Don't you get it? If you don't stop re-living the past, you will have no future! Get off it, girl.

If only she had heeded her own warning sooner. Case McKenna might still be around.

Finding a spot to her liking, Amy sat down and opened the tattered box. Many of the photos were of people she didn't recognize, old photos bearing dates from the 1960's and 70's. Near the top was the larger, color photograph of Matt Hastings looking young and vital in his Nehru-collared shirt and love beads. His smile was infectious, and Amy suddenly realized why this handsome man looked so familiar. Why hadn't she seen the resemblance before?

The baby pictures charmed her maternal heart, both delighted and depressed her. It was hard not to think about her own lost child, and yet she wanted to look at every snapshot of Case's babyhood.

Here, the first day of kindergarten; another, a smiling display of a missing front tooth. The sea bass that hung from a scale beside him, nearly to his ankles. An intrepid William Casey Jenner sitting on the gallery railing.

"Happy Mother's Day, from Your Son," read the decaying, probably school-made greeting card of now-faded construction paper.

In the bottom of the box was a wedding photo. Liam Jenner waved from the steps of a church, his charming, youthful bride grasping his other hand. Amy shook her head slowly. She replaced the photos and put the lid back on the box. She wondered if Case would ever be ready to see its contents.

He found her on the beach. She wasn't hard to spot, her yellow linen dress a bright spot against the endless expanse of sand. Sitting with her knees drawn up, facing the surf, Amy was focused on the horizon.

"This seat taken?" Case asked.

Amy turned a startled face upward, but did not answer. Case sat beside her in the sand, and both returned their gazes to the sea.

"I owe you a big apology," Amy said at last.

"Not really."

"Yes, I do. I should never have meddled in other peoples' lives. You tried to warn me. God! Yesterday was so awful."

Case shook his head. "That's what I came to talk to you about. You might as well have it all." From his hip pocket, Case pulled a packet of yellowed, folded notepapers and handed them to her. She looked at him in surprise.

"What...?"

"Go ahead. Read it."

Amy unfolded the aged papers and began reading the first page. As her eyes traveled over the painful, awkward scratchings of a ten-year-old boy, she paused to glance at Case momentarily, but his eyes remained fixed on the churning waves before them.

Point Surrendder, California, May 10, 1984
Cleaned all of the windows in the lantern today. Also, got the poptop out of the motor gears that fell in last Friday night from Dad. The light is turnning good now.

Dad is still sick. He has been sick ever since mr. Hastings died off our cliff in back. I feel real bad. Mr.hastings was a very nice man. He gave me a Matchbox car for my birthday last year.

Stayed home from school again today. Still haven't found Mom's phone number. Maybe she will call us. But I don't really want her to.

Dad will be better next week.
William Casey Jenner, Assisttent Keeper

Point Surrender, California, June 1, 1984
The people from school called today. I pretended I was still sick. Dad is sleeping most of the time. Last night, the light would not turn on and I got scared. But I figgured out if you switch all of them at the same time, it will go on.

Mom called. ~~She told~~ I don't remember what she said.

The huggest ship I ever saw past by tonite

when I was on watch. It had red running lights and was at least 1000 feet long.

Dad ordered more groceries today. I hope he askd for soap. He never forgits to get beer.
Will. C. J., Assissdent Keep

Newburg, California, June 10, 1984

Civilian keeper at Point Surrender lightstation was pronounced dead on arrival at Roth General Hospital at 21:54 hours. Mr. William R. Jenner, apparently the victim of a fall down the tower steps, died from injuries sustained thus. Keeper Jenner's young son witnessed the fall and due to the storm related power outage, was forced to walk up the bluff and to the next dwelling approximately 2 miles for help.

Although disputed by his son, it is the opinion of the M.E. that Mr. Jenner had imbibed a large amount of alcohol prior to the fall.

Mr. Jenner's former wife, a Mrs. Leta Mansfield of Las Vegas, Nevada, has been contacted about the care of her son. The younger Jenner will reside temporarily with Mr. Emery Davis, a neighbor and family friend.

It is recommended that a complete inspection and investigation be initiated to determine the future value of Point Surrender lighthouse.
CPO John Daniels

June 14, 1984

Today I am leaving to go to my mothers house in Las Vegas. I wonder if she will even remmember me. I have not told anybody about what happened, about how my father said he wasn't my dad at all and about how he fell because he was trying to push me out of the way. I just keep remmember over and over how he looked on the floor, how messed up he was, his head all twisted to the side like that. I couldn't stop starring at him.

The journal pages ended without a final signature. Amy carefully folded the papers back to the way they were and handed them back to Case, who refused to take them from her.

"I don't need them anymore," he said quietly.

Unsure of what to do, Amy held the packet in one hand while hurriedly wiping her tears away with the other.

"I am so sorry. It must have been terrible for you."

Case offered a sardonic grin. "Yeah, it could've been better." Looking down, he made little concentric circles in the sand. "I couldn't understand why she left. She just...left. While I was asleep. I used to...used to go up in the tower and watch for her to come back." He chuckled softly. "My dad, he just started unraveling. He kept the things she'd left behind. For me, it was a dark time. He loved that damned lighthouse. Lived and breathed it.

When she left, he just let it go."

He looked at Amy then, reached over to pull a strand of hair away from her cheek.

"I used to see Matt Hastings on my way to school. Then I stopped going. Had to stay home, take care of my dad. Matt came by one day, said he'd talked to my mom, and that we could go see her if I wanted to. About then, my dad–Liam–he drank all the time. I waited until one afternoon he wasn't so drunk, and I asked him about going with Matt to Vegas."

Amy sucked in a breath. She suspected what had happened next.

"So..." Case focused on the horizon, heaved a sigh. "Liam got royally pissed and stormed into town, on foot. I waited in my usual spot, perched up in the tower. When he got back, it was dark and Matt and Emery Davis were following him. I couldn't hear what they said, but Matt kept after him. He held out his arms, like he was begging. I was scared. Worried. I'd never seen my dad–*crap*. I'd never seen *Liam* so mad. I hustled down the steps as fast as I could. I'd gotten pretty good at it, actually. But by the time I got out there, Matt was gone. Home, I thought. I was disappointed. I really wanted to go with him. To escape."

"Oh..." Amy slipped her hand onto Case's shoulder. "I can't imagine..."

Case looked down, wet his lips. "I didn't think it was possible for things to get worse, but of course they did. They found Matt's body on the rocks. Liam wouldn't talk to me about it. I kept thinking about Mom waiting for us in Las Vegas, that we'd never come and she wouldn't know why. A couple of months went by, and I finally got up the nerve to ask him about what happened to Matt. He got wild, yelling, accusing, you know, the whole nine yards. There was a monster storm that night. We were up there." Case seemed mesmerized as he gestured toward the beacon on the cliff.

"That's when he fell," Amy offered. "You were with him. Oh, God."

"The Coast Guard put me on a train to Vegas with a ten dollar bill and all my worldly possessions in a knapsack. They said she'd be there. Of course, no one met the train. I had my mother's address on a scrap of paper, so I used the ten to get a cab to an empty fleabag apartment that reeked of pot. When she did come home, she seemed unimpressed by my sudden appearance–and you gotta remember, here's an almost eleven-year-old kid who's spent all but two nights of his entire life in that round building over there. I knew nothing of crack, or slots, or even neon lights."

Amy couldn't help a remorseful smile at Case's first impression of Las Vegas. "You must have been terrified."

"Oddly, I wasn't. The whole time I rode on that train, I thought about what I would say to her, what she might say to me, but it was so different when I finally saw her. She was ragged, stoned–I didn't know it at the time, of course. I was still reeling from the change in my supposed father's behavior. I probably thought the whole world had gone going crazy. So I was afraid to ask her about my father, about what he meant. I don't think I really wanted to know.

"She didn't have any food in the place, except for stale crackers, beer, garbage. I waited five days before I finally demanded she talk to me; I was getting pretty hungry. She finally agreed to send me up to Aunt Rose's."

Amy waited patiently for Case to continue, but when he didn't, she spoke up. "She told me a little about that. She regretted it."

"She got one of her cronies to drive us to the bus station. She probably sold something to get me a ticket to Washington. It was the last time I saw her, standing in that dingy bus station, barefoot, wearing a tie-dyed dress and sunglasses."

"Wow," Amy said softly. She looked at Case, steeling herself not to move toward him, not to take that almost-eleven-year-old boy into her arms.

He sighed, and turned toward Amy. "Rose was the best mother a kid could have. She didn't have any kids of her own." He chuckled at the memory. "Even when I was twelve, we used to bake cookies together. She took me to the park, the Space Needle, we rode ferries everywhere. When I was thirteen, she met Steve McKenna and married him. A year later we moved out to Coeur d'Alene, Idaho."

Amy nodded, silently thanking God that Case had finally found a home.

"Steve's a great guy. Helped put me through med school. He never formally adopted me, but I adopted him. I needed to leave Will Jenner behind."

No longer able to restrain herself, Amy placed her hand over his, squeezed. "I feel so bad for dragging all that out. I had no right. I hope you can forgive me."

The sun's warmth battled the ocean's cool breeze. It was a day like any other day, and yet nothing like any day he'd lived yet. Case took Amy's hand between both of his and looked into her eyes, shaking his head slightly. He wanted to tell her that it was a good thing. He wanted to tell her about the tremendous weight that had been lifted, about the exorcism of demons that had finally brought peace to his troubled soul. But it all sounded so trite, so cliché.

"It's really okay. Things are...okay. I never really stopped wondering about my father, about what had gone on all those years ago. It feels better, knowing."

Tears filled Amy's eyes as she clearly remembered the events leading to his admissions. Most specifically, the night of the storm and her fall.

"That night, in the lighthouse, when I..."

Case pressed his lips tightly together, recalling the heart-wrenching shock of watching another loved one tumble down the staircase. "It was déjà vu, all right. But you know, this whole experience has been like...like when you rip off a bandage. It hurts really bad at first, it's a shock and if you survive it without a heart attack, the sting fades away pretty fast." He rubbed the back of her hand, absently stroking away her grief with his fingers. Amy smiled brightly through her glistening lashes.

"I never told you why I came back here that night," Case continued, once more turning around briefly to view the freshly painted tower behind him. "I wanted to tell you, to apologize for running out like I did. I didn't want you to think I didn't like kids or something like that. I don't really know kids, I wasn't much of a kid myself, you know?"

Amy slowly reached out to him, placing her hand against his cheek.

"It really would have been all right," he said softly. "I could have gotten used to the idea." He pulled her hand away from his cheek, considered her palm before pressing it to his lips. He closed his eyes, returned her hand slowly to his cheek. "I also never told you how sorry I am about your baby. I won't pretend to know how terrible that must have been for you."

"Stop it! You're making me cry again," Amy said, still smiling. Then, dragging her fingers down his jaw line and off his chin, she laced her fingers with his and laughed. "Life's been a real thrill ride lately."

Case got to his feet and brushed the sand from his jeans. Amy picked up the shoebox and stood also.

"So I imagine you'll be heading home now?"

"Car's all packed and gassed up. I'm on my way. I just wanted to see you, tell you that stuff, you know." He paused, shoving his hands into his front pockets.

"Thanks," Amy murmured. "I really appreciate that. Did you say good-bye to your Aunt Irena?"

Case rolled his eyes briefly, grinning at her. "I'm not too sure about that woman. I'd like to put a little distance between us for now. How about you? You hanging around here for awhile?"

"Me? No way." Amy shook her head. "Brian is doing so well, and he and Judy have moved in here now, so I'm a fifth wheel...and besides, this place still gives me the creeps."

"I get that. So what will you do?"

"I'll probably go back and see my dad again, but I'll have to get my own place since he now has Nola there. Maybe I'll find work down there somewhere."

Case nodded, and there was a minute when neither spoke. A breeze ruffled Amy's dress. She smoothed it down, shifted her legs. A moment was upon them, a moment that would soon be gone and she would begin the trek up the path. Back to the lighthouse. She turned to go.

Case swallowed, then touched his forehead. "Oh. I almost forgot! I heard about a school looking for a new kindergarten teacher. 'Course, it's a pretty small school, nothing fancy, and the kids are probably bratty..."

Amy stopped and turned her head. "Bratty kids don't scare me," she said with a grin.

"I know of a place not far from the school where you could hole up. You'd like it, too–no ghosts, no secrets, no dark past...only future."

"Really? Tell me more."

"There are these pines, see. Lots of them. There's this really cool little cabin, it's kinda old, with a huge deck on the front. A kitchen just dying for a decent cook. Windows that need curtains...a cozy but so empty bedroom on the back of the house..."

"Wow. Sounds interesting. I do have some experience with refurbishing old houses."

"There's also this lonely oceanographer who needs more in his life than an arrogant walrus and a bunch of greased up penguins."

Amy's eyebrows lifted, but the whimsical smile stayed on her face.

Case sighed, ran a hand through his hair, and gestured vaguely toward the cliff above. "I happen to be going that way, if you'd like a ride."

"A ride. Just a ride?"

Case held his hand over his brow and stared at the horizon, a smile forming on his lips. She wasn't making this very easy, but the man on the bluff behind her was holding his arms out to the sides, palms up. His smile broad, his message clear: *It's now or never, son. Suck it up!*

"I know you haven't had the best luck with relationships, Miz Winslow. But I'm lately thinking I'm pretty overdue on finding myself a partner. We've both been to Hades and back the last few months and maybe…maybe Grogan's Head would be a good place to start over. It would be worth…worth a try…"

Case glanced back toward the bluff. He got the thumbs-up gesture, and his father turned and strode away. For the *last time*, Case was suddenly certain.

Amy was still clutching the shoebox and her smile evolved into a solemn stare. "Start over," she repeated. "You and me."

"Yeah, you know, like put all this behind us. Like regular people who meet and fall in love and get married and…have kids. You know. Like that."

The smile slowly found its way back to Amy's lips. "Worth a try," she said softly. "Can you give me some time to think about it?"

Case shrugged. "Uh, sure. Like how long?"

"Oh, say, a minute or two?"

Amy started for the rocky path leading up the bluff to the lighthouse. At the base, she turned, shading her eyes with her hand as she looked back at Case. He was grinning at her in the bright sunlight, hands on hips.

"This is where they jumped, you know," she called out to him.

"Who jumped what?"

"Jacelyn and Morgan. The story of Point Surrender."

"Am I supposed to drag out my white flag and wave it?"

Amy laughed, sat the shoebox on the ground, and ran back to him, throwing herself into his arms with confident abandon. That he wanted her was no longer a question in her mind. She was determined that no question should remain in his.

The kiss was enduring and substantial. Amy's feet hovered somewhere between heaven and the sand below.

He released her slowly, and she reluctantly pulled away. She picked up the shoebox and thrust it into his arms. "Hang onto this. I have to write a note! I'll only be a moment."

"Amy?"

"Yes?" She paused on the trail, still smiling and breathless, her bright yellow dress fluttering happily in the wind.

"Do you still have that little blue car you found in the closet?"

"Of course."

"Bring it. My father gave it to me, you know."

Amy nodded at the man who had lost two fathers, and quite possibly his heart, at Point Surrender. She would make it her purpose in life to make sure that for Case McKenna, the losses would stop and the love would begin.

Epilogue

Point Surrender, March 1, 2007

Today is the beginning of a new Winslow era. Jenna Amanda Winslow was born this morning at 8:05 A.M. at Roth General. Mom Judy and baby are doing fine. I'm elated beyond words and can't wait to bring them home.

Heard from Amy last night, she and Case will be here next week to finalize the Hastings estate. Good timing! Too bad about old Irena. She was an unhappy sort anyway. Can't say I miss her, though. No one could believe she actually left the property to Case. He has big plans for renovating the house and reopening the Inn next summer.

Maybe now Amy will give in and marry the guy. Wouldn't mind having a doctor in the family.

I guess Dad and our new "step-mom" Nola will come up next week too. Good thing we have the Hastings House to ourselves now!

People ask me if I miss the Coast Guard, but I don't. Being a lighthouse keeper is way too much fun. And building boats with Emery isn't half bad.
Brian Winslow, Civilian Keeper

THE END

ONE OF A KIND, A MOMENT IN TIME
PHOTOGRAPHY FROM THE HEART
J T MAC PHOTOGRAPHY

Jeannette and Tom McDonald's first cameras were acquired in their early teens. This is where the journey of photography began. Some of Tom's early photography was taken in Viet Nam as a gunner on a riverboat in 1968-1969. His photos portray the war in a unique fashion.

For years, Jeannette and Tom's photography have been original ideas and references for paintings of well-known artists in the Northwest. Only after years of encouragement from these artists and friends did Jeannette and Tom start publishing their own work.

The artists offer one of a kind originals and small limited edition prints. They also have expanded their photography by printing 90% of their own work, along with collecting old barn wood from all over the United States to build their classic barn wood frames for much of their larger pieces.

One of the most interesting facts regarding their photography is it doesn't pertain to only wildlife, landscapes, floral, Native American, or western pieces, but instead incorporates all of these into a collage of freshness that's needed in this day and age.

Another interesting and fresh idea is the combination of watercolor paper and canvas for their photography. The photographs are printed on watercolor paper and canvas, some in full color; others are black and white with a personal hand tinted touch making each piece one of a kind. All watercolors and canvas editions are 50 or less in an edition size or one of a kind originals. Original prints are sold with the negative to assure the buyer that there is only one image of their purchase.

This technique is new and exciting, not only for Jeannette and Tom, but also to the photography world in general. There are very few photographers doing one of a kind originals or this small of an edition. This causes their work to be very collectible.

Jeannette and Tom travel on an average of 20,000 miles a year looking for that perfect sunset, sunrise, or other prize-winning photograph. Amidst their travels, they do an average of 15 to 20 fine art shows a year. The winter months are spent in the Southwest participating in art and wine festivals in the Scottsdale/Carefree, Arizona area, with most summer shows taking place in the Pacific Northwest.

Jeannette and Tom are one of very few husband and wife teams active in the art world today.

Photograph for cover art provided by J T Mac Photography

About the Author:

"Everyone needs a little romance in their lives," Anne Carter will assure you. "Some need more than others." She should know. A storyteller since middle school, Anne and her younger sister would dream up a new chapter to a romantic saga each night before going to bed. Soon, writing became an obsession. In addition to romantic fiction, her credits include young adult mysteries, short stories, poetry, and non-fiction. Raised in Southern California where she, her husband, and three children make their home, Anne interrupts her passion occasionally to restore old photographs, officiate at weddings, and possibly put dinner on the table.

Long a lighthouse fanatic, Anne spent several days holed up inside the Dimick Lighthouse at Port Townsend, Washington, while writing POINT SURRENDER, her fourth published romance. "There's nothing like an authentic setting to get the muse to appear."

Visit Anne Carter at
www.beaconstreetbooks.com.